CUTTER

CUTTER

THOMAS LAIRD

Constable · London

First published in Great Britain 2001
by Constable, an imprint of Constable & Robinson Ltd
3 The Lanchesters, 162 Fulham Palace Road
London W6 9ER
www.constablerobinson.com

Copyright © 2001 Thomas Laird

ISBN 1-84119-419-0

Printed and bound in Great Britain

A CIP Catalogue record for this book is available from
the British Library

Acknowledgments

For Katherine Leigh, Anne Karoline, Andrew Robert and Janet Marie. And for Krystyna Green, who delivered the stuff that dreams are made of. A tip of The Farmer's fedora to Nick Austen, who shared his wonderful suggestions.

Finally to Robert Raymond and Vivian Mildred . . .

To all the above, many thanks and much love.

Chapter One

She runs like someone who knows her business. The full stride, the long legs pumping fluidly. Pumping right toward me. She is only a block away. She'll be right in my lap in just seconds, and I'll reach out from behind this convenient thorny elm and I'll have her.

Why do they run at dusk? Don't they have any fear about that rush of darkness that comes on so quickly at this hour at this time of year? It is mid-fall. The day dies in a hurry at around 4.30 p.m.

Two hundred more feet and she is on top of me. I reach into my gym bag and I remove the bottle. I hurriedly pop the top and pour the ether onto the wad of balled-up T-shirt. The odor rises so rapidly that I'm almost woozy, but I cork the bottle and I hold the saturated pad downwind from myself.

Fifty more feet and she'll be here.

The blade is in my right hand. I've taken it from my leather jacket's pocket. No scent emanates from that finely honed steel.

I can't tell the color of her running shorts nor can I discern the hue of the jacket she wears. It is already too dim. The sand and the water are behind her now and the beach has been deserted for the better part of a month. It is late October, the middle of this preparatory month of the year. Fall is like the fluttering inside a cardiac's chest. They say that readiness is all. But I can't remember where I read it.

1

She is fifteen feet away as I rise from my crouch. In three strides I appear before her in the middle of her running lane. The young woman cannot stop in time to avoid me. I lurch at her and I clamp the soaked sleep-laden cloth over her suddenly oval-shaped lips.

My runner doesn't even have time to scream.

Chapter Two

He was reading poems to me as we headed toward the Lakeshore. Doc, the PhD copper with the degree in English Literature from Northwestern University in Evanston. He was reading poetry to his guinea homicide brother detective. Some Polish woman who'd just won the Nobel Prize for Literature in Stockholm, Sweden. I told him the Swedes are better known for big tits and manic depression, but he never skipped a beat, he just went on reading to me until we arrived on scene.

He was driving our new squad car – a navy blue Taurus that any street cheesedick could make as a copper ride in less than a heartbeat. But we're homicides, so we didn't usually have to sneak up on anyone's ass.

We saw the lights and the yellow barrier ribbons as we came to a halt. I saw my temporary partner from a few years back. Jack Wendkos. He worked a double homicide with me when Doc was supposedly retired in order to finish his thesis at that very expensive university, north of the city. Doc never landed a teaching position, so he came moping back to homicide just in time to help me finish off several murders at a place called Cabrini Green. It was the time I lost two women inside twelve calendar months. First my wife, Erin, died of breast cancer. Then the woman I fell in love with later on found a way to get herself removed from my life via a street punk named Abu Riad. But that was another thing altogether.

'Jack. How've you been?'

'Jimmy. Just fine. I see the senior partner is still breathing.'

'Hiya, sonny. What've you got for us?' Doc cracked.

'I don't know that I can describe this one for you, Lieutenant Parisi.' Wendkos grinned. It was one sorry-assed grin, too.

'That bad?' I asked.

He headed toward the victim.

'Jesus. Holy Jesus,' Doc lamented. I mean he truly sounded sad, moved. And he'd seen more stiffs than I had by a far piece.

The plastic had already been removed from her remains, and I felt as if the air had been sucked out of my lungs.

'Oh my,' was all I managed. I couldn't come up with any on-site quip.

She was torn open from the throat to the pubic hair. Now I knew why all the uniforms were keeping their distance from this victim. They didn't want to become ill: it was considered pussy to lose your dinner in front of a trio of homicide investigators.

I noticed the half-dozen or so stab wounds below the slit that had eviscerated this young woman. I also saw that her eyes were closed. Interesting. Either the knife guy closed the lids, which I doubted, or she was knocked out while he did his cutting.

'Yeah. Her eyes are closed. I can see that,' Doc told the forensics officer. 'See if you can get any prints off the lids or off the eyeballs.'

The evidence copper was not enthusiastic about getting very close to our corpse. He looked like he was becoming a bit green. But he was part of the same fraternity we were and he clenched his cojones and decided he was not going to back away like some of the uniforms had.

4

Doc put his latex on and so did I. Jack Wendkos had the gloves on when we arrived.

'Beautiful girl. She was until a little while ago, anyway,' Wendkos said.

'The ME is en route?' I asked Jack.

'Yeah. He's on the way. I'm sure he'll look into an assault. But other than the stab wounds and the gaping slice, it doesn't appear that she was cut or abused elsewhere. At least I couldn't make any bruises, contusions or whatever.'

Jack was a blond Polski with an oft-broken nose from his days in Golden Gloves. He took a second at his peak, and the guy who took first in that same bout ruined an otherwise GQ-handsome puss. He'd look like an actor if it weren't for the mauled beak.

Dr Gray pulled up just then. He strode slowly toward us.

'Why is it that we never meet socially?' The doctor grinned. 'I always get to say hello to you all in front of some flat-on-her-or-his-ass stranger ... What've we got?'

He never waited for an answer. He always went right at it. When he found out what he was after, he had some of the quickest response time I'd ever seen from his branch of the department.

'We'll have to wait to see on the sexual contact, if there was any. I can't make a quick visual, Jimmy. Even with the klieg lights it was too hard to see. But it looks like he was a cutter, not a putter.'

It was his little bon mot for a rapist. No one ever laughed. Including Dr Gray. He was a very serious medical examiner.

When we'd scoured the immediate area, we wrapped it up when Gray said his preliminaries were finished. The doctor came up to Gibron, my partner, and Jack Wendkos. It seemed that Jack had been assigned by our red-headed Captain to assist us.

'She is missing some equipment, Jimmy. Boys, there are

5

some missing parts in this stiff. I know because I took Anatomy. Got an 'A' in dissection, too.'

'What are you talking about?' I asked the ME.

'There are a few organs missing is what I mean. As in major organs that are required to keep the motor running. As in liver, one of her lungs, and the big pump, as well.'

'Her heart?' Jack asked.

'Yes indeed. The crux of her very being. The very subject of all that Valentine's Day malarkey. The pump that pushes that serum through her arteries – at least, it pushed all that blood around sometime earlier in the day . . . I'll give you a call, Jimmy. Doc. See you, young Officer Wendkos.'

He walked toward his car. He never turned back to us.

'Don't even say it,' I warned Doc.

He wanted to hit me with the FBI attitude. But he had nothing good to say about the FBI and neither of us liked working with the Fibbies. The only Federals we really respected were the US Marshal's people. Most of the hackers and cutters we got were not nearly as flamboyant or bizarre. We got guys who sliced and diced and chopped, but had an average IQ of about twenty in the hole. No super-villains or geniuses.

'So is it a sex thing or a control thing or is it all or none of the above?' Doc mused out loud.

Jack Wendkos snapped his latex and Doc and I involuntarily jerked to attention.

'That's a good way to get your ass shot off on a site like this.' Doc smiled. It was another particularly lame grin he shot us.

'Sorry,' Jack told us. Then he walked toward his vehicle. 'I'll see you both downtown in a few minutes.'

Doc removed his gloves smoothly and quietly.

'So you don't think this cutter eats what he kills,' Gibron murmured.

I snapped off my pair of latex, and it caught my senior partner off guard, just like Jack had.

'Goddammit, that ain't funny at all, Jimmy P.'

6

He looked spooked, truly scared, so I didn't press my luck. This had been the most silent crime scene I'd ever worked.

The specialists had the body bagged, and they were putting her aboard the retrieval vehicle. Some people – old-timers – still call it a hearse.

Chapter Three

There was a war for me. There is always a war for a man in this country. It was fought over the usual. Property. Texas Tea, more specifically. Oil. Mideastern black gold. We killed a quarter-million Iraqis. It was like popping mallards in a barrel.

I was a medic. The medical field seems to have been my calling. No pun intended. It took me just six months to get myself canned from med school. It seems I had a drug problem. I say 'seems' because I wasn't the one with the problem – my customers had the addictions, I didn't. The people at the U were not at all forgiving. They threatened to put the police on me if I didn't leave the school immediately, so it wasn't as if I had a choice. Which led me eventually to where I am today. You might say I'm an 'arm' of the medical profession.

It was a pity that I washed out of the business. No one's better with a knife than I am. I can cut you and you don't feel the incision until you see yourself leaking all over the floor. I'm that good. No shit. That good.

What I do is called immoral, but I don't see it as any more horrible than what we did to those poor raghead bastards in the Gulf. They came out of their holes with their hands high in the air begging for us not to slaughter them. They were just as innocent as the innocents I meet up with in my new business venture, so who's to say what's murder and what's justifiable homicide? I'm no lawyer, but I don't see much distinction between the killings. The government said it was all right so we capped a quarter-million sand niggers. I do a little business on my own and I'm like that gay blade from Victorian England. You have to admit that the line I walked across is rather blurred, don't you?

It is what I do, after all. And a very good living it is. All I need is a little ether and one workable blade. There are no middlemen on my end.

The remarkable thing is that they all come running, literally running, to me. I never have to seek possibilities. They find me as surely as if I were a human magnet.

All I need to do is wait for them and suddenly there they are. Right at my feet.

And the best part of the whole sweet deal for them is that it is absolutely painless. They never feel the initial incision. Their sleep is always, always undisturbed.

Chapter Four

We were waiting in the weeds because Doc was sure that this guy would hit again. We were not playing by the rule that said we waited until he struck repeatedly so that we could start putting together a pattern. Killers like this guy wanted to come back to a location where they felt comfortable. The Lakeshore was a great place for a hit because there was plenty of natural cover for someone like our guy. Trees, brush, vegetation of all kinds. Plenty of places to lurk behind. Anybody on their own was like the antelope that brought up the drag on a herd. He got picked off as a straggler.

Doc had his headset on and was listening to his jazz station from Evanston. I was the ears for the first hour. Jack Wendkos was parked with another detective in a car near the edge of the beach.

The police decoy's name was Edna Millett. She was just out of the Academy, so I was nervous about the whole concept of staking her out like that African antelope at the ass end of the herd. She had volunteered for this, and there was no reason for our red-headed Captain to deny her request. Not with all the sexual harassment and discrimination suits that were flying around the City. So she got her wish. Edna was armed, but it would only take a second to slash her throat, and the killer would be back into the weeds before we could come help her.

The ME, Dr Gray, had explained to us that the stabbing wounds below that gutting slit were done post-mortem. In other words, the cutter waited until after the fact to tear her corpse up a little more. Our copper shrinks told us it was a sign of rage. Doc thought our psychiatrists had an uncanny sense of the obvious.

'No shit, the guy was angry. Who cuts open a live human being, helps himself to her major internal organs, and then gouges the living shit out of her thighs and lower abdomen? No, this guy is definitely an unhappy person,' Doc cracked.

Wendkos raised me on the hand-held radio.

'Anything, Jimmy?'

'Doc is listening to Thelonious Monk. He always tells me who it is I'm not hearing. Him and his headset.'

'Let me hear from you. I'm getting nervous over this kid Edna . . . When is she due?'

'In about two minutes. You got any shakes from where you two are sitting?'

He was paired with Neil Pierson, a brother Homicide.

'Nothing. Slow night.'

I could hear Wendkos's partner rustling some papers. Either a newspaper or some fast-food wrappers. It was hard to tell over the hand-helds.

I clicked off.

'Dave Brubeck.' Doc pointed to his headset. '"Blue Rondo à la Turk".' He smiled.

He started bobbing his head like a teenager whose ear was attached to a boombox.

Then we heard a rustling about twenty yards straight in front of our position, which was behind two thick oak trees.

'It's a little early for Edna, ain't it?' Doc asked when I tapped his shoulder twice.

He tore off the headphones and clicked off the radio in his jacket pocket.

11

'Edna? Where are you?' I asked into the headset I put on. Edna was hooked up with a small earpiece and a microphone on top of her bulletproof vest and windbreaker.

'I'm about two hundred yards from your position by the trees . . . You *are* at those twin oaks, right?'

She sounded as nervous as I was. She was a twenty-four-year-old kid. An ex-stewardess who thought cross-country flights with geezers who told sexually suggestive jokes to her were a giant drag. So she entered the Academy and became a copper.

'We're right where we're supposed to be. There's someone else between us and you. Copy?'

'Where?'

'About fifty yards to forty yards in front of us. You want us to check him and abort?'

'I'm running out of distance. I should be almost on top of him.'

'Fuck it, Edna. If it feels wrong we'll pop him before you go another step. Say it now. Hurry!'

'I'll keep going. Pull up behind him. Copy?'

'We're coming out, Edna. Keep your eyes open and palm that fucking Nine.'

I radioed Wendkos we had a shake. I told him the approximate location of that sound I heard, and then the four of us were closing the ground between the noise and Doc and me. Wendkos was approaching the intruder from the east; we were headed north. There was a lot of undergrowth between us and Edna and between us and whatever was a few feet in front of us. It was a black night. No moon. Total cloud cover. But we couldn't hit whoever was crunching through the vegetation in front of us because he would bolt, and then we wouldn't know if he had bad thoughts about our young ex-stewardess.

Forty yards into our sprint and I heard her.

'Don't you move!' she shrieked loudly enough for Doc and me to hear clearly. But we still couldn't see her. Too much greenery still obscured her.

In fifteen or twenty more strides we were in a clearing

12

and we could now see Edna. She had assumed the shoot position, her hands and arms extended before her. She had the Nine gripped in both hands, and it was pointed straight ahead of her at a kneeling figure.

When we finally got close enough, we saw that the kneeling man was wearing only a T-shirt and a pair of gym shoes. When Doc flashed the big light on the guy, we saw 'Why Bother?' printed on the back of the white T-shirt.

We rushed around him and saw that he had no pants or underwear on. He was quivering like a pooch that had been left out in a thunderstorm.

'Jesus, don't shoot me! I di'n't mean nothin'!'

Then he vomited. Right over Edna's expensive running shoes. I had this revulsion churning inside me. Edna was a pretty girl. Brunette. Well put together. And she'd left all those nice, sterile flights across North America to wind up in a pitch-dark park by Lake Michigan so that some cheesedick wienie-flasher could expose himself to her and then puke all over her toes. It didn't seem dignified to me. It didn't seem worth all that trouble for a woman to make it through the Police Academy.

'I should shoot you for getting sick all over this nice young lady,' Doc told the half-naked quiverer.

'Please don't shoot me!'

'Shut the fuck up!' Doc snapped.

Wendkos and Pierson had finally arrived.

'We got lost in these weeds,' Jack apologized.

'You didn't miss a thing,' I told the two late arrivals.

Pierson started to snigger.

'You aren't really gonna shoot me, are you?' the kneeling man whined.

'Take off your shirt,' Doc demanded.

There were three flashlights trained on this johnson-waggler.

'Huh?'

'Take off that shirt or I'll shoot you right in your prized possession,' Gibron told him.

13

The shaking man tore off his T-shirt.

'Now wipe the lady's shoes. And I mean clean.'

Three more uniformed patrolmen emerged from the surrounding trees and bushes. They watched as the flasher cleaned up Edna's Adidas footwear. The flashlights were still aimed at her shoes as he finally finished the job.

'Now put that T-shirt back on,' Doc concluded.

'You can't be—'

'Motherfucker, you get that thing on your back or I'll kick your sorry ass all the way downtown. When we get there, *then* you can take it off,' Doc Gibron explained.

I saw the perp wince as he put the shirt back on, just as Doc had ordered him. Wendkos cuffed him, and then Doc and I walked him back to our Taurus. Edna was riding back to the downtown headquarters with us.

The flasher got into the back seat with me. I didn't want this reeking, butt-naked asshole sitting next to Edna on the long ride. I saw that she was grateful as I indicated that I'd be sitting in the back seat with her very first perpetrator.

This guy was a pee-pee-wiggler. Nothing more. We went back to the park and found his pants, but there was no sign of a knife. He didn't appear to be a cutter. We charged him with assault and public indecency and with a couple other minor beefs, but he was not our guy.

He had no ether on him, either. He would have had no place to keep all the things our man had used in the killing of Genevieve Malone, the girl who went down in that same stretch of woods by the beach.

Randall Osborne had a sheet, though. He'd exposed himself twice before. Been nailed both times for short hitches in County. But no trace of violent behavior, so we had apparently come up empty.

The ether showed up on the corpse and in the blood work-ups Dr Gray had done at the morgue. So we knew our cutter put them to sleep and then did what he did to them. As I say, Doc was convinced that this wouldn't be a one-time Charlie. The man did a very workmanlike job of

14

removing Genevieve's innards. That was all pro work-manship. The thing that disturbed me was the little rage number with the post-mortem mutilations. It was like this guy was of two minds. First he took care of business, and then he thought he owed himself a little something for all the effort and for all the potential danger. If he just wanted to kill and maim, why take all the trouble to be fastidious about the initial cutting? And then get sloppy and brutal with the remaining thrusts? I didn't like mystery homi-cides. I enjoyed the no-brainers, just as my partner the good doctor did.

Randall went to jail and Edna was beginning to wonder if she could ever get the stink off her Adidas shoes.

'Stick 'em in the washing machine,' Doc suggested. The three of us were in my office. It was very late. Way past the end of our regular shifts.

'Are you kidding?' she retorted. 'These are three-hun-dred-dollar runners. I'll do these by hand.'

She was a pretty girl. Reminded me of another pretty police employee that I was two hours late meeting up with. Natalie Manion, our evidence expert. The redhead and love of my middle-aged life.

Edna left the office, but the cheesy odor of vomit lingered.

'Open the fucking window,' Doc groaned. 'I couldn't say it before because I thought I'd embarrass the kid.'

I went over to the window that overlooked the Lake and propped the window open with the crank that extended the glass outward.

A fresh breeze from Lake Michigan wafted into my cubicle.

'The Captain pisses and moans when we open these. He says it upsets the fucking thermostats,' I told my partner.

'The Boss didn't have two pukey shoes in his office,' Doc countered. 'You think I jumped the gun by putting together this little ambush at the Lake, Jimmy?'

'I don't think so. No. I trust your intuition.'

'This guy might like to expand his horizons, his hunting grounds. I was hoping we'd get lucky.'

I nodded. Doc knew that I thought his call was a good one. If we had caught the prick tonight, we could've saved a life. Suddenly the scary thought was inside us both. I could see it on his face. There would be another cutting very soon. Maybe elsewhere, maybe right back where we just were, at the Lakeshore. But this time we wouldn't be there because manpower cost big money. Everybody knew that dirge.

Doc got up wearily.

'I thought we had a good shot ... I don't like clever killers, Jimmy. They try too hard to be smart, evasive. I got the feeling we just dialed up one of that very kind. Get ready for the long haul, Jimmy P.'

He waved and left my cubicle. The odor of the retch-covered gym shoes had finally departed the premises, so I cranked my window shut. But the fragrance of the Lake and of the beach lingered.

My phone rang. I knew it was Natalie and I knew I was in a pile of something that made Edna's shoes smell like a springtime garland.

Chapter Five

Fog occurs when two air masses overrun each other. I heard that somewhere. Perhaps it was the weather man on TV. But in the late fall you'd expect a lot of overrun since those two opposing forces – fall and summer – are having it out for the last time until the next go-round, a few months later.

It certainly is a convenient atmosphere for my line of work. It was almost as convenient as the thick environment of the woods where I last did business, down by the Lakeshore.

I spent an hour in advance of this detail, walking out along this so-called Gold Coast. It was one of the most affluent areas in the city. Downtowners and yuppies of all stripes inhabit these city blocks. If I were a thief – which, I suppose, is sort of what I am – I could make a very fine living in this neighborhood. If you pay attention to the kinds of security these people employ, you can devise ways of getting at these Gold Coasters. Usually it is a doorman or some security guard.

In this instance I've already eliminated the employee who oversaw the entrance of this multi-level dwelling. He was the fellow with the very sore throat who lies behind me at this very moment.

I'm waiting for the blonde, thirty-five-ish female who left to go out about three hours ago. I've been following her for about three days, and I've learned her habits by this time. She likes to go to a late dinner at one of the expensive Loop restaurants.

Usually it is a sports-theme bar-eatery. Then she returns home by no later than one since she is a lawyer in a firm, also in the downtown district. She does not allow herself to become attached to any of the several males who circle about her as she takes two or three cocktails at the bar before she is seated for an always-solo dinner. When she returned for two or three nightcaps at that same pre-meal bar, it was time for Delores Winston to hire a cab and go home to her Gold Coast apartment.

I couldn't catch her on foot, alone, so the best plan seemed to be to take her here in the entryway to the building. It is a small cubicle. But it works well because it appears that most of the other residents of this complex are well into their senior years and none of them keeps late hours like our counselor, Delores Winston.

I knocked on the door and asked Jason, the fellow lying behind me on the floor, for directions. He was very helpful. He opened the door to answer me. Then I flattened him with a thrust from the base of my right palm, and while he was gurgling something or other at me on account of his badly broken nose, I bent down, took him by his long brown hair and slit his throat from ear to ear. He tried to stem the flow with both his hands, but the dam had broken and Jason expired in a few minutes. Most of the blood gushed down onto his scarlet sport jacket. It was a little difficult to spot the stain in this dim lighting.

I too am wearing a scarlet sport jacket in advance of the return of Delores the attorney. And if anyone should defy an observance of habit and come home late, I suppose I'll have to kill them as well. There could be quite a pile of bodies in this entryway by dawn if Delores doesn't move it along.

Ah, but her cab finally arrives. I can only barely make her out through the fog that is wafting in off Lake Michigan. The driver hustles around to the door to let her out. Apparently he had an eye for a large gratuity. Then she is floating toward me. I keep my head down as she puts her gloved left hand on the door handle. I help her open the glass entry, and before she can cry out, I have the wad of ether clamped over her pretty mouth. Her eyes widen as she tries to struggle, but I have one hand over her mouth and the other squeezing her throat. The fumes do their thing and Delores is slumping to the floor next to Jason the doorman. Just as she goes out, she notices the body next to her own. I can see the recognition crossing her dimming eyes.

It is about 1.15, I see, as I look at my watch. Time to get to work.

Then it occurs to me that I've been all business and no pleasure. I think I owe it to myself to reap the rewards of my work. Certainly once I finish with this flat-on-her-ass lawyer I will not be able to enjoy her. I hadn't seen the need for romantic contact with my previous client, but it seems as if this one is special. She is about my age, whereas the other girl was too young. I have no inclination toward females in their twenties and younger. They are far too immature, too inclined to chew gum and smoke cigarettes. At the same time. They are too inclined to look at sex as some kind of physical release. Women in their thirties and older, however, seem to understand the spiritual side of human sexuality. They have reached their sexual peaks and so they experience much more fully what this carnal contact is supposed to entail. It is not just a fuck to them, I'm saying.

It is too bad that Delores won't be around for this brief encounter. I'm willing to take a chance, here, by delaying my work, but I'm not foolhardy enough to stick around for an entire symphony.

I tear her dress from the neck to the crotch with my nine-inch blade. Then I rip away her bra and panties as well. Delores is very well maintained. She is in full blossom.

I pull her over to Jason, and I position her rear on top of Jason's midsection. Angle of entry. If she were awake she'd realize my little enhancement of pleasure. Just looking at her prepares me. She is a beautiful, ripe woman.

I pull down my zipper, I elevate her legs, I kneel down close to her, and I begin.

Her mouth is wide open, but she does not snore amid her slumbers. I tell myself that I can't take the time I would enjoy taking, that I must end this before someone stumbles upon us, *the three of us. And I wonder if Jason is sensing the urgency I now have at finishing. He is our still-warm cushion. He pads us from the cold concrete floor beneath the three of us.*

Then I am coming in Delores. A sweet throb. But not nearly as sweet or as prolonged as I had imagined. It is because I am rushed, I'm certain.

I stand and pull up my fly. There is a salty, sea-water odor in the close air of this entryway.

I pick up my knife and look down at the stretched-out body of Delores Winston, prominent Loop lawyer. I aim my thin-nosed blade at the point beneath her breastbone and I make my first incision. It is a red line that extends, now, to her pubic patch. I am almost reluctant to cut her any deeper than this delineating line that stretches from breasts to puff of pubic hair, but time grows very short. There is no more of it to waste, standing here desiring this blonde woman again.

I place the tip of my ultra-sharp knife at my starting point, but this time the knife goes in. Goes in deeply.

I can hear the very soft giving-up of Delores Winston's flesh as my tool embeds itself in her chest cavity.

Chapter Six

Natalie Manion was the woman who came into my life just as I thought my life was ending. I lost my wife, Erin, to breast cancer, and then I fell in love with a woman named Celia Dacy. Celia'd had her son murdered at a housing project called Cabrini Green and I was the lead investigator, along with Doc Gibron. We got involved in spite of my knowing that getting entangled with a person involved in a case is strictly out of bounds. But I fell in love with her only to find out later that Celia had capped three of the primary suspects in her son Andres's murder investigation. So I lost my wife and I fell in love with the most beautiful killer I had ever encountered. Then Celia got herself topped by going after the nastiest gang-banger in the Cabrini district, and I was there on scene holding her as the life evaporated out of her.

To say that it put me out of commission was to understate the experience.

I met Natalie Manion while I was working the Dacy homicides. Natalie was working in the lab tech department. But now she was about to graduate from the Academy so she could become a street policewoman. She said she wanted to work Homicide with me.

I told her that she should plan on a different section in the Department because Chicago PD frowned on fraternization between co-workers. She said she didn't care. We would fool them by appearing aloof. But it was all bullshit because everybody on my floor knew I was in love with Natalie Manion. They accused me of robbing the cradle with the redhead because she was twenty years younger than I was. None of which phased this lovely, auburn-haired woman. She had been in the Air Force for four years, and she also had a master's in Criminology from her alma mater, Northwestern. She was just a little bit extraordinary, as I said.

I was at her apartment at 7.00 a.m. She went on shift – her first practice tour – at 3.00 p.m. We ate breakfast together and then we made love and then I had to get home to help take care of my teenaged daughter and my almost-teenaged son. My mother lived with us in our North Side bungalow. We were a couple of miles north-west of Wrigley Field, even though I had been a White Sox fan since 1957.

'You tired, Jimmy?'

I smiled at her. 'We're always tired.'

'Screwy shifts. But I'll be out on the street in another two months, come graduation.'

'That's what I'm afraid of, Natalie. Little red-headed you, out on these lovely streets. With all those very bad hombres. You're going to give me high blood pressure.'

'You've already got hypertension, Jimmy P.'

Leave it to her to know the medical term.

'I forgot,' I apologized.

'I thought I was good for you, Jimmy.'

'You are.'

I took her up out of her seat. We were sitting next to each other at what she called her breakfast 'nook'. I never sat across from Natalie. It was too goddamned far away from her.

I pulled her up to me and kissed her until she insisted she couldn't breathe.

'Go back into evidence or you'll scare me to death,' I told her.

'We've been down this road before, guinea. That's a negative, Lieutenant.'

There was no use. It was just as she said. I lost the argument in a humiliating fashion. She creamed me. She was better educated and smarter than I was. She would likely make a better investigator than I was. Natalie would succeed at anything she wanted to succeed at.

'So come on. Tell me about it. I haven't got a weak stomach.'

I looked at her carefully as we got back to our chairs. She refused to make love in her breakfast goddamned nook. Said savages mate where they eat.

'We find two bodies. The woman on top of a male. She was naked, eviscerated, just like the first. The guy beneath her was the doorman. His throat was cut, ear to ear. He probably died in a hurry. She was dosed with ether, but this time he did her sexually. No semen. But the cute son of a bitch left us a Trojan wrapper inside the woman's split-open torso. He took the liver, a lung, and the big pump. Same stuff, except that he didn't mutilate this one. Other than the "surgery" he did on her.'

'Why do you think he didn't cut her up more?'

'He had sex with this one, or so we're led to believe. At least it was the message he left behind.'

'So what're you and Mr Gibron looking at?'

'Known sex offenders. Rapists. Assault guys. The usual starting point. And then there's this parts-removal business.'

'Is he taking organs and selling them?'

'Could be. Unless he's got another use for them. Maybe it was just psychosexual. We're not getting much help from the shrinks at work. They're not sure what this guy's really after.'

'What if it was a woman, Jimmy P? A woman who wants you to think it was a man.'

'The attack on the door guy. He was popped with enough force that we thought it was a male. And the first girl, Genevieve Malone. She was struck in the face and

leveled. We don't think a female could knock down someone as athletic as Malone was with one punch. Someone
strong had to stifle both victims with that ether. It told me
it was a male. By the sheer weight and bulk and muscle.
But I could be wrong.'

'Aren't you politically correct.'

I looked at her and she knew we had talked enough
shop. Our time together was too precious, too sacred, to
waste it on business. Until we got our schedules in sync,
we were loving each other on a hit-and-run basis.

'Marry me,' I told her.

'That's number 286,' she smiled.

'Number 287. Marry me.'

'And I told you I will. When I—'

'Graduate, get settled on the job, and find out what
section you're assigned to. I can't wait.'

'Neither can I,' she admitted as she kissed me hard on
the lips.

'Will you relent, then?' I asked.

'I probably will. Let's talk about something else,' she
insisted, as she led me to her small bedroom.

We had three possibles, via the computer. Sex offenders
all. Two had a history of violence. All three had spent
time in jail.

We ran into Marco Karrios at his nearby North Side
home.

'Hello, Marco,' Doc smiled.

Karrios was walking down the flight of steps in front of
the three flats where he occupied the middle apartment.
Marco was educated. Worked for himself in stocks and
bonds. No one had hired him because of his record, so he
was fortunate to be a middling genius in the stock market.
He lived in a decent if not affluent hood, but he drove a
new BMW.

'Do I need to call my lawyer?' the blond, muscular man
asked us.

We were standing in the wind. The hawk was blowing in from the northeast this afternoon. Straight off the Lake.

'This is simply a friendly talk,' Doc informed him. 'You want a mouth, you could be hung up here all day. We just have a few questions and then you can boogie.'

Marco thought it over. He had been arrested three times. Twice the charges were dropped. We thought he had intimidated the two teenaged victims into backing off, but we could get no cooperation from the girls or their families. So he walked. The third time the victim was a thirty-year-old legal secretary. She did cooperate, but the judge was a limpdick and gave Marco two years for a minor sex beef.

'Okay. Let's make this quick. Time is money, gentlemen.'

'It says in your file that you were in the military. That right?' Doc asked.

I looked into the blond guy's eyes. I watched his shoulders and torso. I was looking for some body language. Something.

'I was. That's correct.'

'You serve out of country?'

'Yes. I was in the Middle East.'

'And you went to medical school, it says here,' Doc continued.

'And I flunked out,' Marco responded.

He shifted his shoulders and shrugged, but I was not sure if he was simply uncomfortable with Doc's directness.

'You flunked out?' Gibron asked. 'A smart guy like you?'

'I wasn't fit. I never really wanted it. My parents were big on having a doctor in the family. Greek immigrants, you know?'

'A blond guy like you? A Greek?' Doc smiled.

'Lots of Greeks are blonds. Depends on which part of the country you're from.'

'Can you account for your whereabouts on these two dates?'

Doc shoved the documents in front of him. Karrios stared at the two for a while, and then a smile formed on his lips.

'I was with my girlfriend. Both dates.' He grinned.

There was no movement from him this time. His body settled firmly in place.

'Where does your girlfriend live and what's her name?' Gibron prodded.

'Ellen Jacoby. She lives with me. Would you like to have a talk with her? She's home right at this moment.'

Now it was a full, bright smile. He showed Doc and me all those teeth, and their whiteness almost shot out a glint, a gleam of their own.

Ellen Jacoby concurred when confronted with the dates. He'd been with her all the time on both evenings in question. She was a brunette. Not pretty. But seemingly very sexual. There was something seeping out of her. She had long, dark, curly hair, and she sent out some very strong signals. I could see why Karrios overlooked the cosmetic beauty.

'Is that all you wanted to know?' she asked, eyeballing me until she obviously expected me to break our inter-locked glances. But I outlasted her, and she finally stared in the direction of her man, Marco Karrios. When the two of them locked up, eyeball to eyeball, Doc nudged me and we got the hell out of there before those two started dropping their pants on the spot.

Outside, Doc asked the obvious.

'You like him?' he queried.

'No. But I like *her* a lot better.'

Gibron laughed briefly, but then his face went serious as we made our way back to the car.

Chapter Seven

I went to funerals. The idea was that killers sometimes liked to relive their crimes by being around the mourners of their victims. I didn't remember ever catching somebody at a funeral or at a wake, but I figured I would take any edge I could get. Someday it might work out.

But not at Delores Winston's service, out here at Oak Hill Cemetery on the far South Side. The only attendees were a mother, a sister, Doc, Jack Wendkos, and me. It seemed that Delores had been a loner in life, and that was the way she was going out, too.

No one looked remotely like a potential cutter. Unless the guys working for the mortuary were double-dipping as moonlighting killers.

Delores's mother, Frances, thanked the three of us for coming on out here.

'I know you don't have to do this,' she smiled sadly.

'Actually we do. We come out to have a look at the folks in attendance, Mrs Winston,' I explained. 'But we would've come anyway. We get more involved in things like this than most people imagine.'

She looked a bit confused, so I didn't try to clarify anything.

'I'm very sorry for your loss,' Jack said as he extended a hand to the bereaved mother.

Doc nodded and shook her hand, and then we walked toward the parking lot and the two cars we'd arrived in.

I was telling her the truth. Delores was not just a number on the board for Doc and me. Or for Jack, either. It became personal. When I started doing the reading on each of the victims I investigated, the first thing that hit me, over and over again, was that each of them had a history. Every one of the dead had a mother and a father, at least initially, and every one of them spent nine months *in utero*, and they all popped out the chute thereafter in order to learn to stop dirtying their underwear, to grow up, to make friends, to play ball or ride a bike, to mature, to have a life – and then to have some murderous piece of shit end it with a knife or a gun or a lead pipe or whatever. Yeah, they all had a background. I knew because I read about them. I did research on each one of them. And then some miserable son of a bitch stopped time on them and the file closed.

That was when Doc and I entered the picture.

I was thinking this guy was in business with the organs. I don't think he was a Jeffrey Dahmer cannibal. I can't imagine him storing the vitals in some freezer as a trophy. Some of the shrinks who advised us downtown had that theory about our man – who had now acquired the name 'The Farmer'. I don't like nicknames for murderers. It gave them too much opportunity for gaining space and headlines in the newspapers. They got a 'rep' and then they had to live up to it, again and again. It all fed their fires.

'We checked the hospitals,' Doc concurred. 'We had some of our people see how many body parts are being used as compared to the number of surgeries they had on the books. And then we hit our contacts to see if anyone's doing a side-order business, because you know this guy is not exactly working legit.'

I grimaced at him and he smiled.

'We'll never find anything by asking the hospitals. If they're getting illegal supplies, there ain't going to be any paper trail,' Doc admitted. 'So who'd know all about a highly illegal activity like black-market body parts?'

He was grinning at me.

'I find that remark highly racist, Doctor.'

'All you guineas are so goddam *sensitive*.'

Billy Cheech – William Ciccio – was the cousin of an Outfit guy that Doc and I had launched into Joliet Prison a few years back. Danny Cheech was the Don before he was busted. Busted for having several Loop restaurant-goers gunned to death in a botched attempt to kill some piece of shit Ciccio wanted gone. We finally got him before an IRA assassin got to this Outfit asshole.

Billy was on the periphery with the Chicago version of the Mafia. He and Danny and I were all distant cousins. Which was nothing my side of the *familia* had ever been too proud of. But I always liked Billy. And my little cousin had always had the bad habit of confiding in me when he thought the outlaw side of the clan had gone over the edge. In other words I had used my own cousin as an informant from time to time. Nothing big. I didn't want him to get wasted because of his generosity in providing his coz with information that could be harmful to Billy's health. The days of *omerta* – total silence – had gone. Gotti was in the pen and Sammy the Bull had a book out, I heard. There was no Don Corleone 'honor' on the streets. There probably never was. These guys did their grannies if the price was right. Honor among thieves and murderers was Hollywood's version of these wastes of flesh. They had no honor. They were businessmen without a code to do business by. I had never found them romantic or amusing or attractive.

Billy Cheech was a little simple, and that was why he talked to a cousin he knew was a homicide investigator. All of his associates thought he was goofy, too, but he was related to the one-time big boss, Danny, so they gave the silly kid a little room to be stupid.

Doc and I ran into him at the garage where he was allowed to change oil. One of his cousins owned the place, of course. He was under the hood of a Jaguar at the moment. This oil place catered to the wealthy, it appeared. There were BMWs and 'Vettes and a few Lexuses.

'You stealing from the rich now, Robin Hood?' I asked him.

He banged his head on the way out from under the car hood.

'Jesus fuckin' Christ! . . . Jimmy! Cousin! And you got the good Doctor with you!'

Doc had told him twenty times to stop calling him the 'Good Doctor'. Billy got under Gibron's hide. I had to drag him with me to visit my second cousin every time I was looking for a little freebie intelligence on the Outfit.

'You wanna oil change for that piece-a-shit fuckin' Ford?'

'Nah. The Department takes care of the maintenance, Billy . . . You got a minute?'

His jocular mood vanished. He knew why I was here now.

'You wanna get some lunch, Jimmy? Doc? It is that time of the day anyhow.'

Billy excused himself to go wash up after he slammed the hood on that Jaguar that was worth more than my mortgage.

He was back in a hurry. His hands were still filthy, but it was what I put up with for his freebies.

We drove to the Garvin Inn in Berwyn. It was a half-hour from his garage, but he was Billy Cheech and nobody was going to bitch about his two-hour lunch break. It was one of the perks of being connected, of being with a crew.

Garvin's was where Doc liked to take our noon breaks, no matter what time of day it really was. We could afford better, like at those overpriced theme hamburger joints

30

that cost you $8.95 for some browned ground chuck, but Gibron liked the brats and the Polish sausage and I never argued with him because there was something about the smelly-assed environment in Garvin's that appealed to me after all these years. I had never taken my children to Garv's. It was a male bar – except on weekend nights when the softball players dragged their wives and girl-friends (sometimes simultaneously) in here for an after-game brew.

Garvin limped toward us. The leg was courtesy of the Nazis at the Battle of the Bulge. Old man Garvin had fought with Patton, but I thought Patton was the weak sister of the two.

He took our order and limped away.

'So, Jimmy. What's the order of business today? Huh? What do you wanna know from your coz that won't get me dumped in the fuckin' Lake with concrete in my wingtips?'

'You been reading about the murders of those two women? You know, the ones who were what they called 'mutilated', down by Lakeshore Drive?'

'Yeah. I think I recall readin' about it. But you know we don't kill fuckin' civilians, Jimmy P. It is bad business. I'm not talkin' out of school or nothin', but you know I don't get involved in no shit like killin's. I'm small-fry, cousin. You know me.'

'I'm talking about some guy who might be marketing some real expensive goods. Like internal organs.'

Doc belched on his Diet Sprite, and then he excused himself to Billy with a grin.

'Oh man, I don't know about nothin' like that. You know how the crew is. They steal shit. They love stealin' shit. You know. Stuff at airports, trucks, trains. They like hoos and drugs . . . But killin' women for their hearts and kidneys and shit? I don't know, Jimmy P. Sounds like some freelancin' business to me. It was too, whatchoocall, 'high-profile'. These city crews don't like fuckin' head-lines. They like the dark. This is too fuckin' bright.'

31

'Your mama ever wash your mouth out?' Doc grinned at Billy.

'Jesus Christ, Doc. How come you're always on my ass?'

Doc went back to his brat, now that Garvin had brought the food and limped off down the bar again.

'Nah, Jimmy. I don't see this thing as our kinda thing. *Cosa nostra*, ya know?'

'Keep your ears open, Billy. There could be a few bucks in it for you if you help me out.'

'I'm not a rat, Jimmy P. I don't mind helpin' you when it don't hurt me, but I ain't no fuckin' rat – excuse my fuckin' French, Doc.'

'This guy's done two women, Billy,' Doc told him. 'He cut them open like a couple of fish and left them sprawled out naked. He gutted them like you'd tear open an animal. Then he carved out their insides and took off like the weasel he is.'

Billy Cheech looked down at his Polish sausage and at his beer with a look of disgust on his swarthy Sicilian face.

'Look. I hear anything, I'll let you know, cousin,' Ciccio told me. 'I suddenly lost my fuckin' appetite,' he growled toward Doc. 'I better get back to work.'

Doc smiled at him and suddenly clapped him on the shoulder.

'A member of a crew with a weak stomach. A new wrinkle,' Gibron teased. 'Sit back down and finish your lunch. Your boss isn't likely to call time on you ... We could use your help, Billy Cheech.'

My cousin looked my partner in the eyes, and then he sat down quietly and finished his meal.

Natalie was ready for the streets. That was what she told me after she finished her prep tours. I was at her graduation from the Academy with my mother, my two kids, and with Natalie's mother from Sioux City, Iowa. Her father died ten years ago. This was her whole family now, she said as she hugged me after the ceremony. She took off her white gloves, here at the rented arena where new coppers get their badges, and she put her hands in my hair and she rose up and kissed me. I felt embarrassed at first because my family had never seen me kiss anyone but my wife Erin, but the sensation fled and I was kissing her back. When we separated, I saw a smile on my daughter's teenaged face and on my mother's, Eleanor's, face too. My mother had been cheering on this relationship ever since I came home with the news that Celia Dacy had been killed by Abu Riad's bodyguards.

'She is very good people,' Eleanor informed me after first meeting Natalie Manion. 'You hang onto her. You need someone just like her. In fact you need *her*.'

Now Natalie was a member of the fraternity. She was really one of us. I could see her going plainclothes very quickly. She was intelligent, she had the education, and she had the experience from forensics. She would move up in a hurry, and her gender wouldn't stop her. I felt like I was about to be left behind in her rise to the top, somehow.

After the whooping was over, I took my family and Natalie and her mother to Mangione's for dinner. It was the best Italian food on the North Side. We all ordered the lasagna. I bought us a few carafes of red wine, and then I made a toast to her.

'You won't need anybody's help to go where you want to go. You'll make it all on your own. You are a first-rate rookie, and you'll make a first-rate detective in the near future. There are nothing but good things ahead for you, Natalie. And I love you.'

Then I took out the little box and put it on the table in front of her.

'What?' She smiled.

'Check it out for yourself, Officer Manion.'

'What is it, Daddy?' my daughter Kelly begged.

My son was thoroughly bored and he poked at his lasagna. My mother was already in tears, and so she hugged Laura, Natalie's mother.

Natalie opened the box and spied the ring.

'Oh my. Oh my,' was all she could whisper.

I knelt down next to her. She was sitting on the end of the booth, next to me.

'I love you, Natalie. No fooling. Marry me ... I lost count. How many times have I asked you, now? ... Will you?'

She looked at the ring, and then she looked up at me.

'Yes. I will. Anytime you want me to.'

I bent to her and I had my face against her stomach. Then she urged my face upward and she kissed me. When I stood, all I saw was feminine weeping. My daughter, my mother, and my mother-in-law-to-be. My son Michael was unmoved. He held his head with one hand and he continued to poke around at his meal. He was in his tough-guy mode, apparently.

The people in the half-dozen neighboring booths began to applaud, and so now I had to buy drinks for everyone in the vicinity.

Something new came over me. It was an unusual sensation for a man who dealt professionally with death. I felt like I was nineteen again. Not even out of college. I felt the way I did when I proposed to my children's mother. Here I was pushing fifty. I thought I could never breathe the same kind of free air that I had inhaled when Erin had said yes. That was the day the world made sense. Every part fit the puzzle. Things were finally sane and I knew why it was I'd begun breathing at birth. *This* was the reason I came out of Eleanor. This was why we all came from where we began. This moment told it all. The rest was nuts. The rest was crazy and unreadable.

Now it was Natalie. Now and tomorrow and every lucky day I had left. She made me able to throw my legs over the side of the bed every morning for as many mornings as there were left. I would never be an old man again. Not like I was after Erin and Celia left me. She came right into my way exactly when I needed her to, and here she sat before me. A man was never this fortunate. I wanted my family all to pinch me hard, make me know this was no dream, no illusion.

'Kelly. Michael. Natalie is going to be my wife. Not your mother, but my wife, and, I hope, your friend. She is a fine person and she wants to love you.'

My daughter slid over in the booth and embraced my fiancée. Michael sat impassively.

'Come here, Michael.'

I stood away from the booth. He got around the women and came to me. Now he was the one in tears. We walked two paces away from the table.

'Will you try to be happy for me? I know she's not Momma. There is no other Momma. But I love her, Bud. I do.'

'I miss Mommy.'

I choked back my words and there was nothing to say. Suddenly he broke away from me and he went to Natalie and kissed her softly and briefly on the cheek. When he sat back at his place, I sat down next to my future bride.

I looked over to my twelve-year-old boy. Everyone was quiet.

'You're a good man, Michael. You make your old man very happy.'

I took the carafe and I poured everyone a drink.

'I want everyone at this table to be as happy as I am for a hundred years.'

I took a swallow of wine and then I kissed the redhead fully on her lips. Everyone in the immediate area had been watching all this as if it were some kind of video, and so they applauded us once again. So I was bound to buy them another drink.

Michael had finally found his appetite, so he began to dig into his lasagna in earnest. The women and my daughter were too busy embracing each other, so finally I had time to cut myself a piece of the food before me.

I could taste the pasta and the sauce as if for the first time in decades, even though Erin and Celia had only been gone for a few months. A little over a year and a half, I thought it was. The colors were brighter in this room. I could smell the scent of Natalie even though the garlic odor permeated this Italian restaurant. Everything seemed to be pulsing. I was out of the prison I had been in. My incarceration had been self-imposed, but I was out. Past the walls and the restraints. It was something I couldn't even explain. I could feel the blood moving in my veins. I could hear my own respiration and I could sense everything inside me that was alive. And I thought, 'Here I am.' For the first time in a very long time, I was exactly where I wanted to be.

The brand-new police officer, still in dress blues, looked over to me and I was thawing in a luxurious relaxation.

'Let's run away tonight,' she whispered in my ear as she bent toward me.

Chapter Eight

*The herd swerves around the fountain and then makes its bovine way toward the south end of the shopping center. There are **sales** today. Some of these beeves have been here since dawn, walking the mall. It is their only source of entertainment. There is no sun and sky and landscape other than this. They drive hundreds of miles to Minnesota to arrive at the Mothership of Malls. Sales today! Deals!*

I see a brunette ahead who interests me. She seems to fit the age range. Thirty, thirty-five tops. Maybe a little younger. But she'll do.

I won't be able to approach her here, inside, but it is getting toward closing hour and eventually she'll make her way to her car. The crowds are beginning to thin. I'm on the second level, so I can see the numbers dwindling rapidly. It is a Sunday night. They have to rush home to watch their Movies of the Week. They have to prepare for another workweek. They put in forty-eight sets of five so they can retire to the fucking Wisconsin Dells in July or August. They mark the days on their calendars at work – perhaps in red ink. All year long they watch the X's accumulate until the merciful arrival of their four weeks vacation at some resort where their drunken neighbors will roll through the streets waking everyone up before dawn. They'll go lamely fishing for fucking walleye or some such fish, sitting out in a boat and shivering at sunrise, and they'll row the rented boat back to the dock, empty-handed. They're not outdoorsmen anyway. They're pencil pushers from the city on their four weeks' break from morbid monotony.

The brunette turns right and heads down the stairs toward the first level. If she leaves now, the parking lot will be too congested for me to do what I came to do to her. Or to someone a lot like her. She is replaceable. If not her, then someone else. I am adaptable to the situation. It is part of the trade. It is amazing how similar we all are when we're opened up with a knife. All that cosmetic beauty vanishes. We're just an ugly series of waterworks, plumbing.

She stops at a leather-goods outlet. She is not ready to go yet, then. I stop in front of a chain bookstore so I don't get too close to her. She hasn't spotted me yet.

The brunette is in the bootery for twenty minutes. There is nothing left for me to peruse in the bookstore's window, and the crowds in this mall have thinned almost to zero. It is time she made her move to the lot.

Which is what happens only two minutes later. The brown-haired woman exits via the front door and makes a beeline for the parking lot. She goes back up to the second level, and I am right behind her.

This one has her best features behind her. No tits that I can make out. A pleasant enough face, but nothing extraordinary. She'd be workable if I had the time to take pleasure in my job, but the whole scenario of a parking lot puts a number of restrictions on what I can and can't do.

When I walk out the door on the second level, right behind her, I see that it has begun to rain. Rain is a sign of good fortune. Poor visibility, nobody fucks around by their cars. They get in, they get out. Which is what almost everyone has already done. The lot is almost deserted as she walks toward her Chevy Cavalier. It is a new model, appears to be black. She is middle-class but thinks of herself as sporty. There's a white racing stripe across the side of the car.

She is also all alone in this sector of the lot. The lights are on, but the driving rain keeps everyone's head down, in the other sections, as they race toward their rides. The brunette is struggling with her keys. Can't seem to find the lock on the car door. I'm ten paces behind her, and she still hasn't heard me coming. The rain is now accompanied by thunder.

Finally she engages the lock and the door is flung open. I'm three paces from her lovely ass.

She scoots into the driver's seat, and I've got my left hand inside the gym bag I carry with me. I've got the ether now, and I'm getting the bottle and the balled-up T-shirt out as she is about to close the door.

Then the brunette discovers she has caught her jacket. She reopens the driver's side and sees me. The woman is obviously startled.

I've got the ether-soaked cloth in my left hand, and I'm reaching for the knife.

Her bulldog roars at my intrusion and lunges toward the driver's side back window. He almost propels himself through it, judging by the thump he creates as he hits the glass.

Then the brunette squeals, I see the dog trying to hop over the front seat onto her lap, and I'm turning and running. Running as fast as I can through the monsoon raging down on me. I slip but I don't fall, and I'm thrashing through the puddles of rainwater, praying that she hasn't let loose that goddamned dog.

I'm thirty yards from my own vehicle, on the other side of the mall, when I begin to laugh. As I reach my ride, I finally turn to see if anyone has followed. But no one has, of course. The brunette is on her way at top speed out of this parking lot. She might call 911 when she gets home. Perhaps she'll use her cellular from here. In either case she won't be able to describe me. It was raining, pouring, and lucky for me she never saw my face in the lightning. Only now, as I sit in my vehicle, does the flashing illuminate everything back to daylight.

'Trouble?' my driver asks me.

Chapter Nine

We got a message that a woman had been accosted in a
shopping-mall lot by some guy who followed her out to
her car. This kind of thing happens frequently, but the
item that caught our eyes was the bit about the gym bag.
She said he was reaching into a bag for something. Then
her doggy cut loose at this figure standing in the rain, and
suddenly the guy was a ghost.

Her name was Stephanie Manske. She works as a
secretary for some hotshot downtown – which was why
the news about her traveled so rapidly. The hotshot
wanted to know why security was so lax in this mall on
the northwest side, and he made a stink, and someone in
our department overheard another copper mentioning the
particulars, and bells began to ring in this copper's ears in
regards to 'The Farmer', and here she was.

'You didn't see his face very well,' Doc repeated.

'It was raining real hard. And he startled me. He was
just, like, *there*.'

'You notice how tall?' I asked.

'About six feet. I think. He was hunched up a little,
reaching into that gym bag or whatever.'

'Wearing a hat?' Doc asked.

'No . . . but I couldn't make out the color of his hair

because it was plastered down to his skull . . . It might've been blond. Maybe brown. I'm sorry I can't do any better for you.'

'Hey. We're happy you're here to tell us anything,' Gibron told her.

'You think this guy was—'

'We don't know, Stephanie. We have to take everybody very seriously,' I answered.

'I thought it might be that guy in the paper, too. He could've been reaching for a—'

'Maybe not, Stephanie,' I interrupted. 'This could've been something absolutely innocent. And then your dog could've scared hell out of him.'

'That's why I keep Longsworth in the car. I got molested when I was a teenager, and it's never going to happen again.'

'I'm sorry to hear that . . . Is there anything else you remember about him?' Doc continued.

'All that was left was watching his backside as he beat feet around to the back of the mall. I was so scared I got the hell out. Then I called the police as soon as I got home. And I told my boss, Tony, about it two days ago.'

She was not pretty, but she was not unattractive, either. And she was twenty-eight. Just about the same age as the first two victims. But Stephanie survived her encounter with him. She saw his face, if only for an instant, and he might have been the way I said it before – just some innocent mook trying to ask for directions to Cicero or some goddamned place.

But I didn't think so and neither did Doc. It was him. It was *he*, Doc would correct me. It was our man. The Farmer. Whatever his name was. He was looking for some more stock. Some more of the stuff I was sure he was peddling. He'd got a body shop opened, and it wasn't the kind where you need a blowtorch and a welder's mask to do business. Stephanie was like the steaks and chops behind the glass in the butcher's shop. This guy was

41

about ready to do business with her, only she wasn't the customer. She was the product.

We cased that same northwest side mall for four hours the next day. Went from shop to shop, asking if anyone had seen this man who Stephanie had described generally, and the shopkeepers were just as fuzzy in their memories as our potential victim was. Who could blame them? They saw thousands of faces a day. A number of whom were male, about six feet tall, and either brown- or blond-haired. With a blank for a face, as well.

'I don't see the attraction of these places,' Doc lamented. 'They're like rows of warehouses of shit.'

We – Jack and Doc, four uniforms and I – came up empty. There seemed to be no pattern to the killer's hunting grounds. There were only the women in common. White, near thirty, at least all of them were somewhat attractive. One was raped; one was not sexually assaulted. The third got lucky because of Longsworth the pooch or whatever.

'Who's he supplying?' Doc wondered aloud, inside the Taurus. We were still parked at the mall.

'Hospital. Black-market surgeon. Unwitting hospital?'

He didn't like my answer.

'It is too dangerous, Jimmy, going to a legit health-care place. They'd lose their asses. You gotta ask yourself if they'd think it was worth it, jumping over the waiting lists for some murderer's goods.'

'Then who's he selling to? And how?'

'You are now surfing the Internet.' Doc Gibron smiled.

'Holy Jesus.'

'Yeah. I'll bet he's advertizing here, somewhere. Trouble is, these little shits, these cyber motherfuckers, play games with codes. I'm not nearly computer-smart enough to track him through all this. But we've got people who are.'

Matty McGinn was the resident whiz kid for the CPD computer services. He was the guy who caught the hackers who messed with the ATMs and the banks and with anybody else who jacked with machines and man.

'You know anything about computers, Lieutenant?' Matty grinned.

'I know less than my kids. I know how to turn on and turn off the one my daughter and son use at home. That's it. So we're depending on you, Matthew.'

'The FBI has a very fine system, and we work with them and with their people quite often, Lieutenant Parisi.'

'You can call me Jimmy,' I told him.

Doc snorted, so I whacked him on the elbow.

'Thank you ... They'll be using a code on the Internet. The way pornographers and kiddie molesters do. They'll be aiming at a specialized market, of course, and I think you're right in assuming that no legitimate area hospital's involved. But you never know. We'll try to see if we can find anything strange that's advertising some kind of special service or product. This guy might be doing all of his trade outside the city, the state, or even the country.'

'Yeah. The thought had occurred to us,' Doc snorted.

'He is a geezer. Anti-machines,' I explained to McGinn.

'I know. My parents are just like that. My dad still corresponds on an IBM Selectric. He has had it for twenty years and won't give it up even though I bought him a nice Apple PC for his sixtieth birthday.'

Doc snorted again.

'This was your idea, old man,' I reminded him.

'I have outlived my usefulness,' Doc whined.

'No, you haven't, Detective Gibron. You're the one who put me onto him, if he's in here, and you and the Lieutenant will be the ones to arrest him. I just make the machine do our bidding. It really is as simple as that.'

43

'I'm starting to like this kid,' Doc said as he slapped McGinn's left shoulder.

Matty blushed. It accentuated his orange red hair and freckles. He was a dead ringer for Ron Howard as Opie Taylor on *The Andy Griffith Show*.

Nothing came out of computer services for five days. I called Matty McGinn on the fifth day and he told me it took weeks and months, sometimes, to dig these cockroaches out of the woodwork. They could be very clever about their codes, he reminded me.

So I reminded myself that it had been detective work that had solved my previous cases, not some damned machine 'that did our bidding'.

We had only interviewed one possibility, so far. That cute bastard, Karrios. There were two left to interview. Doc and I were going to round up that pair today.

Dawson Repzac was our first conversation of the day. He was a two-time loser on molestation charges, but the previous arrests were ancient beefs.

He was about the right size for the guy Stephanie had seen in the parking lot at the mall. We had his jacket sitting in front of us when we talked to him in the box.

'Do I need a lawyer?' the sandy-haired ex-molester asked.

'Probably. You got probation coming up?' Doc teased.

Repzac was not smiling.

'I am clean. I mean, I am immaculate.'

'You were a war hero. Served in Vietnam twice and in the Gulf War. You were infantry in Vietnam and then you worked as a medic in the Gulf. That right?' I inquired.

'I carried the litters in the Gulf. That's all.'

'How come you didn't carry a gun in the Middle East?' Doc asked.

'I killed enough people the first time.'

44

'You were a lifer until after the Persian Gulf thing,' I said.

'I quit after that pissant adventure. Yeah.'

'You're well educated,' Doc added. 'Went to Illinois Chicago. Studied biology ... What? You want to teach? Go to medical school?'

'I wanted to avoid Vietnam. Then I changed my mind and volunteered after I graduated – Have you guys had enough fun yet?'

'We're investigating a double homicide,' I told Repzac.

'You mean the two women who were cut open? What would I have to do with something like that? I got hauled up for statutory rape. Twice. It was consensual. I tried to break it off because I found out she lied about her age. She told me she was eighteen. Hell, she looked twenty-five. But she was fifteen and she wasn't getting carded at the bar where I picked her up. What I'm saying is *why me?*'

'You're not the only guy we've talked to. We talk to a lot of people. You know that. You've been through the system, so why ask a dumbass question like that?' Doc groused.

'Okay, okay ... Is there anything else you need to ask me?'

'No. Thanks for coming in,' I answered.

Then I opened the door for him.

When he was down the hall from the box, Doc looked over at me.

'You get the feeling you've just been lied to?'

I watched Doc's eyes, but neither of us blinked.

Chapter Ten

Jimmy Preggio was the third guy on our list. He was the hardcore of the three, so far. Like the other two he was very intelligent, and like the other two he had a record for sexual assault. But his jacket was very short, other than the information on the two crimes for which he'd served four and a half years.

He was blond, about six one, and he fitted the general description that Stephanie Manske gave us for the mall parking lot thing.

Doc and I picked up Jimmy Preggio in a pool hall on Milwaukee Avenue. He was with several of his brothers, and it got a little tense when I saw his buddies start to grip their cues a bit too tightly.

'We want to talk to you, Mr Preggio,' Doc explained as he showed the guy his badge and ID.

But the three clowns with Preggio were standing still, with some very fierce body language.

'This is a homicide investigation,' I told the three onlookers. 'Any of you guys here on probation?'

They headed for the bar without a blink.

'I oughta use that line more often,' Doc grinned.

There was a clear, blank, serene look on Preggio's handsome puss. He wasn't troubled by any of this. He'd been downtown before, but never on a homicide deal, as far as I knew.

'Are you going to cooperate with us, Mr Preggio?' I asked again.

'I will. I never had any other intention.'

There was a gym bag under the pool table. Frank's Pool was a twelve-table operation here on the North Side with a small lounge up front that catered to the local hoos and to the pimps who ran them. Word was that Frank, the owner, was heavily connected with the Outfit, so every time he got shut down he got reopened within days.

'Is that your gym bag, sir?' Doc asked.

'Yes. Yes, it is.'

'Then you might want to take it with us.'

Preggio looked at Doc as if Doc were speaking Russian. But then he bent down, reached under the pool table and retrieved the bag. It had 'Indiana Pacers' stitched on both sides. A black bag with scarlet lettering.

Doc shot a quick stare my way, and I returned his rapid look.

'You'd be breaking your probation if you were hanging with known criminals, Mr Preggio,' Doc told him.

Preggio was sitting at the rectangular table here in the box with the two of us. Jack Wendkos was standing outside the one-way mirror, watching.

'You remember where you were on these three dates?' I asked.

I put the sheet on the table in front of him. It listed the dates of the two murders and it also had the date of Stephanie Manske's encounter.

'I really don't know if I can recall my whereabouts on those days.' He smiled. It was a sort of grimace that formed on his lips and cheeks. Then his face went unreadable again.

'You need to try a little harder, Jimmy,' Doc warned.

47

'I'm sorry. I could've been any number of places on those days or nights. I move around quite a lot.'

'I noticed,' Doc said, picking up his jacket, 'that you're a very vague kind of guy. I mean, there isn't a whole lot of information on you in this file. Except for the basic birth-day, social security number business. You want to fill me in on what happened since you popped out of momma?'

Preggio shot an angry glance at Doc at the mention of 'momma'.

'Did I say something to offend you?' Doc smiled.

'I had a great deal of respect for my mother.'

'What about the old man?' Doc went on.

There was another red spark in Preggio's eyes.

'Oh, I bet I did it again,' Doc told him.

'You do not make light about parents.'

'Yeah. I know. I had two of my own. I was rather fond of them both. But then, their son didn't grow up to be a piece of shit who paws little girls.'

'Detective, what is it you want to know from me?'

'He wants to know where you were on those three nights, asshole,' I joined in. 'How long's it been since you had a talk with your own probation officer, Jimmy?'

'All right. On the first night you have there I was with my girlfriend Theresa ... On the second night I don't remember. And on that third date I was right back in that pool hall with those same three fellows that you so cleverly intimidated, Lieutenant Parisi.'

He smiled at me as if he'd just beat me in a hand of blackjack.

'Second night you don't remember,' I mused aloud. 'You mind if we take a look in your gym bag?'

He glared angrily at me. Then he looked back at the Indiana Pacers satchel. He fixed his gaze on it for a long count, and then he returned his stare to meet mine.

'Go right ahead.'

Doc grabbed the bag and slapped it up on the table. Inside it were two white cotton T-shirts and a bottle of liquid.

48

Gibron opened the bottle carefully and sniffed at it from a half-arm's length. Then he pulled the container closer, and finally took a sip.

'Good water,' Doc said.

'That sip just ruined a dollar seventy-five's worth,' Preggio complained.

Doc reached into his wallet and took out two singles. He tossed them in front of Jimmy.

'Thank you, sir. You're a gentleman.' Preggio smirked.

'And you are not and we still want to know where you were on all three dates,' Doc snapped.

'I told you what I remember. Are you going to charge me with anything? Because if you're not, I'd like to leave.'

'Watch your back, sweetheart,' Gibron warned him. 'You break that parole and I'll be right behind you.'

Preggio rose and walked out of the box after he grabbed hold of his sports bag.

Doc sat back down and looked up at me. He appeared all tired out and he looked about as dejected as I was.

'We have nothing, Jimmy P. We have three mooks who all fit the description. I gotta tell you that this last guy intrigues me, and he interests me the most because we know the least about him. I don't like those dark spots. Those little creases where nothing shows up on the monitors, you know? What about this guy's schooling? What about military service? He was probably old enough to have fought in Vietnam, although he would've been eighteen at the tail end of it. He was old enough for the Gulf or Grenada. And that makes him fit the same categories that the other two clowns fall into. We're looking for how he learned to use a knife as proficiently as the guy who did the two women. Something to do with medicine. The first two were medical corps. What are the odds this guy was a medic too?'

'Pretty lousy, I'd say, Doctor.'

'Yeah. I agree. But there are guys in the Outfit who can cut you as neat as most any surgeon, Jimmy. These guys

49

know how to handle stilettos as well as any MD wields a scalpel. And what about a guy who's a butcher by trade? They can cut meat, as grotesque as that all sounds.'

'A butcher?'

'Sure, guinea. Maybe we're being sidetracked by all this military stuff. These street cutters can tear you open and have you wrapped in white paper as quick as any educated surgeon at Rush-St. Luke's.'

I gave him the questioning look.

'Well, maybe *almost* as skillful. You follow my drift?'

'Yes, indeed I do ... Which of the three do you like, Doctor Gibron?'

He stopped and stared down hard at the table top.

'I don't like any of them. I thought all three had it in them. That's what scares hell out of me, Jimmy P.'

Natalie's first duty was patrol. On foot. It was the new thing at the CPD. We were hitting the streets with our shoe leather. Getting to know the inhabitants of the barrios, of the neighborhoods. It was supposed to better connect us with the people we served. And it had shown some positive results, so I didn't suppose I could dismiss the notion too lightly.

But it scared me to know she was walking the streets of places like Hyde Park on the South Side. Hyde Park contained the University of Chicago, but it also held some of the worst gangbangers on that side of the city. They were patrolling in tandem, but even with a partner at Natalie's side, it scared the shit out of me.

We were in her apartment on the North Side. She was only about two and a half miles away from my house, but I was living for the day when I moved her into my place. It was six thirty-two in the a.m., and I was about ready to go home after my shift. She was working midnights as well. At least we had more time together this way.

'You wearing your ring?' I asked.

'I don't wear it on shift. I'm afraid I'll lose it on the

50

street. And I'm never going to misplace *this* piece of rock, Lieutenant, sir.'

Her auburn hair was one of her best features, and she had lots of qualities.

'Or don't you want those other coppers to know that you're engaged to an 'older man'?'

'Yes. That's it! You've grasped it!'

She swooped over to me and flopped into my lap.

'We'll get married in spring. Say April,' she told me. 'Kelly will be one of my bridemaids. It'll be small, just close family. Which for me means my mother and sister and that's about it. And then we'll hit a beach somewhere for two weeks . . . You want more children, James?'

She noticed that she'd just rattled me thoroughly.

'We hadn't talked about that one,' was all I could mutter.

'We can't wait too long, Jimmy. We don't want you to be a daddy at eighty, do we?'

'I don't think so.'

'Well?'

'Well . . . I'd like kids with you, Red. I just never spent any time thinking much about it until now.'

'I think we should wait three years. Get my career jump started, and then we can have one or two. Two, I think. Don't want an only child, do we?'

'I've already got a son and a daughter.'

'But I meant a child of *ours*.'

'I know, Red. It is fine with me. Let's just get to the altar first. Is that all right with you?'

She kissed me and laughed. She was still aboard my lap.

'I'm going on decoy duty for The Farmer.'

She stood after she'd said it.

'They already used a rookie on him. I told them they needed someone—'

'More experienced. I know, Jimmy. But if I want to make progress toward a shield, I've got to get experience on the streets.'

51

An argument took form somewhere in me, but I knew I couldn't use it. She was a policeman, policewoman. She was in the same club with me. It was what we did. So how was I going to tell her she couldn't?

'I don't want you to worry, and I'm sorry I just heaved me and it into your lap like that, but it is something I need to do. I want to help *you*, too, Jimmy. I want to help you catch this son of a bitch, and it is the only way I can figure to do it.'

'I can't tell you no. You knew that before you told me.'

'You aren't going to be angry about it, are you?'

'No, I'll just worry. Now I've got you on my back too, don't I?'

I pulled her back down to me and I kissed her. I urged her face toward my chest and then I bent over and kissed the crown of her lovely red-brown head.

'You couldn't be a goddamned schoolteacher or an insurance rep, could you?'

She clutched hold of me tightly, and then she straightened and looked right into my eyes.

'Well, now you know exactly how I feel when you walk out that door toward those streets. Now you know exactly what it feels like for me.'

Billy Cheech was waiting for Doc and me at Giardino's. It was a pizza joint on Rush Street, near the entertainment district. We had Jack Wendkos with us, too. Jack had been doing a lot of the side legwork that Gibron and I would've had to do on overtime. The Captain was grooming Jack for bigger things, and I thought the Boss had made a fine choice with this young guy. He was good people. Tough. Smart. And honest, as well.

'I get to go to all these great places with you two,' Jack cracked as we walked into Giardino's. This place was known for their Sicilian-style deep-pan pizza.

Billy Cheech waited at the bar, but we moved him and

ourselves off to a table in the back of the place. There were green and blue Christmas tree lights strung all throughout the place. There was also a blown-up poster of Marlon Brando as Don Corleone on the back wall, right behind us.

The waitress came up to us immediately. She was young and ripe and she was wearing a half-unbuttoned blouse that allowed the better part of her dairies to protrude in a very enticing way.

'That's a fuckin' thirty percent tip, that there alone.' Billy smiled.

I raised my hands, palms out.

'You don't like to fuck around, do you, coz?' Billy moaned.

'So tell us, Billy. We're kinda busy right now,' Doc added.

Jack took a sip of his iced water, but he was still looking out for that well-endowed waitress to return.

'I thought I got a shake, Jimmy P.'

I watched his eyes as he raised them from the red-checked tablecloth.

Jack and Doc were watching him closely now.

'Word is that there's a guy selling very hard-to-get items to overseas buyers. He's using some of our people to help him make contacts. I mean, the source I got was kinda vague about the details, you unnerstan, but the kinda cash this guy's makin' does draw attention to certain people. And I can't tell you my source, cousin, because it would fuckin' get me killed.'

'You got any idea how he's moving his goods?' Doc asked.

The big-bosomed waitress returned with our pitcher of beer and four glasses. Jack had lost his interest in her, but Billy was watching her breathe. It was like he had his eyes pasted to her chest.

'*Maron,*' he murmured.

'So?' I asked him again.

'Somethin' to do with computers.'

I looked over at Doc. We needed to fill Jack in about McGinn, our computer nerd.

'They got some kinda code they use over that fuckin' Internet, you know?'

'What code?' Jack asked him.

'Shit, I don't know – I dropped out after the tenth grade. All I know is that you want to look for Imperial Products of Bridgeport.'

'That's the listing they're hiding behind?' Doc queried.

'If I get any deeper, Jimmy P, you'll be my pallbearer . . . It's all I got. I ask any more shit and they're gonna know I'm passin' it on.'

'Okay, Billy. That's good. We don't want you dead,' I told him.

'We're still *familia*, Jimmy P. Even if you got a really shitty way to make a fuckin' livin'.'

'Yeah, we're still family, Billy. And you gotta take care of yourself. You did good, partner. Let me buy you a pitcher of your own.'

'Fuck, no. I get hammered, I'll flop the fuckin' lift at work on top of my dumb ass. I got to eat and run. This is a long drive from the shop.'

The overripe server again showed up with our order, and Billy and Jack Wendkos scoped her every wiggle all the way back to the kitchen. Jack got up and caught the chestnut-haired beauty before she could return to her station. She was smiling and Jack was smiling, and then Wendkos returned to the table.

He sat down and began to eat.

'Well?' Doc wanted to know.

'She's gay,' Jack said through a mouthful of deep pan.

'You're fuckin' strokin' me!' Billy bellowed.

'Yeah. I am,' Jack replied.

Doc let out a belly laugh. I had to join him.

Then the blush left Billy Cheech's cheeks.

'You fuckin' cops. You're always fuckin' with people.'

Chapter Eleven

The computer nerd prevailed. We got the call from Matty McGinn on a Tuesday morning just as Doc and Jack and I were about to go off duty from midnights. The kid'd been up all night with the information we received from Billy Cheech, and he didn't let go until he found it.

We walked into Computer Services at 7.12 a.m. Matty looked as fresh as if he'd just arrived at work, but I knew he had been around his computer for going on sixteen hours.

'I found it just two hours ago. I tried to get a hold of you on the street, but they said you were doing surveillance,' McGinn told the trio of us.

'What'd you find?' Doc wanted to know.

Jack Wendkos was standing behind the red-headed kid, looking over his right shoulder.

'Imperial Products of Bridgeport has a very specialized clientele. They sell goods that are available nowhere else – except, I think, in southeast Asia on the black market. So they've got no competition ... It took me three hours to get past their code. See, they front themselves by saying they're selling ceramic works of art. You know, junk stuff you'd put on your coffee table or whatever. But when you get past the first series of phony pitches, and when you continue showing interest in them, they start with a series

55

of questions that find out what you're really interested in. They ask you if you'd like to see a brochure of what they have to offer. And you have to see that brochure in person. They won't present it on the Internet, naturally. So I set up a meet with one of their 'representatives' for Thursday afternoon. Two o'clock, at Brookfield Zoo.'

McGinn looked at us as if he'd just watched his young wife deliver a healthy set of twins.

The 'representative' was supposed to meet us at the giraffes. Someone was supposed to show up wearing a kelly green windbreaker – that was Jack Wendkos. Doc and I and twelve plainclothes detectives were going to surround whoever showed up, and there were another ten patrol cars waiting outside the zoo. They would be charging in on my command.

It was late fall. Almost closing time for Brookfield. It had become a bit cold for most of the animals to survive outdoors, and they were shutting the place down until spring.

We were all dressed as casually as possible. But we had to wear jackets to cover our weapons, as always. I had my Nine under my black windbreaker, and I had the .44 Bulldog strapped to my left leg, just below the knee. And I was carrying a switchblade in my left-hand jeans pocket, contrary to department policy.

Doc carried two pieces as well. A Nine in his shoulder holster and a .38 Police Special in a holster at the small of his back. He carried a blackjack in his pants pocket too. Jack was armed with a Nine at the shoulder and another Nine on his opposite hip. We didn't arm ourselves quite as heavily for a standard tour of the streets, but The Farmer had everyone behaving a bit more cautiously than usual.

It was an overcast day. There was a hint of precipitation in the air, as the weather guy might say. At least there

56

wouldn't be any sun glaring in our eyes if we had to use any ordnance on this cutter.

And it might not be The Farmer who showed up. He might send a rep, just like the Internet message said. I don't know why, but I had the impression this guy worked solo and that he was going to be here in person.

Doc walked over to the concessions and bought a hot dog. We were making our way slowly toward the area where they housed the giraffes. I had taken my kids here twenty times, at least. But every time I returned, there was a new wrinkle. They added something I had never seen before. The dolphin house was off to our left, at the center of the park. There were shows indoors with the porpoises every half-hour, but those events might have been canceled after the summer became the fall. I couldn't remember.

The lions and tigers and bears (oh my) were ahead of us, and behind them were the long-necked varmints we were looking for.

Wendkos, with his bright green windbreaker, was directly in front of us. He was eating popcorn and trying to become unnoticeable. Which was hard for him to do, especially with the female population. As I said, he had Hollywood looks, and women were constantly mistaking him for Val Kilmer or for some other blond La La Land hunk. Since he'd separated from his wife, I assumed he'd been leading a very active social life. He never talked about women, however. Too bad, because everyone in Homicide wanted to know if he'd scored with the well-built waitress we saw at the pizza joint. Doc had made a legend of that young woman's mammaries by now, and it was like a continuing series on TV, finding out if Jack ever got his hands on her goodies. He didn't talk, though. Said it was wrong to talk about 'private matters'. He was pissing a lot of coppers off. Many of us lived very vicariously.

We approached the bears' enclave. The polar bears lay

57

on the concrete, undisturbed by the plainclothes police-men who ambled past them en route toward the lions and tigers.

'Let's go by the monkey island,' Doc pleaded.

He smiled and took the last bite out of his hot dog. Then he slurped down the ice in the bottom of his Coke cup.

'I love to watch them abuse themselves. I swear they do it to insult us human critters.' Gibron smiled.

'I do not understand your amusement at watching some ape pound sand in public,' I told him. 'You want to see a bunch of whackers, go down to City Lockup around 11.00 p.m. The jailers have to wear earplugs.'

'Ah bullshit, guinea.'

'Nah. I swear that's what they say—'

'There are the giraffes. Right ahead,' Doc said. The smile was off his face.

These animals were housed on the eastern edge of Brookfield. We had guys heading toward them from the north, south, and west. The cars were parked just beyond the giraffes, on the east perimeter. There were fifteen- or twenty-feet-high chain-link fences that separated man from beast here. I saw the other coppers walking slowly toward Jack Wendkos. But they stopped short to give the man in the green coat some space. We saw no one else in front of that tall barrier.

The giraffes were elegant and awkward, all at once. They stared very interestedly at Jack and at the rest of us who stood twenty and thirty yards behind Wendkos. The other plainclothesmen started to move about, to appear as though we were not congregating behind the man in green. Doc and I sat down on a bench, with Jack thirty yards off to our right. The other police were walking past Wendkos and the giraffes and were about to make a cordon around the area so that a crowd didn't form around the homicide detective.

There was still no one else in front of the long-necked

creatures we had come to observe. Until a woman with a baby carriage approached from the west. We couldn't see what was in the stroller. There were blankets piled on top of whatever it held.

Doc nudged me and I nodded.

'It is two minutes after two,' he whispered.

Doc talked quietly into the tiny microphone on his jacket collar. It was about the size of a pimple, and it was the same color as his windbreaker. We all had the small audio phones, flesh-colored, inserted in our outer ears. He was telling all of us to watch the woman.

'She might be carrying, under those blankets. Nod if you hear me, Jack.'

Wendkos's head bobbed very subtly, but he kept staring straight ahead at the giraffes.

The woman with the stroller came up behind our man. She tapped him on the shoulder.

'Would you happen to have a light?' she asked him.

We could hear her clearly. Jack's microphone was hidden beneath the flap of a collar on his kelly green jacket.

'No. No, I'm afraid I don't smoke. Don't you think it is kind of dangerous to smoke around a little guy?' he asked the woman.

She was wearing a scarf and big black sunglasses. Her knee-length black leather coat had its collar pulled up at the back to block the breeze.

'I don't believe in everything the government says. Do you? My aunt lived to be ninety-six, and she smoked a pack a day. I thought it was all just the paranoia of our age.'

It appeared that her lips curled upward into something like a smile, but then she abruptly pulled away from Wendkos. And just as abruptly she halted once more and turned back to the detective.

'You know, you look a lot like . . .'

The microphone didn't pick up the end of her sentence. Then she did retreat for real. She pushed the stroller ten yards, stopped again, and this time she leaned into the carriage and removed a squalling child, dressed in pink, and embraced the kid until it ceased squealing.

'You look a lot like who?' Doc said.

'Liberace, sweetheart,' Jack piped back at him. 'Fucking woman wants to gas her own kid with her stink. We ought to arrest the bitch. Attempted murder.'

'Hey. Cool down, big man. It's early yet,' Gibron said.

The other detectives continued to make a casual circuit around the giraffe enclave, so Doc and I got up and moved too. We walked back toward the concession stand because I was hungry and thirsty, having missed lunch in the rush to get everybody and everything here on time. And I was too wired to eat back then anyway. But now the boredom of the stakeout settled in, and the pangs had hit me in the middle.

I ordered a hot dog, fries, and a large diet pop. It came to six bucks. I winced at the young girl behind the cash register, but she couldn't understand my consternation at their high prices. Doc got a drink too, and we sat at a table with a rainbow-colored umbrella.

'Maybe McGinn didn't give them the right high sign or whatever, Jimmy. Maybe they smelled us coming. Maybe he sniffed us out. I don't think this one *wants* to get caught.'

'I want all you guys to pull back on Jack. Give him some room. Stay out of the immediate area until he thinks we've got an authentic shake,' I ordered into my microphone. They all replied that they copied, and from here, about 150 yards, I could make out clearly that lonesome bright green jacket standing in front of a cluster of brown-and-white-dotted giraffes. We could be on top of him in ten seconds if he called out, so I knew we had to give him a wide berth.

I continued to check the locations of my coppers as I finished my expensive lunch.

'What would this have cost at Garvin's? Two-fifty?' I asked Doc.

'You're still living in the fifties, Beaver. Get with the program, guinea,' he quipped.

'Hey,' Jack said. He didn't utter anything else.

'Oh-oh,' Doc said as he stood.

'What the fuck. *Oh-oh?*'

I was trying to finish my glass of diet pop.

Doc nodded toward our man. Someone dressed in one of those sweatshirts with a hood was coming at Wendkos from the west. The coppers who were also coming at Jack from that direction had sniffed out our new arrival. They were closing toward the policeman in green and that new face at this moment. The plainclothes guys from the north were hurrying on down, too. I threw my wrapper into the trashcan, and Doc and I were hustling toward the pair.

Sweatshirt person stopped ten feet from our detective in the windbreaker. The new arrival stared straight ahead at the inhabitants of the twenty-feet-high fenced enclosure.

But we didn't hear anything from Wendkos's microphone.

Doc and I were fifty yards from Jack. I could see our fellow policemen closing to about the same range, so I said, 'Stop.' And everybody halted. The cops wandered off toward neighboring benches, but the figure in the hood hadn't been watching our approach. He had his eyes on the attractions in front of him.

Doc and I sat on a bench that was perhaps thirty-five yards from the duo we were watching.

Doc whispered, 'Stand there, Jack. We're right here.'

'It's a woman,' I heard Wendkos whispering back. But he didn't dare add anything to the statement.

'*Woman?*' Doc mouthed, almost silently.

'They are so graceful, aren't they?' a new voice began.

Wendkos turned toward the hooded woman.

'Yes. They are.'

'I like the jacket. It is my kind of color.'

'You do? I wore it because I was supposed to be meeting a business partner here.'

'Business?' the female voice countered. 'What kind of business would intrude on a lovely fall day?'

'My business is very special. I have a customer who has very extraordinary needs, and I'm supposed to meet someone who deals in very exotic kinds of products.'

'What company does your friend work for?'

Wendkos hesitated. He must have wondered if he was being hit on or if this broad was checking him out for references.

'Imperial Products of Bridgeport,' he told her. I wondered if he blinked when he said it.

She straightened up noticeably.

'Funny you should mention that name.'

'Why? Have you heard of them?'

Then she appeared to become a bit more animated. She turned about and looked all around her.

'I said, have you heard of them?'

She started to withdraw.

'She's made you, Jack! Grab her!' Doc demanded

As Jack reached out, she bolted away from him.

'Close her in!' Doc barked into the microphone.

The woman in the hooded sweatshirt was into full gallop toward the west. Then she spied the quartet of men headed her way, and she turned in a hurry and attempted to come back toward us. She saw that the north, south, and west were all clogged with policemen, and so she raced toward the only direction left. She hit the twenty-foot fence in a hurry, and then she began to climb.

'Stop!' Jack yelled.

'Jesus Christ!' We were all groaning from the loudness in our ears. I pulled the flesh-colored device from my ear as we ran toward the woman scaling the fence.

She was halfway up the twenty-foot chain-link as Wendkos arrived. Then Jack was up on the links too, and we were almost to him.

The hooded woman climbed as if she was an athlete, a gymnast. Very lithe, very smooth. Then she lifted a leg

62

over and she scrambled down onto the ground where those enormous giraffes stalked. There were six of them in the enclosure, and from what I had read about them, they could be very nasty beasts when they were provoked.

Wendkos had reached the top of the fence when Doc told him to get the hell back down. We had patrol cars outside the far fences. They'd get her, Doc tried to persuade him.

But Jack was coming down on his side, and I found myself on that same fence, going up. Doc screamed at me. He called me something obscene, but I couldn't make out his words, only his inflections.

I was over and down in a minute or so, and then I was racing across the open field. The giraffes were off to my right, and I could feel them watching the two of us chasing this hooded female who was ahead of us both.

Jack stumbled and fell. I caught up to him, helped him up. He had ripped his jeans open at the knee and his leg was bleeding.

'Let's go!' he shouted.

The woman had a hundred yards on us. The fence she was aiming at was another hundred yards away. She sprinted like an athlete, too. She was way ahead and I knew we didn't have a chance of catching her.

I grabbed Wendkos by the back of his green windbreaker and I forced him to halt.

'Stop, Jack ... Whewww! Stop. It's no use. Doc's radioed the guys outside to take her.'

Then I looked up and I saw two of those towering creatures striding determinedly toward us.

'I think we better just stand still,' I told the junior officer. 'What?'

He was still examining the wound on his kneecap.

The giraffes were thirty feet away and closing. I was reaching for my Bulldog. It had the better stopping power of my two weapons. I bent over and tore it out of my ankle holster. The two long-necks approached us slowly now.

'I really don't want to hurt you two boys,' I told the lofty animals.

Jack had his Nine pointed their way too.

'I really don't want to shoot you boys. Please stop.'

They halted abruptly, about ten feet away from us.

'Go on! Get!' Jack yelled.

'Please shut the fuck up,' I told Wendkos.

'You want to explain to the Captain why we shot two Brookfield Zoo giraffes, Jimmy?'

'I'd rather it was them than me, if it comes down to it.'

'HEY!!'

The 'Hey' was followed by a piercing whistle. The giraffes turned toward the south where they saw one of the zoo attendants at a shed. Then the two loped off toward him, like a pair of trained Dobermans.

After the animals arrived at the shed, I could see them bending over a bale of something. Hay? I couldn't tell what it was.

The attendant in his tan zoo shirt walked up to us.

'You two guys want to get squished? You know how close you came?' he asked us. 'Jesus Christ. I mean, do you *know*?'

Chapter Twelve

'We found this at the base of the back fence,' Jack said as he held out a hooded sweatshirt to Doc and me.

Doc took hold of the garment.

'She got away clean, Jimmy. The bold bitch took off the hood and walked right on past the patrolmen outside the fence.'

'How could they let a single female walk on by without even stopping and questioning her?' I asked.

'General stupidity, I guess, Lieutenant. I don't know what to tell you,' Jack lamented.

Doc was so angry that I knew the two of us had better give him some space. So Jack and I took a walk down the long length of the twenty-foot chain-link fence that our girl had recently flown over.

'Did you see her face?' I asked the younger detective.

'She was wearing shades. And the hood was drawn tight. All I could see was that she was young, probably in her mid-twenties, late twenties, and she was white. Sort of pale, I'd say. I'm sorry I can't do better, Jimmy. I only saw her full-front for a few seconds. She looked to be about five feet four, maybe 115 pounds. Hard to tell about the body size with that floppy-assed sweatshirt on top of her torso . . . Jesus. How could she skip on by those guys!'

'Let it slide, Jack. Like you said, it happens. Now we

know he's got help, at least. How close she is to our guy, I don't know.'

'She sounded fairly swift, for the few words she said to me. I mean she sounded witty or intelligent. She was no bimbo. You could tell. She was being, like, playful, I guess you'd call it. She only said a few words, but that's the impression I got.'

'Let's wander back toward Doc. Maybe he's cooled off by now.'

We walked in silence the block or so back to Gibron.

He was sitting inside our unmarked Taurus. Still seething, it looked like. Jack got in the back seat.

'She's working tight with this guy, Jimmy,' Doc said.

'How do you figure?' I asked.

'She got away because she had a plan. I don't just mean scaling the walls and running like an Olympic queen either. I mean she didn't appear panicked. She was cool when we squeezed her. Some messenger girl would've laid down and cowered with all those cops after her ass.'

I thought he was right and I nodded in affirmation.

'Which doesn't excuse those goofy uniforms from letting her slide. They should've grabbed anything moving on the edge of this goddamned zoo.'

He started up the Ford, and we were on our way back downtown.

'We haven't had a nibble. Not even a flasher. I feel like I should be disappointed,' Natalie told me.

We were in bed at her apartment. Then she told me she still wanted a spring wedding and she also went off on all the particulars involved in the nuptials. She was a Catholic, as I was, and she wanted the official ceremony in the Church, which was also fine with me.

'Don't feel disappointed. I know this'll piss you off, but I hope you never lay eyes on our man, except through the media the day we put the irons on him and his girlfriend.'

66

'Girlfriend?'

I probably shouldn't have told her, but I knew she could keep her mouth shut, and it was not likely the media creeps would be all over her to become a source on the case.

'He has at least one, someone who's working with him.'

I told her the adventure of the giraffes.

'Are you crazy, Jimmy? Climbing a fence and going into an area with big, scary—'

'Isn't that what you're doing, staking yourself out for The Farmer?'

I had shut her up. For once in my life, I had stopped her cold.

'Point taken. But at least the guy after me is somewhat human.'

I watched her eyes. Then she knew we were wasting time talking shop again.

I kissed her eyes once she'd shut them. Then I kissed her throat, her breasts, her belly, her thighs, and finally her toes. Which caused her to giggle. When I came back topside, she was not laughing anymore. I kissed her lips and I found her tongue. Then I mounted her and I raised her thighs with my arms beneath her upper legs. She lunged at me quickly, and we maintained a locking embrace for an extended moment. We were frozen there, and even though we were both aching by now, neither of us wanted to disengage.

'The ad on the Internet has disappeared,' Matty McGinn moaned. He looked as if someone had hit and run over his pet pooch.

'You mean the Bridgeport advertisement, I assume,' Doc told him as the trio of detectives stood behind him at his station in Computer Services.

Matty nodded.

'Ain't your fault, kid,' Doc commiserated. 'We had him

and we lost him, and it had nothing to do with you ...
Maybe they'll come back with something else. They aren't
going to stop business, young man.'

He clapped the kid on the left shoulder and we walked
out of his office.

'Next?' Doc smiled.

'We go back after those three Lester the Molesters.
They're the only leads I can think of,' I told him and Jack,
out there in the hallway.

'I hope your keen sense of intuition is on the money,
Holmes,' Doc told me, 'or we'll be watching three cheese-
dicks while the real guy starts in on slicing and dicing
more thirty-something white women.'

Gibron went down to the exit and held the glass door
open for Jack and me.

'Why is it thirty-something white women?' Jack asked.

I looked him in the eyes, and then I looked over to Doc,
still standing there like the doorman.

'Why indeed?' Doc asked, back at my downtown cubicle.

'Why not younger, or older?' I shot back.

'I don't get it either,' Wendkos joined in.

Doc was staring out my window, toward the east and
toward Lake Michigan.

Jack and I sat opposite one another. I was behind the
desk.

'If he's supplying organs, why not go with younger
women?' Doc asked. 'They'd be even healthier, wouldn't
they?'

'Maybe it isn't about the organs' age. Maybe it's just
about the kind of woman he wants to cut,' Jack suggested.

'I think he may have you there, Holmes.' Doc smiled at
me.

'So you're saying you think he's got a history with some
female in her thirties. A white woman. Attractive. At least
minimally. She did something that's triggering his
wanger.'

68

Doc nodded at my proposal.

'So if we're right about why, how does that help us nab this prick?' I proffered.

'It doesn't help us nab him. But it might let us know we've got the right collar when we catch up to him,' Gibron told us.

I looked over to the board with my cases written in red and black ink. The reds were outstanding homicides. The blacks were recently solved investigations. The two latest reds were Genevieve Malone and Delores Winston. I tried to visualize changing the color of the ink that listed their names, but I couldn't picture it. I couldn't see the change happening.

I looked over to Doc and Jack. I nodded, the three of us rose, and we headed out toward the elevators.

Dawson Repzac had a live-in lover. We found out about her from his apartment building's owner. The owner didn't give a shit who lived with whom, he told us, but he liked to remember the faces of the people who inhabited his properties so he knew who to look for if there was any damage done to his flats.

The girl was the right height. We saw her coming into Repzac's as we staked his place out on this Thursday night. She was just the way the owner described her. About five feet five, 120 pounds. Not a beauty, but pretty. Nice rear end, light in the chest, as Jack might put it.

An hour later she waltzed out with himself, with Dawson Repzac. We watched the two of them get in the Toyota that the girl had pulled up in.

Her name was Janice Ripley. We got that from the landlord, too. He knew all their names – even the cohabitors. He was a very careful man.

They took off from the curb, going east. We waited a beat, and then the three of us in the Ford with Doc behind the wheel were tailing them. They were moving out of this near north neighborhood toward the Lake. We saw

Lake Michigan as we approached the beach. Then Janice turned right on Lakeshore Drive and headed south. We were keeping our distance, but we had to be careful not to lose her since we were the only car behind her. We hadn't got the juice on Repzac to pull a massive triangular pursuit, so we were alone on this one. If she lost us, we were lost.

Doc started to become nervous when we were at 79th Street.

'Shit, she's headed for Indiana,' he told me.

'Seems like she's got no inclination to turn off,' I agreed.

'So?' Jack wanted to know.

'We follow her a few more miles, and then we're out of our jurisdiction anyway,' Gibron conceded.

When we saw her heading south, riding in the middle lane, we knew our pursuit would gain us nothing. So Doc turned off, headed west, and we figured we'd give them a free ride. We'd return to Repzac's tomorrow and try them again.

Preggio appeared to be a loner. Except for his pool buddies. We didn't see him with a woman.

'Maybe he's gay,' Doc suggested as we were parked outside that same pool hall on Milwaukee Avenue.

Jack Wendkos was downtown, checking out leads in another investigation he was involved with.

I looked over to my partner and I saw that he was yanking me. Neither of us thought this shithead was a homosexual. He had that swagger that women love, and I couldn't see him refusing all that feminine attention that his great physical build must have attracted.

No, he was a ladies' man. But we simply hadn't seen him with female companionship yet. The investigation process involved a whole lot of endurance. Many times it was a matter of who crapped out first – the copper or the perpetrator. You couldn't let them outwait you. That was one of my mentor's first lessons to me when I began to work this job. Doc Gibron was my mentor.

'He's here for the evening,' Doc groaned.

He closed his eyes and slumped back down on the passenger's side. He was wired to his jazz station, and I heard him click the pocket radio on.

I was wide awake. It was my shift anyway. I didn't like to listen to the radio on stakeout. It was a distraction. So I watched and I imagined myself with Natalie. It passed the time.

But Doc was correct. Preggio was not going anywhere. I could see him shooting eight ball through the big picture window at the front of the poolroom. He played game after game. Pretty soon it was midnight, and our afternoon shift was over. I pulled away from the curb, but Doc never woke up until I approached the Loop.

We saw the girl at Preggio's crib on the northwest side. He lived in a surprisingly solid middle-classe neighborhood. I had pictured Preggio living at the Y downtown or somewhere like that. With transients. For a good-looking guy, he gave out these seedy vibrations, compared to Repzac and Karrios. The reason I was stuck on these three suspects was Stephanie Manske. I knew the man who approached her in that mall parking lot was our guy. I didn't have any physical evidence to back me up, but I knew it in my guts. It was The Farmer who almost opened Stephanie up in that lot. If it hadn't been for that mutt with the cutesy name – Longsworth – she would've been the third name in red. I was certain of it. These three all fitted the physical description she gave of the soaked man with the bag that she encountered, and I didn't know how else to narrow the field down. There was virtually no physical evidence. No fingerprints, no witnesses, no semen, no hairs. Nothing. Nothing left but what I had as a feeling in the middle of me.

71

The girl was too tall. She had to be five seven or five eight. And she was too busty. Too heavy up top. She had long red hair that Jack Wendkos would've spotted immediately.

'This isn't the one,' Jack agreed. 'But that doesn't mean he's bonking only one princess. Maybe the guy's got a stable, for crissake.'

'You didn't expect this to be easy, did you, kid?' Doc chirped from the back seat. 'They're playing Brubeck and his version of "West Side Story",' Doc said as he put the headset back on.

'Easy, no. I'd like to kick the shit out of those uniforms who saw the right female walk right past their noses. This should've been over that afternoon. She would've got us The Farmer, and we'd have black ink on your board, Jimmy.'

I waved him off and watched Preggio's lights come on. I could see the silhouettes against his sheer curtains. And then I saw it.

'There's somebody else up there,' I told my partners.

Doc snapped off his portable and sat up.

'Look,' I said. 'Three of them. And the newest member is female. And a few inches shorter than the redhead. Wouldn't you say, Jack?'

'We got a full house, Jimmy P. Karrios, Repzac, and Preggio. They're all real popular with the ladies.'

Then the light in the living room upstairs was extinguished, and the three shadows cast on the curtains disappeared.

We had a pair of detectives around the clock on Preggio's place. The coppers saw the smaller female emerge from the apartment building at 8.26 a.m., the report read. I was in my office at noon, going over that document. They scoped the girl's license plates and followed her home. She was Caroline Keady, and she lived in a very affluent location – Lake Forest. Apparently with her parents. The

72

old man was a corporate lawyer. Mommy was an heiress in her own right.

'Caroline's got shitty taste in men,' Doc said after he reviewed what I had been reading. Today was Jack's day off.

'She's doing a sandwich with Preggio and the redhead. Rich bitch from the ritziest neighborhood in the city, and she's slumming with a molester and some whore,' I said.

'Yeah. Juicy, ain't it?'

But Doc was not smiling.

'We're stretching this out on your intuition, Jimmy. How far does all this extend?'

'I'm open for suggestions.'

'Don't read me wrong. I'm just saying we might want to leave some options open.'

'Like what, Doc? I'm all ears.'

'Like working with that Fibbie profiler the Captain mentioned. I like your gut feelings, guinea, but I think we ought to work this thing with more lines in the water.'

'Okay. So we talk to the profiler. That's good with me.'

'You're not pissed off, are you, dago?'

'No . . . But I still think we've got the fucking shark in the tank. I still think our boy's in this group of three.'

'You're probably right. But let's make this shrink work for a living. Okay?'

I nodded. Then he told me he was buying at Garvin's. Brats and beer for everybody. It was impossible to stay angry at this would-be professor. He knew our case against my three guys was non-existent, and he was being as gentle as he could with me. I was wondering if I was getting senile at fifty. Or maybe it was the upcoming wedding next spring. Or perhaps I was too anxious about Natalie being a decoy for The Farmer. I didn't know which, and maybe it was all.

'We're gonna find out that you were right on the money, but right now, fuck it. Man has to eat.'

He threw me my jacket and I flopped the three files onto the top of my desk.

73

Chapter Thirteen

So, we have close calls. The police have found us, probably through the Internet, and they almost catch her at Brookfield Zoo. She was prepared to die if they had caught her. She tells me that, over and over. She is prepared to die for me, for us.

She wants to know why I torture her in bed. Why I do the little things I do. Who is it that hurt me so badly that I have all this bile saved up in me that gets aimed at her? She says she wants to know. Then I have to strike her. I slap her across the mouth and I plunge into her, and she doesn't know which reaction hits her first – the pain or the pleasure. I try to explain to her that what I do is intentional, that it merely fuels her desire for me. Not knowing which is coming. Pain or pleasure. They are both unique experiences that I want to show her. She cannot quite understand that the awareness of one of them simply heightens the expectations in the other. I try to explain to her that pleasure and pain are part of the general dichotomy. She complains that she doesn't know what I'm talking about, but when I explain what 'twoness' means, she seems to grasp some of it. That is what I find exciting about her. Not her grape-sized nipples, not the mound of black pubic hair, nor the flatness of her ripe white belly. Not the melon-shaped breasts nor the lovely handfuls of buttocks nor the pouty, full lips. Nothing about her physically is all that extraordinary. It is her willing-

ness to subjugate herself to my desires. It is her ability to try and learn what it is I'm attempting to teach her.

I lunge at her and her eyes widen. I lunge again and again and she cries out. It is all right for her to be noisy. We have another place apart from people. We're miles from the city. Sixty miles west of Chicago, just outside the bounds of a state university. We're close enough to be inside the city limits in an hour, and we're far enough away for the privacy we need. We live, sometimes, in this old farmhouse. I bought the ten acres that surround the place with the money I'd saved in the military. My war was good for something, after all.

She cries out again and so I stab at her deeply and she comes. She comes hard. I can tell by the way she lifts us both off the mattress. She was a gymnast in high school. She has abnormally powerful thighs. When she wraps them about my waist, sometimes she can cut off my air. Until I slap her. Which sometimes only encourages her to tighten her legs about me. I forget the things that turn up her heat, occasionally. Pleasure and pain. Sometimes they are interchangeable.

We've tried bondage. We've tried cutting off her air at the moment of orgasm. But she doesn't enjoy being choked as much as I'd hoped.

She is a useful woman. I owe her a great deal in regard to my business. Her connections have made this venture get off the ground. The people she knows. The places she took me after we first met. Some of her qualities are indeed priceless. There is also her knowledge of computers. If it hadn't been for her, we wouldn't have the immediate access to the marketplace that we have.

Or had. Now we have to change our advertisements. We'll have to recode our ads because it's obvious the police have invaded our cyberspace.

She said she felt them as they closed in on her. She couldn't see them at first because they gave her a great deal of space between her and the cop in the green jacket. But then she felt them moving in. And just as they were about to nab her, she hit the fence. Luckily the animals on the other side were giraffes. If they had been more aggressive predators, she would've been

75

killed. And perhaps the two police who scaled the fence would've gone down with her.

The thought of her being ravaged heats me up. I'm hard again, even before I've had time to withdraw. I start at her again. We're heaving on top of the bed. Her hands are still tied to the bedposts, but she's raised her legs toward the ceiling. I don't know how she sustains her position. Perhaps it's the gymnast in her.

I'm pummeling her, but she doesn't cry out. There is a determined look on her face. It's as if she's refusing to acknowledge the beating I'm giving her. Finally I can withstand her no longer, and it's finished.

I flop on her, exhausted, and she screams loudly. It's as if she's defeated me in some kind of contest.

I raise myself above her and see that she's smiling, so I kneel and then I slap her across the mouth. There's a trace of blood at the corner of her lips. She probes the wound with her tongue and tastes the sticky, salty, sweaty fluid at her mouth. Then she smiles up at me again.

I have to hurt her. She's begging me to do it. So I reach down to her and do it, this time, with my hands. I begin plucking hairs. She will not let the sounds come out of her mouth, but I can see the silent shrieks in her eyes each time I pluck a short, kinky strand.

It all serves to inflame me once more. We're back as we were, and in seconds she is lifting me off the bed, as if she were a magician. We're levitating above the mattress, and I look over at her left thigh. It is inflated and huge, and the sweat glazes her leg as well as her torso and face. I feel like I'm going to slide off her. But we are locked together on account of her enormous female strength, and so I stay in place until she is finished. And this time when the end arrives, I have no energy left to begin again on her. We lie on the soaked sheets, both of us gasping for oxygen. She writhes in pleasure next to me, teasing me, but I'm spent. I undo her bonds, and her arms flop down to her sides. Then she takes hold of me with her hand and, before I can protest, she has her hair and head over my middle.

Suddenly she looks up at me and smiles, but all I can see is her teeth. Her white and perfect teeth. And I don't know whether it's a smile or a grimace. And then she goes back down and resumes working on me.

I want to see if she'll cry out if I yank a few strands of her luxurious hair, but I'm too tired. So I lie back and let her go on and on with it, until she's had enough.

Chapter Fourteen

We had backed off from Karrios. We had spent a lot of time on Repzac and Preggio, so we'd let the first guy slide. Doc and Jack and I decided to go back to our original suspect.

We went to his apartment, but all we met up with was the girlfriend who'd given him the alibi for the nights in question. Her name was Ellen Jacoby, and as soon as I saw her, I knew I'd seen her somewhere before.

'Do I know you, Ms Jacoby?' I asked her as the three of us sat on the sofa inside their apartment.

'No, I don't think so.' She smiled.

'You look very familiar to me, somehow,' I continued.

She smiled again, and I could see what Karrios saw in her. There was a flame underneath her skin. It was the kind of sex that permeates some women who didn't have all that cosmetic flare to operate with. She was a pretty woman, but not a beautiful one. I'd say she was an Italian, except for the name, Jacoby.

I showed her the three dates of the two killings and the near encounter, and she came up with the same scenario that she had when we'd interviewed her directly after talking with her boyfriend.

She had her gaze fixed on me, and it was almost embarrassing. She was ignoring Doc and Jack. Usually when the three of us did any talking with suspects, females couldn't keep their eyes off Wendkos. He was the face-man of the three of us. But she was concentrating on me, and I was wondering if she had remembered where it was the two of us had seen each other. I was very good with faces, but not so good with names. I had to work at memorizing people's names, which was a flaw in a homicide investigator. It was my most glaring weakness, so I had to work at it the hardest and the longest.

Doc was grinning. He thought this girl wanted to jump my old bones. Jack had a nonplussed stare going her way. It didn't appear that he saw the appeal in Ellen Jacoby.

'You're quite certain he was with you all that time on those dates?' Doc finally asked, breaking an awkward silence.

'Yes. I'm sure,' she said. She was looking directly at me.

We wasted a few more minutes asking unimportant questions, but she didn't lose her poise. She was confident when we came in, and she and her story hadn't been shaken since. So it was time to stop wasting time. We'd have to keep an eye on Ellen Jacoby and Marco Karrios – but from a distance. You could bet that Marco and his girlfriend knew all about the subject of harassment.

We offered her our thanks. She kept staring at me with those eyes. Like she was a witch trying to mesmerize me. I almost laughed out loud as I excused the three of us, but suddenly there was nothing funny about her staring. We walked out of the apartment and out to our car.

'That bitch is definitely wrong,' Jack muttered.

'Why? Because she didn't eyeball you the way she did our Lieutenant?' Doc cracked.

'No. It ain't jealousy here, Doc. There's just something wrong with her,' Jack countered.

'I've seen her before but I can't remember where it was,' I told them.

Her face danced in my mind like something dangling at the end of a pole. Like a piñata, with all the goodies

79

inside it. If only you could whack it with a stick and make all the insides come pouring out. There was something besides her face that I remembered, but it was too deeply embedded for me to dislodge it.

'Well shit, I'll be thinking about her all goddamned day now,' I admitted.

'The redhead wouldn't approve,' Doc suggested.

'The redhead's got nothing to worry about. Jack's correct. This female is definitely wrong. But I'm not sure she has a damn' thing to do with our principal focus in this case. And where the fuck's Marco?'

'We forgot to ask,' Jack laughed.

'Maybe she's psychic,' Doc said. 'She willed us not to ask about her beloved.'

'There's something stronger than that coming out of her,' I told my two colleagues.

'I think this girl has put the spell on you, guinea. What do they call it? The evil eye?'

'How could someone named Jacoby have an evil eye?' I told Doc. 'That's a Sicilian thing.'

'Yeah. You're right,' Gibron admitted.

Something stirred inside me, just then.

'What's wrong, Jimmy?' Jack asked.

'I . . . I don't know. I thought I . . . Jesus, let's get back downtown.'

Doc was driving, but he looked over at me in the front passenger's seat from time to time as we cruised south down Lakeshore Drive.

I was preoccupied with Ellen Jacoby all of the rest of the afternoon, but nothing came to me. I couldn't place her. I saw her face and I knew I'd come across her before. And I knew it'd been a long time since I'd encountered her, but I still couldn't fix a date and a place as to where I'd come in contact with her.

I was all preoccupied when I was with Natalie, as well. She asked me what was troubling me.

'It's like trying to think of a word, but you can't recall it. You think you've got it, but it eludes you. That's what

I'm going through with this damn' woman. She's the lover of a guy we're watching.'

'For The Farmer?'

'Yeah.'

'You think she's his accomplice?'

'Maybe not. I just know I've seen the damn' woman before and it's irritating the hell out of me. Doc thinks she's cast a spell on me. She kept staring at me during the interview.'

'She's a witch?'

'No. She's somebody I know I've seen before.'

'Maybe she *did* cast a hex on you, Jimmy.'

'You're the only woman with magical powers in my life.'

'Then why're you so upset about her?'

'I can't shake her. It's like an itch square in the middle of your back, just out of reach.'

'Come here and I'll scratch it.'

She sat down next to me on her own sofa, she lifted my shirt up, and she proceeded to rub my back.

'I'll get over it. I never forget a face . . . Doc called it "the evil eye". Like those old Italian women . . . Like those old black-dressed Sicilian women . . . It still won't come, God damn it!'

She took hold of my face between her hands.

'You look into these eyes. There. Right there. I'll take the hex off . . . See? I can stare and glare with the best of them.'

Then she kissed me, and it was as if Natalie had broken that so-called spell. Ellen Jacoby's familiar face disappeared and I was left with no one but my fiancée in front of me.

I felt a burden had been lifted. I reached up and put my hands over her hands. Then I kissed her.

We kept surveillance on Preggio, Repzac, and Karrios. We also had the whole squad keeping a lookout on any other

81

offender who might fit the bill of The Farmer. My gut instincts did not preclude keeping the file open on potential cutters other than the three I'd got on my shortlist.

The file on Preggio was still incomplete. We were missing a lot of bio information on him, and it was troubling me. I didn't like blanks when it came to a suspect's sheet. And Preggio wouldn't be forthcoming with any information since we'd had our one chat and we had nothing further to haul him downtown for. There was this stumbling block called The Constitution, the Bill of Rights. We had to be aware of those small details where we worked. So if he was not willing to fill in the blanks, we had to fill them in for him.

We started with his prints. You got arrested, you made prints. We ran the prints to the FBI, and guess what? He was indeed military, and contrary to the lousy odds Doc and I established, Preggio was indeed in the Medical Corps during the Gulf War. All three of our boys had ties to Band-Aids and gauze. And knives. And even if they hadn't trained as medics, the Army still taught them how to use a blade. But not so much about how to remove the innards of a guy you were wasting. At least, *I* didn't recall learning how to dissect some sorry son of a bitch I was supposed to be killing. We went through all the combat training before we were shipped off to Vietnam in the late sixties. Luckily, I never had call to use a bayonet. Just the M16, and that rifle with its choice of automatic and semiauto fire was quite sufficient for me.

So Preggio completed the trio. All of them veterans of the same short war. All of them sex offenders with crimes against women and/or adolescent girls. All of them in the same age range. None of them were without current female companionship.

I could still see that sweatshirt-hood racing up that fence at the giraffe enclosure.

The sick feeling of guessing wrong about The Farmer hit me, as it did about three or four times every day. I remembered Doc said we had to leave the door open to other possibilities besides Preggio, Repzac and Karrios. He was right. But my stomach still said it was one of them. Maybe it was my ego, my pride.

The Farmer was down for retooling. He had had a close call with the woman at the Zoo, so now he was retrenching. Changing his ad on the Internet. God help Matty McGinn find him again. I would be pushing it to go back to Billy Cheech for any new information. He was my cousin, so I didn't particularly want to see him get killed. Jail, he deserved. Death, no. He was a petty thief, mostly. He was not a made man and he probably never would be because I didn't think he had the sack to kill people.

Our boy was lying low, waiting for his comeback. And if Doc and Jack and I didn't hurry, he'd be notching number three on the handle of that razor-sharp knife he was an expert at using.

Chapter Fifteen

The old man sipped from his can of Diet Dr Pepper. He was not as old as he looked. He was just sixty-three, but he looked ten years older.

'Dr Gray, do you think our guy would have to have had a medical background?' I asked the ME.

'Not necessarily, Jimmy. Why would you think that?'

He sipped slowly at his soda pop again.

'Because of the skill he showed in cutting out the organs.'

'But that doesn't mean he was a physician in training. A couple of courses in dissection could've got him where he's at ... Why are you stuck on that theme about med school?'

'Because that's how we came up with our three boys. From the computer and from the profile. Their age range is twenty-five to forty, their race is white, and they were all medics in the Gulf – and one guy served at the tail end of Vietnam, right before the fall of Saigon in 1974–5.'

'So the computer made all these hits, and wa-la, here are your three primary suspects. How many guys were on the list before the cut?'

'Something like thirty-eight.'

'Jesus, Jimmy. That leaves thirty-five extras in your scenario. You're putting a lot of faith in that damn' machine.'

'You sound more like Doc every time I talk to you, and now you're scaring the shit out of me, Dr Gray.'

'You'll survive. You're not gonna be shaken by what some old quack told you ... I'm just trying to say that you might be overplaying the hits from the computer on their history as medics. I read all that crap about the ages of white serial killers, and I know it's supposed to work. But let me tell you, Lieutenant, the knife work on those two women is not exceptional. It's workmanlike. Not messy. But not extraordinarily skillful. A good butcher could have done those two jobs. After he'd dosed them, they became like slabs of meat, didn't they?'

'No. Not really, Doctor.'

'Stop being so goddamned *spiritual* with me, Parisi. I'm talking about their physical bodies. I know they were human beings. Give me a little credit. But the task of removing those organs from dead human beings is nothing like the skill it takes to remove all those parts from a living person and the skill it takes to replace those same items and keep said subject alive ... Am I coming through, Lieutenant?'

'Yeah. I think so. I know you guys know your business.'

'We're not meat-cutters, I'm telling you. But the guy who did these two ladies could very well have been on about that kind of primitive level, so I'm saying I wouldn't get all caught up in what a wonderful *surgeon* this clown seems to be to you and to some of the media. They're comparing The Farmer to Jack the Ripper, who might well have been a medico. I say bullshit, Jimmy. *This* guy's a novice cutter. Neat, but no superstar. You want a superstar, watch a neurosurgeon do his thing ... Now, if there's nothing else?'

A meat-cutter. A butcher. All that improbability went right down the shitter. The computer picked these three on common hits. And I was the guy who was convinced the machine gave me three good names to pursue. And Dr Gray ripped me a new anal aperture for being stuck on them, for insisting it had to be one of them.

85

The list of molesters – the original one – had almost forty names. And the only common hits were the race (white) and the age range (25–40), and the military business. And forty was probably a bit too old for the standard serial murderer. My machine detective suddenly appeared to have warts. What if I was spending all this time on the wrong suspects? That singular obsession had been gnawing at me ever since Doc had brought the notion up. The Medical Examiner made my own innards sink when he tore up all my theories about a war-vet medic being the guy. It sounded so good until Gray got hold of it, and now . . .

You went on until the end. All I could do was eliminate the three of them and then start on the rest of the list when I saw that Repzac, Karrios and Preggio were just beeps that matched on the cyber system. Then I would be right back at the beginning.

But it was the women who kept me thinking there was a reason to go back and keep hacking at them. Three women. I knew the woman at the zoo belonged to one of them. Three women who had the general body size, give or take an inch or two of height, to keep them on the playing field.

The woman was the key. If I found her, I found The Farmer.

Janice Ripley, Repzac's live-in, had long, sandy-blonde hair. She was a little tall – about five five. But it was close enough to make her a possible. Jack Wendkos had never made her face clearly. The hood had been drawn and the sunglasses had covered much of her visage. He couldn't be sure exactly what she'd looked like.

Doc and I met with Ripley at Repzac's apartment on the North Side. Repzac was at work, she told us as we entered the middle flat of a three-level. Jack was at work downtown, waiting for the results of possible fingerprints on the hood we'd found at Brookfield.

Her eyes were unlike those of Ellen Jacoby, Karrios's lover. They were more vacant than brilliant. They looked at you, then around you, and then at nothing in particular. I was thinking drugs. I looked over at Doc and he watched me before I began.

'We've asked you about these dates before, Ms Ripley. Before you give us the answer you did last time, I want to remind you that if you withhold evidence in a capital crime you're looking at major heat.'

'Major heat?' She smiled. But there was no amusement in her face.

'That means a lot of years of incarceration,' Doc explained.

'Oh, I understand,' she said.

Now her eyes were focused out the front window, behind Doc and me.

'Are you waiting for someone?' I asked.

'Huh? . . . Oh, no. I was just looking to see if the sun was out. It's getting cold. Winter'll be here before—'

'You understood what I said, did you?' I questioned her.

'Sure. I wouldn't lie about something like murder. I read about the two killings. They were horrible. Just horrible. How could anyone do a thing like that? . . . I know Daw couldn't. He just couldn't.'

'You're aware of his criminal record?'

'Sure,' she told me. 'Daw didn't do it. He had a juvy record, so they just picked him out because he was an easy mark.'

'Are you using?' I asked her.

She sat there, but now she was watching me carefully.

'Hey man, I—'

'Hey, shit. Are you using, Janice?' I asked her again.

'Are you narcin' me, Lieutenant?'

'No. I'm Homicide. Remember? But if you're into things you shouldn't be, you could put your boyfriend – Daw, right? – into a world of shit. Unless, that is, the two of you are already into that world of shit. Is that the way it is, Janice?'

She averted her eyes to the window once more.

'I think I don't want to talk to you guys anymore. Not without a lawyer, anyway.'

'Okay,' Doc told her. He left his card on the coffee table in front of her. 'But if you want to jump the ship your boyfriend's sinking with, call me and let me know ... Janice, you ought to come down and see the pictures we've got. You might want to buy a night-light so you can keep a good eye on Daw before you go to sleep.'

'I don't think I want to talk to you anymore, Detective.'

She stood now, and her glare was angry and resolute. I might've been wrong about the drugs. Or maybe all that spacey shit was part of an act.

'Call if you change your mind,' Doc insisted.

We walked out the front door.

'Was she the fence climber, Jimmy P?'

I opened the driver's side of the Taurus, out by the curb.

'If she was as sober as she was at the end of the conversation, I could see it, yeah.'

We had to drive all the way up to the northern suburb of Lake Forest to find Caroline Keady, Preggio's third member of his little love triangle.

We called on the phone first, just to make sure that we wouldn't waste time and gas for the trip. We also gave County a call before we intruded on their territory. County was very cooperative.

We had to drive a quarter-mile along their driveway before we pulled up to the estate. 'It ain't a house,' Doc told me. This was the ritzy part of northern Illinois. It was where the yuppies settled when they cashed in their stocks and when they inherited Dad's bucks. This was the old rich section of the Chicago area. It was probably the most affluent area in striking distance of the city. There were no mean streets in Lake Forest, but that didn't preclude there being a few mean and ornery human creatures up this far north, just off Lake Michigan.

As we also expected, Caroline didn't answer the door. A butler did. But he didn't resemble Jeeves. He was not British. He was Filipino, with a very pronounced accent. I felt like joshing him about his green card, but we didn't have the time to mess with him.

We waited in the library. It was on the main floor, just past the staircase. Caroline Keady showed up in less than five minutes. Doc was checking out the beautifully bound books that were shelved all around us.

The girl walked in wearing raggy-assed blue jeans. But I saw a very expensive brand name on the rear of them as she turned and closed the doors behind herself.

'This is all very embarrassing. I don't know why I'm involved in this . . . investigation,' she sputtered.

I identified Doc and myself, we showed her our credentials, and then I got down to it as Doc carried on checking out the tomes in leather.

'You know Jimmy Preggio.'

'Yes. Or you wouldn't be here. Right?'

'Look, Caroline. We're not here to flame up on you. We're interested in Preggio . . . You were at his place several times in the last few weeks?'

She was right on the money with her size, complexion, hair color. It was a mousy brown, my wife Erin would have called it. She was not outstanding in the face, but she was attractive, like the other two. And there was a very up-front sexuality about her, as there was with Jacoby and Ripley.

'You're having a relationship with Mr Preggio. A sexual one, I mean,' Doc said, his face still aimed at the stacks.

Caroline eyeballed the doors behind her, just to make sure she had closed them.

'That's none of your business,' she snapped at my partner.

'Yeah, it is. When it's involved in a homicide case it is. So?'

'My father has a number of very fine attorneys—'

'I'm sure he does, sweety. Just answer what I asked,' Doc said, his back still toward her.

'You are very rude, sir.'

'You oughta see how downright snotty I can become in the Loop . . . How will you explain all that interviewing in the homicide department to your dear old Pa-*pa*?'

She appeared furious at my partner, so she turned to me.

'Don't look to me for any help,' I said as I put my palms up at her. 'You just answer what he's asking and we'll be out of here before tea.'

'Look, I have a relationship with Jimmy, yes.'

'Is that why he brings in outside help? To encourage your . . . relationship?' I asked.

'I didn't know that it was against the law.'

'It isn't. I don't think. Unless the redhead was a pro. And I think she was. That's where it might get messy, Caroline. If money actually changed hands. Oh, don't get me wrong. We're not Vice. But I've got a lot of friends in that department.'

I stared at her, and then I saw her visibly weaken.

'What we do behind closed doors is none of your business.'

'That's right. But I'm going to turn every screw I can to get you to pay attention to me, Caroline. This guy Preggio is a loser with a record that includes sexual molestation. He's very dangerous and he might have killed the two women I told you about over the phone. So why not just answer our questions, and then we'll leave you to your privacy?'

Slowly, she nodded her head. And then the three of us sat down amidst that wealth of literature, and I began the interview.

'I like the way she played innocence. She was first-rate, Jimmy. You can bet the bitch is a user, just like our Ms Ripley. And Ellen Jacoby, for that matter. All three are lying down with canines, and they're all likely bearing those little mites caught from just such an occasion.'

90

'Fleas, you mean.'

'Yessir. Precisely ... You like her, Jimmy?'

'She fits the physical description the best of the three ... But I got my doubts after listening to you and to Dr Gray.'

'Don't second-guess yourself.' He looked out the passenger's side as a cold Lakeshore Drive flew past us. 'Like you said, Jimmy P. We have to eliminate these three assholes and their girlfriends, and when we do we'll keep going right on down that list.'

He looked over at me, and I knew he was thinking what I was thinking: We didn't have time to track down a list of forty. The Farmer was going to start hacking and whacking again, once he got himself set up on the Internet for business. We couldn't rely on Matty McGinn to catch him in cyberspace because we wouldn't get any more clues from my cousin Billy: I was not going to get that half-wit member of my family killed by his own people.

The machine narrowed my list to three, and they still seemed likely. Each one of them.

Of the women, Ellen Jacoby was the nastiest. She had killer eyes. But we might have seen Janice Ripley on downers. Maybe she sprouted fangs when she took amphetamines. There was no telling unless you were there. And the recent graduate of Wellington College – Caroline Keady. Was she the corrupt rich, slumming with a piece of shit like Jimmy Preggio because she actually *knew* how deadly he might be? Did that float her fucking boat?

I was getting headaches from trying to sort all these men and women out. What I had to do was simplify. I had to pick a pair, and then go for their throats. This was the selection process that Doc and I talked about. You always had the terror of hopping on the wrong trolley. It was like a confidence game. The dealer had three cards. The Queen of Spades was one of the three. His hands shuffled them so deftly, so quickly, that often you were fooled about where that dark lady was hiding.

91

And sometimes the dealer cheated. Sometimes he palmed the Queen. Sometimes the game was a fix.

'Three little sweethearts. And one of them is giving it up for free to our guy. The more I think about it, the more I like your selections, Jimmy.'

He had just grabbed hold of me before I fell off this cliff on whose edge I had been standing. He had reached out and snatched me before vertigo took over. I didn't feel quite so dizzy now.

'But of the three pairs, it's anybody's guess. I mean really, I don't have a favorite, and that is no shit, Jimmy P.'

The Lake water was grey-blue. Winter was closing in on the city, and the Farmer's Almanac was predicting a bull bitch of a season for us this year. We'd had it easy, the last few years.

'We put twenty-four hour surveillance on the women. We let the males think we've loosened the knot. We watch the girls, and one of them leads us right where we want to go,' I told him.

'Let's hope he's not all copacetic with the Internet, Jimmy. Let's hope he's not quite ready to go back out into the field yet.'

'He felt the heat on his neck when the girl almost got picked, at the Zoo. He'll lie doggo until he thinks the heat's turned down to low. He'll try to outwait us. This guy needs to do what he does, but he'll wait until he thinks he can get away with it a little more easily.'

I felt my confidence soar. All that backsliding with Dr Gray had disappeared. My gut and my head were telling me we were headed in the right direction.

Three women, three criminals.

It came to me as I saw the Sears Tower ahead of us:

What if one of the females had a record? What if one of the girls had a jacket for us to read up on, downtown?

Chapter Sixteen

He was a mass of tubes. Somebody had shot him as he walked out of the lube place where he worked. I found out about it during the second half of my midnight shift.

Doc came down to St Luke's with me. Jack was left on the phones downtown until we could find out what the hell had happened to Billy Ciccio.

He was in serious but stable condition, we learned as we arrived at his room. The doctor was on his way out. Seemed that Billy took two .22 caliber hits, one to his left shoulder and the other to his lower back.

'They woulda put it in the back of my head, Jimmy, if I hadn't heard them come up from behind me out in the alley. Then I started to run and they tried to pop me anyways.'

He looked pale, but not as bad as I thought he'd look with two rounds in his back.

'This is about your thing, Jimmy. I know it is. Somebody thought I'd put the finger on them around here, and they were takin' me out. I know it.'

'Just take it easy. We'll take care of it, Billy.'

Doc stood by the door. He was never a big fan of my cousin, but I could see some concern on my partner's face.

'You'll take care of it? This is one of our things, now. How're *you* gonna take care of things?'

'I'll find out who it was. I'll take him.'

'You ain't gonna clip any of these bastards. I oughta know. I'm one of them!'

'Take it easy, Billy ... The guy who came up from behind you. You never caught a glance at him?'

'Hell, no. I went down and played dead. And I'm fuckin' lucky he didn't waste a coupla more rounds makin' sure I was out. But I heard him hurry past me. I saw the backs of his shoes, and that was that.'

'It's because you talked to me, wasn't it?'

His tired face aimed itself at me.

'I can't think of nothin' else that'd get two .22s in my back end.'

'So I'm going to tell you how we save your ass,' I told him.

'Yeah? I'd like to hear that.'

'Listen, Billy. You want to keep on breathing, the only way to do it is to help me find this guy who's been using the knife. He was the guy with the gun, and if it wasn't him personally, then he's got somebody inside who's working with him. You want to keep living, you better get more aggressive about finding out just who the hell he is.'

'You got me into this, cousin.'

'Saying sorry's not going to help you out, Cheech. This time you'll have to help me and yourself. I never wanted you in harm's way. You know that.'

'So I'm your guy on the inside ... And what else do you want me to find out?'

'I'm Homicide, Billy. I'm only interested in one case. I told you. I'll let the Feds put you and your crew away. You want to steal, you deal with them. But I told you the truth. I never wanted to see you get hurt. And now the only way to make things right is to help me.'

He was far more tired now than he'd been when Doc and I got there. I had to let him rest.

'Will you do it, Billy?'

He looked at me and I saw that he was watering up as if he was going to cry.

'Like I got a fuckin' choice?'

'I don't think the cutter's a member of your crew. He's not Sicilian, I don't think. He'd be an associate, or he'd be tight with a crew member, but he's not a blood brother . . . You have to try and remember who you pumped to get me the stuff about Imperial Products of Bridgeport. The guy you talked to and the guys he talked to. You know how to follow a rat trail by now.'

'Yeah. I do. I just hope I get up that fuckin' trail a ways before somebody gets a better shot at my fuckin' noggin.'

'I'm sorry about all this, Billy. But this guy's been killing other people. Two women and a doorman, so far. We'll keep an eye on you until you get out of here. You call me if you need anything. I'll keep coming in until you leave. Then I won't do any more face-to-faces with you. You won't need a cop up next to you when you go back to the crew. Right?'

I reached out and grasped his right hand. If things had been different, I might've wound up where he was. In the Outfit, I mean. I'd had my opportunities when I was as young as he was, when he joined up. A lot of the guys he hung with I went to high school with. Some of my old classmates were dead or behind the wire now, too.

I walked over to Doc at the door.

'You cops are always fuckin' with people,' Billy lamented.

I looked over at him and smiled, and I was wondering if he'd get back to where he started. Whoever popped him wouldn't be satisfied with scaring the guy. He wanted my cousin dead.

The search for information on the three women led us to a file on Caroline Keady, the rich girl from Lake Forest. She'd been arrested twice for possession of marijuana. Both charges were dropped at the insistence of her very prominent attorneys, I was sure.

The other thing was a weapons charge against Janice

Ripley. She was caught with a .32, trying to board a plane to San Francisco. She was hauled in and then later placed on probation.

We found nothing on Ellen Jacoby. Not even a traffic beef. Which confused me. None of these three were choir-girls. I'd expected to find a little something on each of them. So we'd come up somewhat empty.

Which was the smarts of The Farmer showing. He wouldn't want someone with a sheet being his partner. Paper trails were how you got caught. Statements, documents, IRS return forms. Paper nailed your heinie. So he picked something close to a virgin, as far as the state was concerned.

I was looking at Ellen Jacoby. I knew her face. It was still bothering me. But the memory wouldn't come to me. Her face was maddeningly familiar.

Suddenly I made a tiny connection with her. It had to do with Billy Ciccio. Maybe with his cousin, Danny Ciccio. But that was as far as I could take it. Then it all crumbled in front of me. If I wanted Danny Cheech's help, I'd have to go to Joliet and have a talk with my second cousin, but I didn't have the time right now. Maybe Billy would recognize her from the photos we had of the three women. I made a mental note to ask him when he was feeling stronger.

The women were only a little bit tarnished, and Ellen Jacoby was the cleanest of the three. That was why I liked her. She was a front, not substance. Something had to be underneath her exterior. Something past that 'come fuck me' look that she liked to throw toward any male in her vicinity.

One of these females was hooked to The Farmer. I knew it in my blood. It had gone beyond the gut and into my veins, and if I could remember where it was that I'd first seen Ellen Jacoby, maybe I'd be able to find the Queen of Spades that was hidden beneath one of those three face-down cards.

Chapter Seventeen

All it takes is the word that we're up and running, and I'm back in business again. She tells me we're aboard the Internet and I've set up shop within hours.

College campuses can be crowded, but laboratories and libraries are not the most popular places to be after, say, 9.00 p.m. This college campus is only three miles from our farmhouse, so it is very convenient for me. Ten minutes and I'm there. Fifteen minutes to operate, and I'm on my way home, product stowed.

The geology lab seems to be the most unpopular classroom on campus of this university. There are only two students and one faculty member still here – apart from me. I've secured a gray work-shirt with 'Ralph' sewn above the left breast pocket. I spent last night checking out the maintenance crew, and the school has no particular precautions when it comes to security. Their staff are not ID'd. At least, not with laminated cards attached to their shirts and blouses.

So I walk in with a broom and I avoid the real maintenance man – Carl – who's still working on the labs in the biology wing.

Finally the two female students depart, and I'm left with the associate professor who's come down here to grade papers. It's quieter here than in the library. I've been to the library previously, too.

She looks up at me and smiles, and I return the expression. She's very young for my tastes. Perhaps in her late twenties.

She's probably just received her PhD and she's still a go-getter who grades her own work without the aid of a Teaching Assistant. I feel something like regret that she's the one who's here with me, but the feeling quickly fades since this is a business matter. And she's close enough to the right age. The memories come back, and what struck me as a passing sympathy has vanished. I can see her the way I saw the other two. I can impose that portrait on her face, just as I did with Delores Winston and Genevieve Malone. This geology professor or instructor fits the bill.

I go out into the hall and I walk toward the biology wing, here in the science building. The place is now deserted. It's a Friday night, so all the undergraduates are at the bars or at some dormitory party. Or they're rutting with a mate in their little garrets somewhere. But they have left these premises. I find the maintenance man sitting at the teacher's desk in one of the classrooms in the next wing. I can hear him snoring from the hallway. I pop my head into the classroom, and I see that he is indeed asleep, his forehead resting on the desk top.

I walk back to the geology room. I've left my bag out in the hallway. I reach down and take it up as I prop the broom handle against the brick wall.

When I walk in, I see the blonde teacher has left the room. I begin to panic. How could she have left this abruptly? Then I see all of her paperwork has been gathered and removed as well.

I find my jacket in the bag, and I put it on. It's blustery and cold tonight.

She cannot have gotten far if she's outside. But if I pursue her, there are all the variables of catching her and working on her outdoors. I've got no choice. I've come this far. I've got orders to fill and miles to go before I sleep.

I trot down the hallway and then I bolt out the exit. I stop and look. I don't see her at first.

She's about five feet six, about 125 pounds. Nice tits, even though she tries to hide them under an oversized white blouse. I never saw the bottom half of her, but I can imagine she's got the kind of body I could enjoy, if I had the time to enjoy it.

I walk out into the darkness of the campus. It's then that I make her out. It's beginning to drizzle, so there is no one else out here. If it becomes any colder, this drizzle might turn to ice. It feels frosty enough.

She's walking toward the school's lagoon, her briefcase full of papers crammed up under her right arm. When I close in on her, I can see that her rear end is just as juicy as the front torso. Why would a woman as ripe as this have made a life in the study of rocks?

I close the block between her and me very quickly. There are no lovers down by the university lagoon because of the elements. And because it is Friday night, bar night on this campus, there are no lonely strollers to interrupt me.

The distance is down to a quarter of a block when she drops the briefcase.

'Can I help you?' I ask her. She's still bent over, trying to pick up the mess she's made.

When she stands straight, she shoves her eyeglasses back up onto her nose. Her gesture inflames me. Then I see that she's startled by my presence.

Before she says a word, I have the T-shirt over her mouth and I'm forcing her back into the shrubbery that surrounds the tiny body of water they call a lagoon.

I've effectively muffled her screams. I've got her down on the ground, it's cold and there's always a risk, however remote, that someone might walk right on up to us at any second, but I've got to see her. As she lies on the wet, cold grass before me, I slit open her blouse and brassiere. I was right about her.

Then she moans. I haven't dosed her sufficiently. It happens occasionally. I go back into the bag for the T-shirt.

But I find the moaning more arousing, so I stop and replace the T-shirt in the satchel.

Then I tear her skirt and panties off with my hands. Before she can fully come to I'm on top of her and then in her. I'm lifting her off the soggy, chilled grass and I'm pounding at her, and all the while I can see her eyes coming more alive and alert. My own eyes have adjusted to the dim lighting that the surrounding streetlamps have provided, and I can see her waking gradually. And she knows that someone is inside her,

99

that someone is taking her, and she tries to scream, but she's still too foggy, and she quiets herself as if she's in the middle of some dream, as if she's enjoying what's happening to her. And then I hear footsteps. They are still some distance away from us, but they are approaching.

I cannot stop, as dangerous as I know it is. She's moaning, either in pleasure or in stupor, and I cannot stop myself. I am lunging and crashing against her, and suddenly she's coming to consciousness.

It is then that she cries out. I punch her once, then twice, and then she is asleep again. The footsteps I just heard have become louder. They're closer. So I pull up my zipper, gather my tools, and I get the hell out of here.

'You came home empty-handed?' she demands.

'Yes. Someone came up on us and I—'

'I can smell the sex on you. I can smell her. You had to fuck her before you—'

'What I do when I do my work does not concern you. You know how it has always been, and it will always be that way. Why are you so suddenly concerned about what I do to them, as long as I come home with—'

'But you've come home with nothing! It took two days to plan this, we've got a buyer waiting, and you come here to me with nothing! ... You're wrong. This is not jealousy. This is purely business, and you have fucked up, and I'll be the one who has to explain why there'll be a delay while you find someone with whom you can keep your zipper pulled up ... I don't care what you do to them. Just make sure you don't leave me vulnerable. Do you understand? Do you?'

I slap her and she falls to the floor.

'This is not a time for—'

I undo my pants.

Then I reach down to the floor and open my bag.

'What the hell are you doing?'

Just as she's about to scream, I choke the sound off. It isn't as if someone's going to hear her, out here.

100

I hold her down and I quiet her while I squeeze her throat. Then I enter her. She struggles at first, but her lack of air prevents her from fighting me as strongly as she would normally. She's fading as I finish.

Then I kneel next to her, and I show her the knife. She's coming to and her eyes are widening, but she's still weak from the near-throttling.

I sweep the flat of the blade across her stomach and down onto her pubic patch. I place the tip of the blade just at the edge of her labia.

'You ever talk to me that way again, and I'll use you the way I use them. Do you understand me?'

She's hushed quite nicely, and she nods her head very slowly and very gently.

Chapter Eighteen

She called it a conflict of interest. I called it using my weight. I got to oversee her stakeout for The Farmer because it was my case. She knew that I was the primary investigator on this deal, but she was hoping Wendkos would take over, seeing that she knew Doc and me on a personal level. I explained to Natalie that it didn't work that way this time. The Captain was aware that she and I were engaged to be married, but he also understood about manpower, and manpower was something we didn't have an overabundance of since U2, the rock-and-roll group, had come to town. And this Irish band got a lot of security help from us, and that led to shortages elsewhere, and hence Natalie couldn't get our red-headed Captain to get somebody other than me to head this detail.

'I don't want any special attention,' she said as we left to go to our area of operations.

'You won't get any,' I told her as she rode in the back of the Taurus. She was riding with Doc and me to the site.

The site this time was Watertower. We had picked that mall thing because the time of year was near to the holidays. It was also the time of year when the sun set early. So we let Natalie wander the Watertower shops. We let her amble toward the other stores and outlets on

Michigan Avenue, and we let her walk solo toward her parking lot.

She fit his bill. She was near thirty (twenty-seven), she was attractive, and she would be alone. At least, it would appear that way.

We dropped her off on Michigan Avenue where she picked up her own vehicle. She got in the Camry and headed north to the nearest private parking lot. We stayed discreetly behind her. Three other cars were on surveillance with us.

We knew it was a very long shot. This guy had been throwing darts at a board as if he was blind or as if he didn't care where he landed. But he'd hit the Loop area twice, and I still agreed that most of these serial slayers liked to stay in a comfort zone. When it got down to it, he'd come back home. And if The Farmer was Repzac, Preggio, or Karrios, Chicago was home.

She arrived at a lot just three blocks from where she had originally parked. She drove the Camry into the lower level, and then we had to wait until she emerged. She was gone for a few minutes, so I began to worry that something might have happened in those few seconds when we'd left her unattended. There was a blind spot in every plan, and walking out of the parking lot was that blind spot.

Finally she walked out into the waning daylight. It was just after 3.00 p.m. It was almost Thanksgiving, but the holiday crowds hadn't formed yet. Not until the parade and thereafter. When I saw her come out, my heart literally swelled. I could feel it expand inside my chest. This was my wife-to-be, I told myself, and she was staking herself out like a sacrificial she-goat. But she was also a police officer who had asked for this detail, too.

'She's one hellaciously pretty girl.' Doc smiled. 'If the asshole is in the neighborhood, he's got to notice her.'

'How many women are walking Michigan Avenue alone this afternoon?' I countered.

'We all know the odds on hitting on this thing, Jimmy,'

he told me. Then he slapped my forearm where it rested on the steering wheel.

'The odds are too long. Way the hell too long. I've never liked these things. Too risky. I wonder how many times we've actually been lucky on—'

'Hey, guinea. It's what we do when we have nothing else going our way. You know how it works.'

We pulled into a parking lot only one block away from Watertower. We'd passed Natalie on Michigan Avenue, but she knew to slow down and started looking into shop windows in order to make it very obvious that she was out there and she was on her own. We had Natalie's parking spot covered with eight coppers, so when she returned there were police all around her. This was another blind spot, while we were parking our car. The other detectives were cruising around and past my fiancée, but there were a few moments when she was out there all alone.

I could understand why she had asked the Captain to put Jack Wendkos in charge of this detail. Even I was aware of what a pain in the ass I'd become. Jack was one of the coppers on scene at Natalie's parking area.

Doc got us a spot. We got out quickly and hustled down toward street level.

We walked the block and a half to where we were supposed to catch up to the redhead, and there she was, looking into the picture window at the entrance, right next to the swiveling glass entry door. Natalie entered, and we were walking in after her. There were already four pairs of plainclothes inside, waiting for her. Each pair consisted of one male and one female police officer, so that they appeared to be couples doing Christmas shopping. I knew who the eight officers were. They were all Homicide.

As soon as we walked in, Doc and I saw Natalie board the upward escalator. This building was a house of glass and escalators. Everything seemed to point upward. There were numerous levels, and she rode skyward, seemingly bound toward the top. Anybody who suffered from fear of heights would not much like Watertower. You leaned over the railing, you felt like Jimmy Stewart in *Vertigo* when he kept on peering down, inside that bell tower. Even I tried to avoid looking at what we were leaving behind.

The redhead got off at the seventh level. We hadn't seen anyone squirrelly following her to this point. Just the group of Homicide people looking for a killer who might qualify as that kind of small bushy-tailed rodent.

She walked into a yuppie version of a clothes store. It had overpriced blue jeans that teenagers 'die for'. Forty-buck pants that you could buy in a place that ended in 'mart' for twenty-five percent less. It was the tag the kids wanted on their asses, anyway. I knew because my daughter Kelly loved to come here and drain my bank account.

Some bearded, bald young guy came right up to Natalie. He was wearing an ID, so he must have been an employee. She shed him in about thirty seconds, but she did it with a smile.

Doc nudged me as I pretended to peruse a pair of those high-priced denims.

I looked up and I saw a blond-haired man watching the redhead. He was about thirty-five, I guessed, about six feet one. He fit the general billing that we got from Stephanie Manske, The Farmer's one miss. It gnawed at me, of course, that we didn't know for sure that the guy who came up to her in that rainy parking lot was our guy, but you got to place your bet on one horse eventually or there was no chance at winning any cash.

Stephanie beat the hangman. She saw The Farmer and survived him. She was the only one we know who had, to this point. Was it Repzac or Preggio or Karrios that she saw? With his hair plastered to his head, lurking outside her ride in that thunderstorm? Yeah, I thought it was.

But this wasn't one of that terrible trio. I saw that as Doc and I wandered closer to the redhead. He was definitely eyeballing her.

105

I stopped with Doc and we looked through a pile of denim shirts.

Natalie walked around for a few more minutes. She had made this guy. The sign was a quick flick to the side of her nostril. It was subtle, but I saw it. She knew the blond man was on her trail.

She left the clothing store and began to walk toward the Warner Brothers outlet. The place with all the Daffy Duck and Bugs Bunny stuff. The blond guy was right behind her, and Doc and I were right behind him.

Another pair of plainclothes picked up the trail just outside the Warner store. It was Tracy Jascow and Billy Whiteside. Tracy was very noticeable because she was the best-looking homicide detective we had. She also had one of the highest clear-up rates in the department. Billy was a twelve-year veteran and a very successful copper, too.

All of us were inside the home of Looney Tunes. About three beats after we were in, Blondie approached Natalie. She was about thirty feet away from my partner and me, so we couldn't hear what he was saying. Natalie was not wired. It was difficult to do audio inside these kinds of places. There was a lot of interference in a high-rise mall like this, so we decided simply to maintain visual.

Natalie seemed to shake him off. He smiled, walked off – but he didn't disappear. He kept her in his sights and was pretending to shop at the glass cases that cluttered the floor.

When the redhead walked out, we watched the man. He waited a few seconds, then he went after Natalie. Doc and I and the other pair of detectives followed, a brief interval between us.

She rode the escalator upward, once more. I was starting to get dizzy even though I didn't chance a glance back down over the railing.

'You okay?' Doc asked. 'You look a little green.'

'I don't relish heights.'

Doc nodded. He remembered the case with the murder-

106

ous ex-nun who stabbed an ex-cop on top of a high-rise. The ex-cop flew down at us from the height of all those stories, and then Doc and I had to run up all those flights after her. She damn' near jumped over the edge. I was the guy who had to grab her. As I said, I didn't like heights.

Natalie hit a few other galleries. I saw a second swipe at her lovely nose as she turned sideways on the escalator down, now, and I knew she was aware she still had this guy behind her. It was time she made her move toward the parking lot in order to see if this man's intentions were sincere.

Down we went, but I kept my eyes straight ahead. Doc reached over and gripped my upper left arm, but I grinned to tell him I was all right, and finally we arrived at ground level. Tracy and Billy were still coming down after us.

Once we got outside, I was using the hand-held, and I told the detectives in the parking lot that we were headed their way. I got an affirmative response from Marty Marion, one of the Homicide guys waiting at the parking deck.

'These things never work out, Jimmy. He's just trying to hit on her and he can't understand "no".'

I shot a glance toward him, but we kept on walking back down Michigan Avenue. The six-foot blond man was between us and my fiancée. I was wearing the Nine in the shoulder holster and the .44 Bulldog against my lower left leg, just like the last time we came looking for trouble.

One more city block and we were back where Natalie began. It had gone quickly. Only forty-eight minutes had elapsed since the redhead got out of that lot. She hadn't even accumulated a decent bill for the parking yet. It was not supposed to work like this on stakeout. You were supposed to be prepared for an all-night-all-day marathon. I was not used to this kind of fast pace.

She walked inside the parking high-rise. Our guy was

right behind her, and the four of us were right behind him.

Natalie was parked on the third level up. She took the stairs. We backed off from the blond a bit, because it was becoming a little cramped for space. So we gave him a bigger interval. The level where she was parked was loaded with coppers anyhow.

When we caught back up with the two of them, Marty Marion whispered to me over the hand-held.

'He's going to a vehicle of his own, Jimmy. Red Dodge. New model, left-hand side of the lot.'

Marty got off quietly and quickly because he knew I was not far away from Natalie and the man behind her.

We saw the redhead opening the door of the Camry, her back to all of us. The blond man was off to our left, and he was unlocking his trunk. He pulled out a gym bag.

'He's been behind her from the beginning. How the hell did we miss him?' Doc whispered.

Natalie jiggled the keys in the lock of her car to give the blond time to approach her. The other cops on surveillance would come rushing to her when I gave them the signal over the hand-held.

The six-footer had the bag gripped in his right hand. He walked steadily toward Natalie, and now Doc and I were moving at a trot, coming at him.

'Go!' I said into the hand-held.

I heard a number of car doors being opened, and then I saw the crowd of us descending on the man and Natalie.

'Stop!' I yelled.

The Nine was pointed at the back of his towheaded noggin.

'Drop the bag!' Doc commanded.

He dropped the gym bag.

Then he put his hands high in the air, turned toward me and my partner, and began to beg.

'Take my wallet, but don't hurt me!'

'Shut the fuck up,' one of the other four police told him.

His expression was genuinely confused. He was surprised and frightened. He was either a very good actor or he was about ready to fill his jockey shorts.

'Why were you following her?' I asked again.

'I told you. She was very ... pretty. She turned me down, but I wanted to try again.'

It was a dead end and Doc and I both knew it. There was nothing in the gym bag but a couple of towels, a clean pair of undershorts and a T-shirt. No knife, no ether. Nothing.

His name was Patrick McGaherty and he worked in a health club. Apparently he was not used to being turned down by women. And, yes, he was behind her after she left that third deck in the parking lot. He must have been following Doc and me, and that was why we didn't make him until later on in the surveillance.

So we cut him loose after we checked to see if he had a record. And he was clean. Not even traffic violations.

Natalie was waiting for us outside the interrogation box.

'Nothing?' she asked.

I shook my head, waved goodnight to Doc, and steered my fiancée by the arm toward the elevators.

'We're losing credibility with my Captain, Red.'

'I know. Manpower minus results. I'm sorry, Jimmy.'

'Hell, it's not *your* fault, Natalie. I'm just disappointed this wasn't the guy. He sure fit the bill physically. Right age. Right look. Everything that the profile calls for.'

I was driving her home. We were working the same afternoon-to-midnight shift, so we'd be able to have dinner and spend the night together. My mother was still living at my house – which was an issue we'd have to address after I married the redhead.

'These things are always very shaky when it comes to odds, Natalie. You know that.'

109

'You don't think we're going to catch this man in the act, do you, Jimmy?'

'No. We rarely ever do. Stakeouts work occasionally, but they're really just action for the sake of action. You feel a little desperate, you want to *do* something, get out on the street. Somebody keeps killing people and you can't stop him. You want to be active, get out there and make a play. These guys like The Farmer are control freaks. They hardly ever allow you to turn the tables on them. This guy might kill again, and he might do it right under our noses. He might chop somebody up on the Gold Coast or in the Loop. Or he might move to the burbs, the way he tried to with Stephanie Manske. He was telling us that he wasn't committed to one area of the city. It's the women who are linked. It's their ages, their general appearances. Once we find out why he prefers his particular kind of victim, maybe then we can set him up . . . No, little shots in the dark like tonight aren't going to bring down the big dog, here. He's too goddamned cute, Red.'

I pulled up to her curb. We were both tired. I figured we might skip dinner, sleep awhile, and then do what came naturally and next. I'd take her out for a fancy and early breakfast when morning hit.

There was a new fragrance in the air as we stepped outside the car. It was the scent of snow. We were due for our first snowfall. I thought I'd heard the forecast on the ride over to Natalie's, but I'd still been a little preoccupied with my bride-to-be's first encounter with the bad guys out on these streets. I'd have to resign myself, as the man said. I'd have to learn to live with the idea. She'd be encountering nothing but bad guys when she went to work, from here on out.

Chapter Nineteen

Doc picked up the information from the County Sheriff's Office. They'd received the word from a neighboring county, sixty miles to the west of the city, and the three of us, Jack included, were on our way toward the State University that was located in that area.

She was waiting for us in the teachers' lounge. School was on break for the end of quarter, we had been informed when all this was set up by the young woman we were going to interview and by the local Sheriff's Office.

She had a black eye and a bruise on her cheek. Another pretty woman, nearly thirty. She was almost a clone of The Farmer's first two victims. Like Stephanie Manske, she had survived her encounter with him.

We sat down at a round table in the lounge. A dean was in the room to introduce us to Diane Swanson, an Assistant Professor of Geology here at the University.

'You're sure this is a comfortable place to talk?' I asked as we sat. 'We could go off campus if it'd be easier.'

'No. I want to get back to work. I want to get back to normal . . . He's been in my dreams.'

She looked at me as she explained it to me.

'He's been in my dreams.'

'And in mine, too,' I confessed. 'But I haven't been

where you were, Ms Swanson ... You want to tell us what happened?'

She explained how a blond man had been wearing a maintenance outfit, how he'd come in and out of the lab where she worked, but how she had paid almost no attention to him.

'This is a very safe campus. It's isolated from the town next to us, and we're rather enclosed. We don't have this sort of thing. You can walk the campus at night and no one . . .'

Her voice trailed off.

'There is no history of this sort of thing around here. I was never afraid to work late at night, alone, but now, of course, I am.'

'Yes. I understand,' Doc joined in. 'But we need to get all the information we can so we can make sure this man won't hurt you or anyone else in the future.'

'Do you think he'd come back?' she asked Jack.

'No, Ms Swanson. I don't think he'd come back here. He hasn't hit the same location twice yet,' Wendkos replied.

'Yet?' she asked me.

'It's extremely unlikely he'd return. The Sheriff's told you he's going to keep an eye on you, hasn't he?'

'Yes, Lieutenant Parisi, but—'

'He won't come back,' Doc reassured her. 'He knows you'll all be wary now, and he likes to take his victims by surprise ... Please, just tell us everything you can about him, physically.'

She gave us the same description that Stephanie Manske had provided. Except that Diane Swanson was positive this guy was a sandy-colored blond. The height and body size were identical to the previous rundown. She'd only caught a glimpse of him in the lab, and she'd seen nothing but the nametag on his gray work-shirt as she was knocked on her back by the fumes of the ether. She remembered only vaguely that she'd been sexually molested.

112

The Sheriff found the condom wrapper on her naked body after two students who were passing by saw her lying by the school's lagoon. They found no semen when she was examined at the hospital. There were also no fingerprints on her or on any of her garments. As usual, The Farmer left no calling cards that could help us trace him.

Diane Swanson seemed to be very strong. She displayed very self-confident body language, the way I saw it. She didn't quiver or shiver or weep. At least, not in front of three policemen who were asking her some extremely uncomfortable questions.

'Would you be willing to undergo hypnosis in order to try and remember some more physical detail about this man?' I asked her.

'Absolutely. Yes. I would.'

'We'll get a man down this afternoon, then. I'll call him and ask him to make an appointment with you at a time that'll be convenient, if that's okay.'

'It's okay, Lieutenant ... I want this man out of my head. I want my life back.'

Now there was moisture in her eyes. Her cheeks began to color.

I reached out and covered her hand.

'We're going to get him. He's not going to hurt you again. I promise you he won't.'

She looked up at me and attempted to smile, but she couldn't quite pull it off.

Then the tears began.

'I'm not going to let him win. I'm not. I'm not.'

'No, you're not going to let him. You're right.'

I repeated the information about the psychologist-hypnotist that the Department was sending her way this afternoon, and then she finally managed a smile.

'Maybe he can help me stop smoking,' she grinned.

'You're going to be all right,' Doc told her as he shook her hand.

'Best of luck to you, Ms Swanson,' Jack added.

113

She finally noticed the presence of our junior partner, and there was a slight blush on her cheeks.

We told her we had business with her County Sheriff. Then Jack asked me if we'd come back around and pick him up when we were through. I told him it was okay, and then I watched him approach the geology professor. It seemed he had more to say to her.

When I saw the young woman look up at Jack, I knew that the two of them had made a more than professional connection. And Jack had that strange ability to get through to people who'd been touched by evil. I saw him do it when he was with me during Doc's sabbatical. He got involved with the survivors on scene. I'm not saying he was trying to hit on a woman who had been recently raped. I'm saying he was touched by her. We were supposed to be professional with the human beings we encountered. We were not supposed to get wrapped up in their problems. But I knew from my experience with Celia Dacy that it happened. I almost lost my career on that case, but if Celia came along again, who knew what I'd do? I'd have liked to warn Jack Wendkos to back off, but I didn't feel as if I was the right man to do it. And Doc tried to keep his distance, too, but he'd got himself all unraveled by the murders of two black girls on the South Side a few years back, and he'd had to take a leave of absence for two months to put himself back together again. The shit *got* to you. The people and their faces got inside you. It was inevitable. That was why Homicide cops usually worked in the department for less than ten years. Doc and I had already lasted longer than a decade, and, as I said, we had already had our temporary breakdowns.

Jack walked down the hall with Diane Swanson. I heard her laugh briefly, and I was already hoping the two of them wouldn't wind up the way Celia Dacy and I did.

*

114

We talked to the County Sheriff briefly at his head-quarters. He told us the same story the professor had. It was a safe college town. This kind of shit didn't happen here.

'Why the hell would they let those three out of jail?' he asked when I showed him the jackets on my three suspects.

I was going to show Diane Swanson the photos of Repzac, Preggio and Karrios after the hypnotist tried to open up her memory.

'I don't know why we let predators loose,' I told Sheriff Espinoza. 'I wish I had an explanation.'

Doc shook the Sheriff's hand and then we headed back toward the U to pick up Jack.

'You find anything out?' I asked Wendkos on the drive back to the city.

'Yeah. She's beautiful and she didn't deserve this shit,' Jack said.

'You becoming more than an investigator on this one, Jacky?' Doc teased from the back seat of the Ford.

'I told her I'd be happy to help her any way I can.'

'You're not the local gendarme, Jack,' I tried to explain.

'That's why there's no problem, right? We're not directly involved with her case. It's County, no?'

He was not smiling, but I knew he was glowing inwardly behind that handsome Polish face.

'You're smitten, poor boy,' Doc rejoined.

'She's a rape victim, Doc. Think I'll start out by being her friend, and then maybe she'll let me know if it's okay to continue on in other directions . . . I really liked her. Christ, did you see how tough she is?'

What was there to tell him? Like I said, I was no one to talk about getting mixed up in people's lives. And Doc appeared too tired to continue ragging Jack about the interest he had shown in our latest survivor. Gibron pulled his Irish tweed hat down over his eyes and went to sleep. We still had a long way to travel to get back home.

I did some research on the families of Preggio, Repzac and Karrios. I found nothing on Karrios, although he'd given us the line about how he was the son of a Greek immigrant. *Like the guy who ran against Bush*, I think it was. Anyway, I came up empty on my first try with him.

Preggio's parents were both dead, I found out as I researched the number two suspect.

Repzac's parents resided in the city, so I called the family home to set up an interview with them. When I called, I was surprised to hear that they wanted to talk to me voluntarily. Doc and I got in the car and headed toward the northwest side. Jack was headed back to the U this afternoon. Apparently it was on, with Diane the geology professor. The official reason he was traveling was to 'reinforce' our first talk with the teacher. But all three of us knew that Jack was full of shit and Jack was in love. 'Smitten', like Doc said.

Caroline Repzac opened the door for us. They lived in the middle apartment of a three-flat, here near Wrigleyville.

We walked in and sat in the living room. Mrs Repzac explained that the old man wasn't at home. He worked twelve-hour shifts.

'We're still devastated by what happened to Dawson. I still cannot believe that he would be capable of harming any young girl. But I know he's been straight ever since . . . Would you like some coffee?'

'You don't have to apologize for him, Mrs Repzac. We're not here about his previous problems,' I told her. 'We're here to talk to you.'

'Talk to me? About what?'

116

'About your relationship with your son,' I explained.

'What is this? I don't understand.'

'We want to know if you had any particular difficulty with Dawson, say when he was young or when he was a teenager,' Doc said.

'Are you men psychiatrists or cops?'

'We're policemen,' I told her. 'But we need to know some things about several suspects in a murder case.'

'Murder? Dawson wouldn't – *Murder*?'

'We're not telling you he killed anyone, ma'am. We'd just like to know about his background, and you're the expert,' Doc explained.

'He ... he had a typical teenager's life. There was nothing out of the ordinary. He had no history of ... of molestation, if that's what you mean.'

There was fear in her eyes. I knew she had something she didn't want to tell me.

'Are there other siblings?' I asked.

That one lit her up.

'I don't think I want to talk to you anymore unless I have a lawyer here. I remember how they told me not to say anything to you guys unless I had legal—'

'It's all right, Mrs Repzac. We didn't come here to bully you or upset you. But it'd be helpful if you just told us more about Dawson,' I urged.

'No. That's it. You got no warrant and I'm through talking. You have to leave now.'

I looked over at Doc, but he knew the show was over.

We walked toward the front door. I turned to Caroline Repzac one more time.

'Two women have been brutally murdered. One man has been mutilated also. If you have something we need to know, you'd better call me. Here's my card.'

I placed my card on her coffee table, and then we were out of her door.

*

'She's got something she wants to tell us,' Doc confirmed.

'It has to do with the rest of the clan ... Looks like I need to do some more research.'

We got into the car and Doc pulled us away from the curb.

Maybe he had something traumatic with a brother or a sister. Maybe it had to do with Caroline herself.

Thirty-year-old women. If it *were* Caroline, that would put whatever it was back about twenty or twenty-five years. I'd have said she was in her early or middle fifties. If it was a sister ... A sister made the math harder to figure. So I'd have to get into the computers and the paperwork again.

It was as if Caroline Repzac had been glad we were there, at first. And then something had changed her mind and the door was slammed in our faces. Cold. Slammed shut.

Something had happened to Dawson. Something had happened to one of those sons of bitches. Or to some son of a bitch we hadn't even spotted yet. But the notion resonated in me like truth itself. I just knew I was not going off wrong on this one. It was always the age of the female, the general physical makeup. Those two tiny threads held the whole fabric of this case together.

'Where shall we take lunch?' Doc asked.

Without even looking over at him, I already knew the answer. I headed us toward Berwyn and the Garvin Inn.

The hypnotist came up almost empty. Diane Swanson had never got a clear look at her attacker's face. All she remembered was the name 'Ralph' on the tag on the shirt the supposed maintenance man was wearing. 'Ralph' popped into her classroom and popped back out. She got a look at the back of his head as he left the room. She saw the color of his hair and the height of his body, but she couldn't even be certain about his build or approximate weight.

We heard from the psycho-hypnotist downtown, but Jack Wendkos had been to see Diane in person.

'She's dry, Jimmy. There's nothing there. She never really got a look at this bastard.'

'Whoa. Are you taking all this personally, young man?' Doc teased.

'Yeah. I am.'

There was no amusement in Wendkos's tone.

'Oh-oh,' Doc murmured.

'Yeah, I'm personally involved, but like I already said—'

'It's still on the border, Jack. And I know I'm not the guy who should be telling you, but I took a hell of a risk when I walked over the line.'

'But she was part of your case, Jimmy. Diane's not on our board. She's in another goddamned county!'

'All right. I'm not complaining. But you better keep your travel plans private from here on out. The Captain won't give a shit if we're *indirectly* involved with this woman as a witness in a murder-rape case.'

'Okay, okay. I'll keep it to myself . . . It isn't anything romantic yet, anyway. At least, not on her end. She's scared. No matter how tough she tried to look. She's on the edge and I think I can help her.'

'It's all right with me. I surrender,' I told him. 'Just don't let it get in the way of what we're doing around here. Yeah, I've been where you are. And a lot deeper into it than you are. Just don't let the two of you get in the way of business and I'll hope for the best.'

He was in this personally, all right. I'd seen anger on him before. His face read like an open script. He couldn't disguise gut-level reactions. Like love.

Or hate.

He had a personal thing for The Farmer. This cutter'd hurt one of his own. At least, Jack thought so. I didn't know what the teacher felt toward the man who had nearly ended her life and her career, but my young partner had been bloodied on the inside. He didn't respond for-

119

givingly to that kind of insult. He'd only known Diane Swanson for a few days, but it didn't make any difference. It was what we guineas call the vendetta – *the vengeance*. It was in his eyes, in his voice. It was an obsession that got hold of your insides and twisted them all in one direction. Then there was nothing left to do but go after the point of your hang-up. It was a holy crusade, once it started. All that pain was housed in that pretty professor, and Jack had taken it upon himself to cut her loose, to free her. Falling for a woman did that to you.

I ought to know.

Chapter Twenty

I take her out to the dance floor. The rhythm obliges her to begin to sway. The music is not from her generation. It's a decade older than she is. It comes from the time that I was out of the country. We heard this music over the Armed Forces Network. It's called 'Classic Rock 'n' Roll' to her and to all the other thirty-year-olds who have no music of their own.

The Rush Street bar is loaded with out-of-towners. She's one of them. A stewardess out of the Bay Area. When she began to talk to me at the bar, she asked me if there were any good seafood-sushi bars in the Rush Street district. I told her I didn't know, but I'd find out if she danced with me.

'You know, that dark hair and mustache don't go with your eyebrows,' she tells me when she gets up close for a slow dance.

I feel a burn of anxiety over the lack of a match. I put the hairpiece and the mustache on in a hurry and I neglected to color the eyebrows. But it's too late now. She's not as drunk as I thought she was. No one else in this disco-lounge is sober enough or close enough to be as observant as she's being.

'I have to tell you the truth.'

'And what's that?' she asks.

'I have to wear these things because I get mauled if I don't.'

'Why do you get mauled?'

I pull her closer to me. The jukebox is playing 'Me and Bobby

McGee' at the moment. We're one of the few couples still left on the dance floor.

'I'm an actor.'

'No! You're not!'

She shoves me away playfully. But I pull her back to me. Red and green and blue lights twirl over our heads as if it's a goddamned prom instead of a nightclub.

'Please don't talk so loudly. That's why I have to wear a hairpiece and a mustache . . . I'm Aaron Jacobsen . . . You know, from The Heartbeat of Love . . . You know, the daytime soap opera?'

She watches my eyes. Then she decides to lie in response to the false television show I've just made up.

'Oh my God! I watch it all the time!'

'Not so loud.'

'I'm sorry, Aaron. Why didn't you tell me your name before?'

I look at her with an evil grin, and then she realizes the stupidity of what she just said. She's going along with my story. She seems to be a lot friendlier now than she was when we began talking. It appears that she might not watch a lot of daytime TV. Perhaps she spends her afternoons in the air, working, or at the pools of all those motels she's compelled to stay at while she's on the job.

'I remember your name now. Aaron Jacobsen—'

I put my finger to my lips.

'People hound you that badly?'

'Isn't it obvious?'

'I've seen movie stars on a few of our flights. People can really be obnoxious to them.'

'How long are you scheduled to be in town?' I ask her.

'Oh. Until the end of the weekend. It's a long holdover until Monday, and then I'm headed back to the Coast.'

'Do you have time to spend any of that weekend with me?'

I pull her close again.

'We'll see. Maybe.'

I love a prick-tease. They are so much more fun to work on.

'Why aren't you sure?' I ask her.

'I don't know. Actors. I've dated actors before.'

122

'I'll bet you have.'

'What color is your real hair?'

'The same as it is on television,' I tell her. It shuts her up. She doesn't want to drag herself any deeper into the lie she's kept alive.

'Oh,' is all she can muster.

I walk her back to the bar. I order a double tequila for each of us. She throws the drink down like a pro. One swallow, no lime or salt. So I order another. She puts it down in the same manner and doesn't notice I've left my own drinks untouched on the bar.

'Another?'

'Sure. I'm not driving tonight.' She grins hazily.

'Does that mean you'll let me take you back to the hotel?'

'I don't know. Can you be trusted? What with that disguise and everything.'

'You don't know what it's like to have a lot of people looking out for you.'

'No. I guess I don't.'

'It's awful. I can't go out to eat. I can't walk the malls or go to a movie. Being in acting's not as much fun as you might think it is.'

'I guess so.'

I order her another double tequila without asking her first. One more round'll get the coy out of this cunt.

She's getting toward the end of her flight attendant's career, no matter what the airlines appear to be doing about age discrimination. They all want youth on their flights, and Dee Dee Tremont, the stewardess who sits on the stool next to me, is headed into the twilight of her career. But she's closer to the end than she supposes.

She downs the next drink as she has the first few. She handles her liquor better than most women I've known, but tequila will have its way on anyone. She's beginning to slur her speech, just noticeably. Her head seems to snap toward me whenever I tell her anything. It's only barely noticeable, but it's there.

'Maybe we should head on out into the fresh, cold air,' I suggest.

123

She nods. It's over. That nod was the last decision she'll ever make for herself.

We walk out of the bar and out of the exit and then out onto the street. Earlier I managed to find a parking spot three blocks from the lounge. She wobbles a bit as I lead her by the arm toward my ride.

'I want you to know that I don't believe your bullshit story,' she says.

'What bullshit story?'

'You're not an actor and there is no such television show and I know it because I'm a big fan of the soaps and there is no such goddamned show . . . *But I like your face. Shitty wig and all, you have a very nice face . . . Are you as good in bed as you are with the bullshit?'*

'I'm better.'

'So what's your real name?'

'Peter Arnett.'

Once I get into a lying mode it's impossible to stop.

'That name sounds familiar.'

'I'm a correspondent for CNN.'

She stops and stares at me.

'You . . . you're not gonna tell me who you are, are you?'

'Then the mystery'd be over, wouldn't it?'

'Yeah. It would. Okay, so we'll play it your way. It's kind of a turn-on, isn't it? Pretending to be someone else . . . What do you say we stop and buy me a wig and I'll be Farrah Fawcett. You can be that Ryan O'Neal – before he got all fat and puffed and old.'

'You don't think I'm fat and puffed and old, do you?' I ask her.

She stops and looks at me with the aid of the overhead streetlamps.

'No. You look good. But that wig's got to go.'

'It will. Once we get out of here.'

'You taking me home?' she asks.

'Sure. You're halfway there already.'

We get to the car. I unlock her side and let her in.

'You're a gentleman. Don't get much of that anymore.'

124

'The least you can say about me, Dee Dee, is that I know my manners. I had a very strict upbringing.'

My last words almost lodge themselves at the top of my palate. I feel as though I'm going to gag, but the sensation passes.

I drive out of the Rush Street district and head west on the Stevenson once I've got us out of the Loop.

She's nodding as if she's halfway unconscious, so I get no argument from her about why we're not headed toward O'Hare and the hotel adjacent to the airport.

We're headed toward home. But not hers.

There is a cornfield, minus the crop, directly south of my house. We are fifty miles west of the city. My nearest neighbor is eight miles from my farmhouse.

My significant other is in the city this evening, taking care of business. Just as I am.

I stop the car and I turn off the engine. She wakes as we come to a complete halt. She looks out the window and sees the single light shining from a lamp in my front window. The house is only a hundred yards from this field where we're parked.

'Where in the hell are we?' she wants to know.

'I just took us for a ride. It's a nice, crisp, early winter's evening, and you like to go for rides, don't you?'

She nods, but she's still half out of it.

I open her fur coat.

'Anyone ever throw blood on this thing?' I crack.

She moans something or other, but it's not a sexual moan. Not yet.

I unbutton her silk blouse. She's a very well-dressed flight attendant. I remind myself to save her coat and clothing. My significant other will like Dee Dee's taste.

'Oh, you,' she grins.

She's awakened and she's got the idea now.

She surprises me by going for my fly. She's got her cold hands on me and it shocks me, so I shake her.

'You want to play rough, Aaron?'

'Sure. I love to play rough.'

So I slap her. She looks at me strangely, and then she strikes me on the face. I hit her back with equal force, and she returns with an angry swipe that smacks the bridge of my nose. I think I'm bleeding.

She comes up to me and kisses me savagely and buries her hands in my crotch. She finds me and begins to mold my flesh into what it is she wants me to be. I find that I'm almost distracted by what she's doing.

The stewardess bends down and takes me. She stays there for a long time and I can't find it in me to stop her.

Then she jerks herself upright.

'Turn the heater back on. It's cold in here.'

I do as she commands. Then she takes off the rest of her clothes. She is as I imagined she'd be. The very image appears before me in this dim light of a full moon and the slight glow from my house, those three hundred feet away. But I can see her in this moonlight and she is as lush and perfect as the first two.

She helps me slide my pants off, and then she straddles me. I'm sitting on the middle of the front seat. I'm watching her eyes, trying to remember what it was that I had in mind for her.

Dee Dee rips my hairpiece off. Next she tears off the mustache, and it sears my upper lip as she does so.

I slap her on account of the pain, and she responds in kind. This time I know I'm bleeding. But she bends toward me, her breasts brushing against my hands, and she licks the blood from my nose and lip. Then her tongue jams its way into my mouth and she's slamming at me as if there's no time left. As if she's got to get this thing over now.

I was raised in a very strict household. I told her that, or something like that. I was referring to her indirectly, but I knew what I meant.

She was a beautiful woman. More beautiful than any of these three. More beautiful than that ripe geology instructor I took. She had all of the attributes that photographers look for when they seek models to photograph. That's what she did, in fact. She was a model. And the more mature she became, the more popular she became with all those cameramen.

126

Dee Dee continues to thump at me. She almost slams into my balls and I grab hold of her and slow her crescendo.

'Take it easy. We have a tank full of gas and we've got all night,' I tell her.

She bends to me and takes a nip at my lip. But no blood, this time.

I squeeze her breasts until she squeals, and I'm thinking maybe it's time I replaced my significant other, the woman who lives with me. Dee Dee would be suitable. She's more beautiful, she's got a much better body, she's got a taste for violence . . .

But she's not like me. Or like her. She wouldn't have an appetite for what it is we do. Which cuts the field down considerably when it comes to potential mates and partners. My line of endeavor would likely scare her off.

And besides, I have her out here for a reason.

She continues to jolt against me, and then she releases a genuine shriek. She's finishing. When she ceases to throb on top of me, she looks into my eyes.

'You're still all there, aren't you?'

I nod.

She dismounts, bends over, and then she makes certain my climax is imminent. Just as I'm about to end it, she jumps atop me and sways on me as it comes to a conclusion.

Dee Dee quickly puts her coat back on. I reach over the seat and grab hold of the bag. I put it on the seat between us.

'Extra underwear?' She smiles.

She reaches out and grabs hold of me again, and I respond even though I don't want to. It is all subconscious, but this woman has taken control. And I cannot have that. She may not dominate. When I allow the other to bind me atop our bed, I know I can rip away the feeble knots that tie me. She may think she's in control, but I am always the one in charge and she knows that.

Dee Dee's head is bent over me again and she is preparing me for her. But just as I'm readied, I turn her around and I force her face against the glass of the passenger's window.

'Hey! Don't play so—'

I ram my way into her and she squeals.

'No! Don't do that! No!'

I plunge into her again and her face smacks against the window. This is unnatural, I tell myself, which is why I enjoy it.

'**Unnatural beast**,' she called me, all those years back. But there was nothing unnatural about me then. She was the one who contradicted nature. It wasn't me.

'Please! You're hurting me!'

Three more thrusts and it is finished. She slumps down onto her side of the car and turns to me. She has her hand raised as if she's about to slap me, but she sees the knife in my hand before she can follow through.

'Oh Jesus! Oh my God!'

I tear her fur coat off after I hit her with my fist. My blow lands squarely on her temple and the force stuns her. She's still awake. I want her awake. There's no ether this time. She'll know exactly what's happening to her.

I get out of the car and go around to her side. I throw the fur coat in the back seat after I open her door. Then I drag her out by her hair. I stand her against the side of the automobile and I hit her on the side of the head again.

She falls to the cold ground of the barren cornfield. I open the trunk of the car and I remove the box. I walk back to her, I clutch her long blonde hair, and I drag her fifteen feet away from the car. She's woozy and unable to rise. I remove the stakes and the leather straps from the box, along with the wooden mallet.

I bend down and tie the straps to her feet and her wrists. Then I drive the stakes into the hard, frozen soil. She screams when her head clears. But it is all right. No one can hear her. My closest neighbor is far away, and there are too many trees, too much vegetation, between my farm and the next property for anyone to hear her cries.

She continues to scream, but then she stops and begins to whimper.

'Why? Why me?'

I bring the lantern out from the trunk of the car and I place it a few feet away from her sprawled-out body. She is so beautiful, so complete. She reminds me so much of the other. Same age, same pure white body—

I have to have her again, so I take down my pants and position myself between her spread legs.

'Why? You can have me as much as you want, but don't—'

I hit her to quiet her. But I don't want her knocked out. Until I start removing things, there's no reason why she can't enjoy the whole spectacle.

I hear myself grunting like some mad animal and it further incenses me. She deserves this. This is justice. She's had it coming for all this time and now . . .

I'm spent. But I haven't used a condom. I'll have to clean her thoroughly when it's done. Can't have DNA catching up with me.

'Please . . . Why?' she sobs.

I stand over her. Then I kneel next to her, the knife again in my hand. She watches the tip of the blade as it enters beneath her breasts and the sound she makes shatters the stillness that had only recently enveloped us. She's still shrieking after the first cut.

I stop and look at the full moon above me. It lights my way, and I begin again.

Chapter Twenty-One

'Billy? Where are you? What the hell time is it?'

'You got to get here now, coz.'

I looked at the clock. It was 4.48 a.m.

He told me the address. I had no choice because I'd told him I'd look after him. So I hung up after I told him I was on my way. Billy was spooked. Big time. He must have found out who it was who'd tried to waste him with the two shots in the back in that alley where the paramedics scooped him off the blacktop.

I walked into my mother's bedroom. It used to be our old guestroom. I gently shook her shoulder.

'I got to go to work, Ma. I'm sorry to wake you up.'

'I . . . I thought it was your day off.'

'Not anymore. Something came up.'

She groaned. She knew something always came up with my work.

I kissed her and I went back into my room and finished dressing. I should have called Doc, but I was not going to. It was his day off too, and this was my cousin. And Jack was back for another overnighter at the college where Diane Swanson taught post-adolescents about the history of rocks. It appeared Diane was getting beyond just needing Jack as a sympathetic ear. Wendkos was only recently divorced, so I hoped this was no rebound number for him.

But the way those two had looked at each other when they first met . . . Who could tell? Who the hell knew?

I strapped on the Nine and I slapped the .44 against my left leg. I carried that switchblade in my left pocket, just in case of an emergency.

I was out the door and into our Voyager van. I was not used to driving the Plymouth to work, but this really wasn't in the line of duty. It was family, whether I liked it or not. Even if I had given my word to a semi-thug like my cousin Billy, it was still my word.

He was holed up somewhere on the far North Side. It was damn' near Wisconsin. The driving was fast because of the early hour. It also felt eerie to be on the road before the sun was up. I worked a lot of shifts in the dark, but I didn't work too often by myself at this time of day. It made me rethink not calling one or both of my partners for backup.

It wasn't very likely that this was an ambush – with someone holding a gun to Billy's head in order to lure me out. The Outfit was not big on shooting coppers. They would rather not have the heat. They were not as open and blatant about what they were willing to do in public. And since I was not on the payroll, they had no beef with me.

It took forty-five minutes to get to his location, just north of Evanston. He was holed up in some condo in a very *ricci* – rich – part of town. Billy might have been soft in the noggin, but he had expensive tastes.

I pulled the van to the curb and got out. It was still a while until dawn. I checked the slip of paper with Billy's address, and this was indeed the place. It was an old, wealthy neighborhood with trees and low-slung branches that gave you an idea of how shady and comfortable it must have been here in the warmer months of the year.

I punched the buzzer at Billy's front gate. His voice came over the intercom.

'Yeah?'

'It's the fuckin' milkman. Open up. It's cold out here.'

131

He let me in, an electric buzz signalling the lock's release.

I walked up to the top of the steps where his front door was, and he opened up for me.

'It's early, cousin,' I warned him.

'It could be later than I think.'

'So you got a scent?'

'Yeah. I got a real bad scent . . . Sit down, Jimmy.'

He had a dim-wattage bulb in a lamp on the table next to his front window, but I could still make out that he had lines of sleeplessness on his Sicilian face.

'So who's the big dog that wants to disappear you?'

'You want some coffee, Jimmy P?'

'I wanted coffee, I'd be at the fucking White Castle. Come on. Tell me what's scaring the shit out of you.'

'He's a made guy, coz. And he got permission to pop me.'

'Who is this guy?'

'Jackie Morocco.'

'What's his real name, Billy?'

'John Fortuna.'

The light went on inside me when I heard the actual surname. Fortuna was one of the Young Turks who took over when we sent Danny Ciccio to prison on a multiple murder rap that stuck.

'What's Fortuna got to do with The Farmer?'

'I'm gonna get wasted no matter what I do.'

'Then come on and help yourself. I told you what you have to do to survive, cousin. You tell me what's going on, I take these bad nasties out of the picture. Everybody gets happy if you do the right thing.'

He watched me to see if I was setting him up.

'You wired, Jimmy?'

'You want me to drop my pants?'

'You wouldn't've had time to wire up, would you?'

'Quit wasting our time. Tell me.'

He looked at his own outstretched fingertips.

'Jackie Morocco – Fortuna – has a guy in his pocket.

132

This guy was connected to Jackie because of some bitch, Morocco's little sister. The little sister was supposed to be worse than her brother. She's a killer cunt, I hear. She'd be a made man if she had balls. You know what I'm sayin'? She's a vicious little shit. Into all kinda kinky crap. Sex, I mean. And she's had a few physical-like encounters with a few other women, I hear. I don't mean she's queer. I mean she likes to hurt people. You know? She was up in Elgin when she was a teenager. They kept it real hush-hush, the family did. Very private matter, but I don't know all the particulars ... Well, she comes into contact with this outside guy and falls for him big-time. But the guy's a bigger fuckup than she is.'

'What's her name?'

'Mary Margaret Fortuna ... But she got married when she was just outta high school, and I think she goes by her married name. I don't know the new name, but I'll try to find out what it was. She went by something other than her given names, too. Bitch was a whacker. Hated her family. Hated Jackie Morocco. The word was that her bro was fuckin' his little sis all while they was growin' up under one roof. But it's weird. She never called the cops on him. Although maybe that's the Sicilian in her. She never stuck him in the back with an ice pick, which like I say she's very capable of doin' ... She's just a weird female. All messed up in the head. You know what I'm sayin'?'

'So how does she connect with The Farmer?'

Billy chewed off a fingernail and spat it on the lush carpet.

'She meets this geek right after she gets divorced. He goes off to that fuckin' Gulf War bullshit and he comes home all whacked in the skull. The guy had been in medical school or something and he was a medic over in the Gulf, too. You wouldn't think a guy like that would become a blade man, would you, coz?'

'You don't know his name?'

'No. I was lucky to make the connection with Fortuna's

goofy fuckin' sister. Lotta guys don' wanna talk to me after I got shot. They can smell the wrong in the air. They know Jackie Morocco's got a beef with me. They know there's bad blood between my family because of the way Fortuna took over when Danny Cheech went away.'

'So what's the hook Jackie's got into The Farmer?'

Billy bit off the fingernail on a new finger and spat it out on the same portion of carpet. There were faint rays of sunlight coming through his sheer curtains now.

'This war vet knocks Mary Margaret up.'

'He doesn't do the right thing and marry her.'

'That ain't it, Jimmy.'

'Then what?'

'The guy does an abortion on her. She damn' near bleeds to death. But she don't call out the dogs on the guy who butchered her. She begs for his life. It becomes a matter of honor for her bro, Jackie. So he puts the knife-man to work. He gives him a choice. Come up with fresh body parts that Jackie sells overseas, or else Jackie takes one of his lungs, then a kidney ... You get the picture? He takes a week to kill the motherfucker. See, The Farmer's an amateur when it comes to cutting, compared to his almost-brother-in-law ... But the strange thing was that this lover of Little Sister doesn't try to bolt from the business. Someone offered you a job like that you'd run for fuckin' cover, wouldn't you? This fucker embraces Jackie Morocco and the whole deal like it's the sweetest proposition he ever heard. It even scares Fortuna, I hear. He never figured the kinda monster he was puttin' into motion. You know what I mean?'

'Where do I find Fortuna?'

'Good luck. He's a phantom, Jimmy. He's a capo, but he's damn' near invisible. I was you, I'd try the Feds. They always know where everybody's perched.'

'Why's he so 'invisible'?'

'The Feds been after him for a long time. Fortuna doesn't do hits. Hasn't since he got made. He gets other guys to do his dirty work. Lots of guys think he's a fuckin' clone of Old Man Daley. You know, the old mayor of the city. He keeps his own hands clean. He never leaves a connection to anything he ordered. Shit, the guy's got an education. Went to the state college. You know, the big one down south in Illinois. He's no jamolk. He's mean as hell, but he's not even a little stupid. That's why I say you'd better check with the FBI. They got so much electricity hooked up to us, I get a hard-on takin' a piss wherever I go.'

'So I find Fortuna, I can find the guy with the blade.'

'That's why I called you up here, Jimmy P. You're all I got. I don't trust the Feds. They wanna put me in a hole, just like the hole Danny's in at Jolly J.'

'Jolly J' referred to Joliet Prison. That was where his big-dog cousin was residing for concurrent life sentences.

'You settled in here?' I asked.

'I got a few places to roost. I'm gonna move around every so often.'

'You fixed for funds?'

'I'm all right, Jimmy P. Are you offerin' financial fuckin' aid to me?'

'If you need a coupla bucks, yeah. Sure.'

'Nah, I'm okay. But I appreciate it. Really . . . You think you can bust Jackie Morocco?'

'I want the guy he's hiring out to work the body shop.'

'Body shop. Yeah, I read that in the papers. "Body shop." You don't take Morocco down with him, and you'll find little pieces of me all over one of my safe houses. You gotta take Fortuna too, Jimmy, or I'm dead.'

I sat back against his thick, comfortable chair.

'The FBI'll want in on this, like you said. Doc and I don't much like working with them, but if that's what it takes then I'll do it. This guy's killed enough women.'

'He likes the work, Jimmy. And look out for that crazy hoo that lives with him. Like I said, she might be worse than her old man. They both got that fuckin' foamin'-mouth disease. Whattayacallit?'

'Hydrophobia . . . I'll let you know. You better stay

off the phone here. Use a payphone. Move around, like you said. I can give you twenty-four-hour help, if you want.'

'Yeah. Put a cop at my door, and then you can put a bulls-eye right over my ass while you're at it. No, thanks, Jimmy. I'll shoot the moon on my own.'

'It's up to you. There's the witness protection program, too.'

'I'd rather be fuckin' dead. I want to go back to an occasional boost, coz.'

'I really don't want to know about it, Billy.'

'Hey! Oh! If I can't go back to my old life, then fuck it. I really mean it. I'd rather be a floater in the fuckin' Chicago River in all that green water on St Patty's day.'

I looked him in the eyes and I saw it was not bravado or beer talking. He was sincere. He didn't know any other way to live. There was nowhere for him to retreat.

I slapped his arm as I got up.

'Remember. Use a payphone, and call me at work. Fortuna might know we're family and he might bug my home phone. Don't call any of your old crew. You gotta have a woman, pick one up off the street, but do it at random. Don't hit on anyone you know ... Don't smile, Billy. You know how serious this shit is.'

He smiled in spite of me and came over to me and embraced me.

'Blood *is* thicker than fuckin H$_2$O, ain't it?'

I clasped his hands once more, and then I got out.

Jackie Morocco. John Fortuna. The elusive Outfit capo. He was looking to be the Don when the middle-aged current chief went down.

Terry Morrissey was the local special agent who'd been assigned to help us with Morocco and The Farmer and this supposedly murderous female partner the cutter had living with him.

'He stays on the periphery. Your cousin's right. We've

136

got no photographs of him in the last three years. He's like a vampire. Supposedly only comes out at night.'

Terry was sitting with Doc and Jack and me in my small cubicle downtown on the Homicide floor.

I explained to him that we had The Farmer narrowed down to three choices, but he suggested, as Doc did, that we use the FBI's profiler here in the city. So he made an appointment for us for this same afternoon. He called the agent from my desk.

When Morrissey left, Doc rolled his eyes, but Jack remained seated without any visible response to our new 'partnership'.

'We get too many people on the pile, somebody gets crushed,' Doc said.

'Let's not make this political, Doctor,' I told him.

'I'm not. I just don't want this to become the circus it can become when the United States Government gets its incompetent little feet in our sandbox.'

As I said, Doc and I both were not fans of the Fibbies.

'They got the resources. We really can't say no at this point, can we?' Jack suddenly remarked.

Doc pointed to the junior partner.

'Listen to the yuppie. He knows how to adapt.'

'I'm just saying, Doc, that if we want to go through the Outfit, we're going to need help. Expensive help.'

'I'll go along with the youngster.' Doc finally smiled. 'We're not getting to shore on our own, are we?'

Egos. Politics. Gamesmanship. It was part of the trade, although few of us in the department wanted to admit it. No one wanted to ask for help. Sometimes it just came up to you and sat on your lap until you were finally forced to accept that there was this two-ton fucking ape sitting on you. And the FBI was that four-thousand-pound primate.

'He doesn't do it for the money,' Dr Adamson told the four of us. It was Doc and me and Jack and Terry

Morrissey in attendance, here at the FBI headquarters in the Loop.

'I know,' I said. 'My cousin told me that he was coerced into the family business because he became involved with Fortuna's sister. But it didn't take any force to make him go along with what the business involves. I've tried to figure this guy by the woman he's with. I've tried to tie him to his military record. And what I come up with is that he is particular about his victims. I don't think his employers care much about the physical appearance of the victims; they just want saleable product. It's The Farmer who makes the on-site choices. That's his end of the operation. The Outfit sells the organs on the Internet. We haven't been able to find their new listing after we lost the girl on that surveillance.'

'I'd agree with your tactics, Lieutenant. Especially when it comes to finding out what provokes such rage at his targets. He fits the traditional serial profile, so we don't have an argument about his color, his age, or his general physical appearance. I think you need to go after what it was that made him enraged with this type of female he's pursuing. I'd guess that the original subject is either dead or is, to him, untouchable. Meaning that the trigger of his anger is beyond his reach, and unfortunately it also means that he can never satisfy his desire to strike at her. He'll do it repeatedly and I don't think his lust is going to be sated unless all of you stop him. So I'm saying you're headed in the right direction if you get at the backgrounds of your three principal suspects.'

Adamson was the guy who wrote all the books. There have been a half-dozen movies that have fictionalized him as a character in the films. He has appeared on all the cable shows and the mainstream talk shows. I found him to be less self-important than I thought he'd be. He was direct and succinct, and we were out of his office in less than forty-five minutes.

Morrissey stopped me and my two partners in the hallway outside Adamson's cubicle.

'We're putting out the nets for Fortuna. We're going full-tech after him. Everything that can hold a wire will. If we need to use a satellite, it's been okayed. The Farmer has hit the big leagues. I don't know if he'd be likely to celebrate his new status.'

Morrissey smiled and walked down the hall, away from the three of us.

Chapter Twenty-Two

We eliminated Caroline Keady. She was Lake Forest. Her parents were legitimate. She was off the list.

Janice Ripley had no Sicilian in her background. She came from good WASP stock, just like Keady.

We got nowhere, at first, with Ellen Jacoby. Until we looked at the marriage record. Jacob Jacoby was the first husband. It lasted eighteen months. Then he disappeared and we found, also, that Ellen Jacoby's maiden name was Fortuna – just like her brother's last name. John Fortuna.

We were waiting for them to arrive at their North Side apartment. Another stakeout, another night of late-evening jazz for the Doctor. He was plugged in. He sat in the front seat on the passenger's side. Jack Wendkos was parked a half-block down with Jimmy Johansen, another Homicide guy.

It was two a.m. We were getting stiff and weary. I was wondering if Karrios was going to show up with his partner. She was his way into the Outfit. He knocked up a sister of John Fortuna. Jackie Morocco explained his dissatisfaction with the way Karrios terminated Little Sister's pregnancy, and so Marco Karrios took his lunch pail to Fortuna's workplace every day thereafter.

Changing her first name slowed us down, as well. Apparently she chose 'Ellen' because of a favorite aunt. We found all this out from my cousin Billy when we told him her new name.

It crept toward two-thirty, and still no one was home. It got more and more likely that these two weren't returning tonight. Which made me wonder if they'd got wind that we were onto them. How they'd found out about us was beyond me, but the CPD had paid informants inside it, just as any big-city police force does. It infuriated me to think we were not secure, but I'd been down this road before, and so had my partner.

'These two wolves have sniffed us out, Jimmy P. They're headed for the woods,' Doc said after he removed his earphones.

'It feels that way, doesn't it? How could they've made us this fast? We just popped Fortuna's sister yesterday afternoon.'

'When you call up as much manpower as we have for tonight's joint punitive action, Jimmy, people sit up and pay attention.'

'We got moles in our holes.'

'Yeah. We both knew that. Unfortunately somebody's nose is attached to a Fortuna asshole . . . You want to stay here until dawn?'

'We might as well. This is probably going to be the quietest hood in the city tonight.'

Doc plugged back into his bebop, and I turned my attention to the middle apartment our two killers were supposed to be infesting.

Chapter Twenty-Three

I walk in from the cornfield. I close the door slowly behind myself. Ellen is still in the bathroom, taking one of her forty-five-minute hot showers. She tells me they are therapeutic, but I reply that I don't understand the meaning of 'therapeutic'. She groans when she thinks I'm being difficult.

So Billy Cheech has put them onto us. The cop Parisi is this half-wit's cousin, and Ciccio has pointed them in our direction. John Fortuna hears they're about to clamp us, and we escape by the hairs on our asses. We missed them by about six hours. Very close.

But now they've made me. I'm effectively out of business. They've got my photo circulated on television, newspapers, and to every squad car in northern Illinois. I'll even have to move from my farmhouse here because the sheriff's police might attach me to the rape of that college teacher. They had me hooked into that crime. The newspapers connected her assault to the killings, so I'm not safe where I am any longer.

And I'm not safe attached to old acquaintances either.

Ellen comes out of the bathroom with only a towel wrapped around her dripping hair.

'You'll wet the floor,' I tell her.

'It's okay. We're not staying here much longer, are we?'

She sits in the chair across from me, on the couch. She lets her knees separate.

I walk over to her, and then I kneel between her opened knees. I touch her and she quivers gently. I bend down and I bite her thigh. I bite so hard that the blood rises to the broken flesh. She slaps me.

'Son of a bitch! You don't know when to—'

I slap her back much harder than she cracked me. Her head flies backward and the towel-turban comes off.

She reaches up and rubs the welt on her cheek.

'Jesus Christ, Marco! You fucking hurt me!'

I bend over quickly and bite her on the other thigh. She squeals in pain and tries to lash out at me again. But I catch her fist and then I turn her wrist until she's in more agony than the shots to her face gave her.

'Please . . .'

'Your fucking family got us here, Ellen. All those fucking guineas. They got no idea how to keep their lips tight, so here we are tonight.'

'My brother . . . His people had nothing—'

'They all had something to do with this. They all helped get us where we are. Big John. He's the one who was gonna kill me, until he found out I could be a moneymaker for you and his fucking family. He thought he had me at the end of some puppet's string, but he was looking at it ass backwards. I was the moneymaker, all right, but I used him. It was never the other way round. But you fucking guineas suffer from a massive overdose of ego. You think you're always in control. Well, Ellen, do you feel like you've got your hands on my balls right now?'

I turn her hand a little more and she screams.

'You broke my arm! You son of a bitch, you broke my arm!'

I let go and I see I've probably gone a little bit too far. Her arm dangles loosely. But as soon as I let go of her, I see that she's trying to whack me with her good limb. So I punch her in the mouth with a straight right, and her head bounces off the headrest of the chair behind her. Then I pop her again with another straight right, and she bounces back at me and then falls on her face on the floor after I get out of her way.

There is blood all over her teeth, but I don't see any of those fangs missing from my two blows. I reach over and pick up the

143

towel that flew from her wet head. I bend down and wipe the gore from her mouth. It's still a lovely mouth, so I would not want to damage it.

I pull her to her knees. I slap her lightly to bring her back. When she's awake, I wait to see her strike out at me, but she doesn't. When it appears as if she's clear-headed, instead of clawing at me she begins to unzip my fly. I ball my fist to show her that she'd better not be thinking of biting anything in close proximity.

But she's doing what she does best. Her mouth is her best feature, as I say. When she's got me where she wants me to be, she gets back up on the chair and opens her legs wide. So I accommodate her.

When it's almost over, I reach to her throat and I squeeze. She doesn't like this play. Nearly choking doesn't get her off, and she knows that I know it.

Her eyes plead with me as she reaches the envelope of consciousness. I'm lunging at her, and in spite of the fact that she's running out of air, she's still pumping hard at me. When she finally begins to go out, I release her throat. She takes an exaggerated pull at the air she was being denied, and then the color starts to return to her cheeks.

'Why . . . why do you insist on doing that? Isn't it good enough without all that?' she gasps.

'I can't get hard unless I hurt you,' I tell her.

Something resembling shock crosses her bruised and bleeding face. I look down at her thighs and I see the blooms of blood on her bitten legs.

I bend down again and bite her near one of her open wounds. She tears at my hair and screams. When she nearly yanks my scalp off, I jerk up and nail her twice with two more rights. This time two teeth come loose.

She claws at me again, even though she's almost gone to black. She's vicious and indomitable. She'll take nothing from anyone, male or female. Ellen says it's how she survived her family and the things that John Fortuna did to her when she was a young teenager.

144

I kneel down and bite her repeatedly. She yips like a bitch who's being harassed by a male in heat. I have her blood all over my lips, my face. I press my nose and eyes into her wounds as if her blood is balm.

Then I rise. Her eyes open as I stand erect. I go to the closet and get the knife out of my bag. It is at this moment that she knows this has not been some perverse dance. She knows she's going to die. She knows I'm going to cut her.

I take her hair and I pull her face up at me. Then I cut her throat. But I miss the jugular purposely. She bleeds only lightly. I take hold of her left eyelid and I slice it away from her.

I look down at her destroyed face, at her gory legs. I want her to see herself while she still can. All that noise coming from her has decreased to moaning. When she looks in the living-room mirror, and sees what I've done, I hurl her to the floor. She begins to beg. It's the first time she's ever been reduced to begging. She's John Fortuna's sister. Nobody brings her family to its knees, literally or figuratively.

'Johnny'll kill you, Marco. He'll cut you open like you did all those women.'

'You mean like I'm going to do to you?'

She begins to weep. Then she tries to catch me from the floor with a kick that I easily sidestep.

'Come on. You can't fuck me anymore if you kill me.'

She's pleading. I'm enjoying the moment.

'Marco, please. Jesus, please . . .'

This has gone on long enough. I don't feel safe in this farmhouse. The police will be here soon. It's inevitable. That Chicago cop – Parisi – he'll be on me. He'll find me out here, so I have no options. I've got to leave everything behind me. I mean everything.

'No, Marco, no . . .'

Ellen's flat on her back. I can see the red line across her throat.

'No one'll want you now, Ms Fortuna. No one'll want you. You're ugly. You were always ugly. As ugly as the one before you. That was a long time ago. I remember her. I remember

145

what she did. Nothing washes it away. You know that? You were always ugly, but it was your ugliness that attracted me to you. Did you know that?'

I stick her in the left side. She blurts out what passes for a scream.

'How many times can I perforate you before you run out of noise and blood, Ellen? Huh? How many times?'

Her eyes follow the hand with the knife as I raise it hand and blade above my right shoulder.

It's a long flight to central Mexico. I don't let anyone handle this part of the operation, of course. It is what you might call too delicate – dealing with Guerrero.

His name means 'warrior', I'm told. He is my connection not only to the rich and corrupt in South and Central America and Mexico, but to those in Europe and Asia as well. There is a large community of Americans where I'm headed, and Guerrero insists that he loves dealing with Americans.

I use a private jet, courtesy of the Outfit. It's the least they can do to accommodate our business venture. But the trip always tires me. It reminds me of all the air time I endured during the Gulf War. And the ride is equally uncomfortable coming down here, even on days of clear weather.

My business is pharmaceuticals, as far as the Mexican Federales are concerned. They have been paid off with money from the Cartel that does business with my friends in Chicago. Or at least with the people who used to be my friends. This is very likely my last trip south. I will need to make new arrangements soon.

After the multi-hour flight we land. I am hustled through the terminal by Guerrero's people with no delay. His people are everywhere, here. He has his beak into everything, being the CEO of the Cartel in central Mexico.

After a perfunctory run-through with the Federales, there are big smiles and much politeness, and I'm headed toward Guerrero's driver. Once we get out of this midsized Mexican city, I am blindfolded by Juanito – Johnny – who is a bodyguard of the

'Warrior'. I never see the last ten miles of the trip. My eyes are wrapped with gauze and the gauze is covered with heavy material that makes any glimpse of my whereabouts impossible.

I left her in pieces. I need to make this visit as fast as possible before her body is found. Then, of course, I become a persona non grata with my one-time allies in the city, and of course they will be looking to eliminate me. This is my last business with the Cartel boss, and I'll need his cash to go underground from the Outfit and the personal vendetta from that cunt's brother. I should have killed him too, but he is too dangerous to approach. And it would be a silly risk. After this deal, with her lovely internal works to trade, I'll be fixed for a lifetime.

The mask of gauze is stripped off when we arrive inside Guerrero's compound. I'm assuming it is a fortress of some kind although I've never seen the outside or the grounds. It would simply seem to be the kind of place he'd use for his business and pleasure.

I am seated in his office in a huge, new-smelling leather chair. It is high-backed and executive-like.

Guerrero walks in alone. We are never accompanied in here. There is a video camera behind me, I've noticed. But Guerrero has explained there is no audio. They can see us but they can't hear us. And the camera is aimed at Guerrero's chest so no one may read his lips.

I'm sure he is armed. He is not a stupid man so he does not trust me, just as I have no confidence in him. But to do this business we must take some chances. And I would never allow those Chicago wops to deal with this man. It is my business. I made it happen, regardless of how it all began with her pimp of a brother.

'Buenas tardes.' Guerrero smiles.

He smiles frequently, but there is never pleasure on his face.

He is an Indian. Dark and truly handsome for a mixed-blood Mexican.

'You looked tired, señor. Como esta?'

'I don't have much time, jefe.'

'You are rushed, eh? Why is that?'

'Pressing business, back in Chicago.'

'Ay, Cheecago. I would like to visit it. I am a big White Sox fan. Do you like baseball, señor?'

'No. I don't like—'

'You ought to have a hobby. Such a grim business as yours would make one . . . tense. No?'

'No, jefe. I am fine. But I need to hurry, if you don't mind.'

'I see no reason why this should take very long . . . The goods are delivered. No?'

'Yes. In the usual fashion.'

'It helps to own the union which does the baggage. Eh?'

'Yes. It makes things much easier, jefe.'

'And the fucking Federales. They are expensive, but it is a necessary expense. Just as they are everywhere we take your goods.'

He is smiling broadly now.

'You're telling me my end of the deal is to be reduced?' I ask.

'It is becoming more expensive to fill all these pockets, señor . . . I hear they call you The Farmer. Is that true?'

'Yes. It is true.'

He laughs boisterously.

'It is not a thing of laughter,' I tell him.

The smile disappears. He is very dark brown. Blinding white teeth. Even, perfect teeth.

'You are not thinking of a dispute?'

'I'm being squeezed. Right?'

'Claro!' He laughs loudly.

'I don't suppose I have a choice but to go along.'

'You are very cooperative . . . too cooperative, senor. If you were to reach into your pockets for anything my bodyguards might have missed . . . Or if you somehow managed to conceal a weapon on the way in here, your head will adorn my mantelpiece and the coyotes will eat your cojones. Are you with me, Mister Farmer?'

'How could I have snuck a weapon into here with all of your security feeling me up and examining me beforehand?' I smile.

148

His canine teeth are just slightly too long, I notice. I'm wondering if he is a biter.

'There is always that chance. No one is that good, hombre. No one.'

He is a well-built, fit man. There is no fat on his frame. You can see the muscle beneath his expensive sports attire. Guerrero is wearing all American brand-name sportswear.

'And besides, I've already received the call.'

'What call, jefe?'

'From the brother of that bitch that you sliced up and cut to pieces.'

I find myself rising from the chair.

'Sit down, Mister Farmer . . . Bueno. They have offered me very significant dinero to send you back to El Norte, just so the brother can do to you what you did to the sister.'

'Why are you telling me all this?'

'It's not good business. You are good business. I don't know about your friends, but we have made very fine profits, you and me. And why would I want to fuck it all up? Over one puta, one hoor?'

He watches me to see if there's a rise.

'We were in business together. She was a cunt. That was all.'

'I see. Yes, I understand. But her brother doesn't agree with you.'

'He was fucking her himself.'

'Such twisted people. Like a pretzel, no? You are very interesting people, you northerners. You like to destroy each other no matter what you're doing. In sports, in the bed. It makes no difference. You want to wipe the other away. There is no mercy with you, Señor Farmer.'

'Do we stay in business?'

He watches me carefully. He wants to see me squirm, but I will not.

'We have interests in London, Paris, Amsterdam, Moscow, Beijing, Hong Kong, Manila, Toronto, Berlin, and a dozen more cities throughout the world that I can't remember. We are talking about hundreds of millions of pesos and dollars and

pounds and yen. You think I'd give you up for this puta-greaseball? I don't think so. And I told this Italian bastard that whatever he has between him and you is left right there. I will not protect you, señor. That was the only concession I gave to your master up north. But if he includes me in his vengeance, then I will protect myself, and he does not want a war on this side of the Rio Grande.'

He takes a sip of his iced tea. The glass has been sweating on the table since I arrived.

'I will not protect you from him, but I never said I wouldn't help you evade his revenge. I will. Help you, that is. But you know how it is with the wops. I'm doing it only because it is good business . . . What is it that made you as you are, Mister Farmer? How did you become the crooked thing of beauty you are now? Was it a woman before this puta that you just destroyed?'

'It's none of your fucking business, Guerrero.'

'You don't disrespect me in my casa, Marco.'

He hits my first name with a hard emphasis. He knows my name, but I don't what his real moniker is.

'Yes, Mister Karrios. I have had you investigated. I know as much about you as your friends at the Chicago Police Department do. I have many friends in your city. I have many friends all over the north. And in the world, too. How else could one sell body parts from murder victims? And then you have this habit of defiling the bodies of these unfortunate creatures. Why is that? Was it your mother? Did you have a sister, perhaps?'

His information is limited. He is fishing with sharp barbs aimed at my flesh.

'Were you abandoned at birth, jefe? Like so many of these little street bastards who beg for money in the streets of your putrid cities? Did you start out by sucking the cocks of the honchos on the street corners? Was that the way you rose to power, chief?'

'You assume that you can say whatever you want. It is your way, Marco. You are ignorant of manners. But I accept that. We are businessmen, no?'

'Yes. We are businessmen.'

150

'Then we should both learn to treat each other as partners. No?'

'Yes. Of course, jefe.'

'But do not feel safe or secure. As I said, I will not protect you from your old friends. You are on your own when it comes to personal security. It is simply that I have refused to return you to the north. How you get back, once you are dropped off at the airport, is up to you ... We will need to make new arrangements about dealing with you. There is sometimes not enough money to cover up your crimes against those women. You have become too famous. You should have stayed in the darkness. It is becoming very difficult to make the police and the Federales turn their backs on you. That is what fame will do. It will take away your freedom. You will have to live in a fortress, such as this one, Marco.'

His expression almost turns to sadness, but he quickly recovers his feral smile. It is a smile that intimidates; it does not suggest pleasure or humor.

'If the money wasn't so good, I think I would have a good time carving you up with your own blade, Marco . . . You better get out of here quickly. Your last mess may be your final mess.'

I can see him up in the hills or the mountains with Emiliano Zapata or Pancho Villa. He is the kind of Indian who would prefer to use the machete. He is the man who has moved our goods. He is our international middle man, but he is nothing more than a very dark Indian with an intimidating grimace planted perpetually on his lips.

'Go quickly, then, gringo. You will never see me again. You will deal with other men from now on. You are too hot to make direct contact with me anymore. Go with God, Marco. He is the only one who will have you now. Adios.'

He reaches under the long mahogany table and presses a button. Immediately Juanito is back with us. He is carrying the gauze and the eye cover. Once he's done his job, I'm escorted out of the citadel of Guerrero's castle or fortress or hideout or whatever it is that he lurks inside.

If they're going to cut my throat, this would be the moment. As Juanito leads me out of the door, I'm anticipating the slice of

151

a blade across my jugular. I've done it to others so many times, it would be a fitting way for my end to come. And if my end is to come, a knife would be my own personal choice. The sweetness of that bleeding, the slow draining away of all hopes and ambitions. The sleep that would put its dark hand over my eyes and finally put me to permanent rest. That there is no hell and no heaven is my only certainty. There will be an end to this, only an end. How it will come, I'm not sure. Whether it will be Juanito or Guerrero or Ellen's vile brother or some Chicago policeman makes little difference to me.

Dreamless sleep. Oblivion. They are my versions of paradise. So come on, Juanito. If you have the knife in your hand, use it. Do it quickly. Do it deftly.

Let me float away from this life. Here in this sultry country. It's as good a place as any. Go ahead. Tear me open and let my bowels rush forth, just as I have done to those women. It all ends the same way. Blackness. Dreamless sleep. Oblivion.

Juanito delivers me down the halls and out into the air and into the limousine. When he secures me inside the Cadillac, I feel almost disappointed that I'm still here, still breathing, still in this world.

Where do I run next? In which direction do I aim myself? Where will the wind take me now?

Chapter Twenty-Four

The Sheriff had men around the perimeter, just as we did. This was a cooperative bust, county and city.

Once Marco Karrios's picture made it to the newspapers and other media, it only took a few days for all this to turn up. It appeared that Marco and Ellen had done their shopping at a store in the college town. One of the cashiers made him and her from photos, and then we found the farmhouse.

We were going in about 4.00 a.m. It'd still be full dark. There was not much to illuminate the area surrounding the farmhouse. Just one dim streetlight from out at the end of his quarter-mile driveway.

Everyone had their bulletproof vests on. If he was in there, we expected that he'd know we were coming. There was only one car parked in front of the house. It looked like a Camry, but we couldn't be sure from where we were sitting.

I radioed the Sheriff's people it was time to go. They affirmed, and Doc and Jack Wendkos and I got out of the Taurus. Jack took out his Nine, as I did. Doc removed the .38 from his holster. I had the Bulldog strapped, and I also had the switchblade in my pocket.

We moved up to the house. There were four cars in front and five behind the place. We were in communication with the Sheriff's cops at the rear. We waited until the time we had set, and then two cops hit the front door with the horizontal sledge that we used to pop open doors. The jamb and panels splintered and we crashed inside.

There was no light as we barged in. Doc sought and found the switch in the living room. No one was in here. The Sheriff's police rammed the back door, and now they were in the house with us. The bulb was in an overhead fixture and it made everything in the living room appear garish, nightmarish.

We saw the blood when we scoped out the rug. There were large pools of it and there were ropes of it threaded across the carpet. Someone had lost more than a few pints out here, and it was rather recent, too. The rug was still wet with the stuff.

Jack yelled to me from the bedroom. When he emerged, he leaned back against the wall near the doorway. His face had turned white in a hurry. Doc and I rushed past him into the bedroom.

Wendkos had turned on the overhead light in that room. The room was bright, like in a hospital.

Ellen Jacoby was hung upside down by her ankles. She dangled from the ceiling fan next to the globe of light. She'd been torn open, and her entrails hung out over her chest and face.

Marco had also taken the time to give her a Colombian necktie. He'd pulled her tongue and its connecting tendons out of her mouth and had looped it around her neck. It was what the drug guys from down south did to anyone who betrayed them.

Her throat had been cut, her eyelids severed, and there were too many stab wounds to count. She dangled just beyond the foot of the bed. There was another pool of blood beneath her. This job appeared recent. We hadn't missed him by too many hours, but the ME would let us know how close we'd come.

'This guy's a fucking hound, Jimmy. We got to put him

154

to sleep. She might've had it coming, but then *nobody* has all this coming,' Doc said softly.

The Sheriff himself walked in behind us.

'Oh my lord . . . It's like a slaughterhouse in this room.'

When we'd seen enough, we got out of there. There were policemen all over the farmhouse. There were cops out in that one-time cornfield. But Marco Karrios wasn't here with the rest of us.

'You could go on vacation today.' Billy smiled when we sat down on his couch in the safe house in Evanston.

'Yeah? Why?' Doc asked him.

'Because Jackie Morocco don't allow shit like this to happen to his own family. That's why,' Billy laughed.

'You saw that woman, Billy Cheech, you wouldn't be laughing,' I told my cousin. 'This guy Karrios might think he owes himself an informant, namely you.'

Billy lost the grin and he gulped.

'He tore her up real bad, I guess,' he admitted.

We didn't answer him.

'I thought you said you'd protect me.'

'Yeah. But from who? They're standing in line to whack you, coz.'

'Jimmy. You *are* gonna find this Karrios prick, aren't you?'

'That's why they sign the checks, Cheech.'

'Come on, Doc. You're gonna haul in Jackie too, ain't you?'

'The Feds are in it with us,' Doc told him.

'See? It's a done deal, then. The Feds take out the Big Man and Chicago's finest deliver that fuckin' Farmer guy.'

He gulped again when he saw that neither Doc nor I gave him any solid affirmation.

Chapter Twenty-Five

Sal Donofrio is my contact to Jackie Morocco. He's the guy I did business with. I know it'll be difficult to ask him for any favors after they've heard about Ellen, but I'll make him a fine offer. It's one of those kinds of deals you just don't turn down.

I arrive at his bungalow at 4.00 a.m. I arrive, of course, unannounced. I get through his screen door and his back door with a burglar's pick. Things that Sal taught me. Sal's a made man and a soldier, but his allegiance to John Fortuna goes only as far as Sal's wallet. These men have no codes, other than greed.

But he wouldn't help me out because his boss would kill him if he did, and so I have to put the screws to my one-time contact.

I lean over his bed. His wife is snoring. I jostle him lightly.

'Huh?'

'It's me, Sal. Get up . . . No, no, no. Don't reach for the night table.'

I show him the blade.

He sits up slowly. His old lady continues to snore.

'Whatta you want?'

I motion for him to leave the bedroom.

'Don't reach for anything, Sal, or I'll do you just like I did your boss's sister.'

He's fully awake now.

We walk into his kitchen. I sit him down at the table.

'I need a plastic surgeon. You know the guy I'm talking about. Up in Lake Forest.'

'Dr Richmond?'

'Yeah. I need a new face.'

'And why the fuck would I help you get one?'

He's a forty-year-old guinea. Short, squat. Wears all the usual gold around his neck. You can picture Sal standing out front of one of their private 'clubs'.

'Because I'll tell Big John you helped me. I'll let him know you tried to keep me going even after his sister got all cut up.'

'He won't believe you, you crazy motherfucker.'

'He'll believe me. He knows your end of the take on our business venture. He'll believe you want me to get us up and running again. You're losing a lot of cash by my being unemployed. No?'

'It ain't gonna work, Marco.'

'Yes, it will. I get a new face. I disappear. I give you the same cut you've been getting – without Fortuna's tribute. How's that sound?'

He stares at me.

'Or I could slice you and that Saturday-night cocksucker you're sleeping with.'

I show him the blade.

'You're not such a bad man without your piece, are you, Sal? You ought to sleep with that .45 under your pillow.'

'You talk to the boss and you're dead. You better make sure this prick with a scalpel makes you look a lot different . . . All right. I'll call him . . . You say we're still gonna be in business together?'

I nod slowly.

'We got three orders to fill from Thailand. They're indirects, like always. Some business people from Germany and Switzerland are goin' through our broker in Europe.'

'I'll be back in the saddle just as soon as the stitches come out . . . We have this Dr Richmond under certain restraints?'

'John got him out of a hit-and-run homicide. The good doctor was drunk and he ran over some jogger running on the Outer Drive. He owes us major. It's no problem.'

157

'Call him, then.'

'Now, Marco?'

I look at him and I turn the blade over and over in my hand.

'You are one goofy motherfucker. Why'd you have to do John's sister?'

'She betrayed me.'

'How the fuck did she betray you?'

I rip a slice across his cheek before he's able to pull back. The blood ripples down his cheek.

'Jesus fucking Christ!' he cries out. He puts a hand to the cheek to stanch the blood.

'Women always betray you. She was how they were going to get to me. She was the way the cops were going to find me. If you hook yourself to a woman, they'll find a way to drag you down before they leave you. Haven't you figured that out yet, Sal?'

'Jesus God, you're nuts.'

'Get on the phone. Do it now.'

He continues to hold his wound and walks to the wall phone.

'The bleeding'll stop soon. I just nicked you. Tell her you did it shaving.'

He makes the call. I can hear that Richmond's all pissed off at being awakened.

'He wants to know when, Marco.'

'Now. Forty-five minutes. At his clinic.'

He tells the doctor.

'He says you're crazy.'

'Tell him the Sun Times'll love a story about a surgeon who owes the Outfit big time.'

Sal repeats what I said.

Sal nods at me.

'Forty-five minutes,' he says.

'I usually have a nurse to aid me.'

'You're working alone.'

He nods.

'You understand what happens if anyone contacts the police

158

*about this procedure? You understand what happens if you put
me under and decide not to go through with this?'*

He nods again.

*'Sal will kill your wife and your two teenaged daughters.
And your parents, both of whom are still living. Right?'*

He nods once more and I finally see perspiration on his brow.

*Dr Richmond also serves as anesthetist this morning. He
injects me and we begin.*

*I hide out at Sal's when Richmond transports me there after the
operation is completed. I'll need to stay at Donofrio's until
Richmond can take the stitches out. Sal is not happy to accommodate me, but he's sent his wife to her mother's until I'm not
around anymore.*

*When the stitches come out, I'll have to color my hair. I'm
going to be fitted with contact lenses that change these blue eyes
to brown – as opposed to the way it is in the song lyrics. I'm
going to buy eyeglasses despite my twenty-twenty vision, and
I'm going to grow a mustache and beard. This will all take
weeks, but Sal knows I keep my word. He knows I'll rat him out
to Big John and that I'll kill him and his old lady as well. He
knows how good I am at my work. He heard all the details about
Ellen from their contacts at the police department. He under-
stands how thorough I am. And there is always the element of
greed, which is the final weight in convincing him to help me
out. I'm his moneymaker. It would've been like a pimp killing
his best whore if he'd done me. These guys are close to death all
the time. What motivates them even more than survival is profit.
They are the ultimate capitalists minus the restrictions.
Businessmen.*

*The days go by slowly. Sal brings me videos. I have a taste
for a woman, but it's too dangerous until I've made my
metamorphosis. I keep waiting to see a sign on this guinea's face
that he's going to turn me over to Jackie Morocco, but the days
pass slowly and uneventfully.*

*Then the good Doctor shows up at Donofrio's bungalow to
remove my stitch-work. He is very professional, very artful in*

159

the way he works. There is virtually no pain. When he is finished, he shows me his handiwork in a mirror.

'The swelling and the bruises should be gone soon. A week or two. Here's something for infection.'

He hands me a bottle of penicillin.

The doctor leaves us, and I start packing.

'I'll be in touch about that triple order within two weeks. Make sure you tell them the goods are on the way,' I tell Sal.

'You better keep your end of the deal, Marco. You squeal on me, you won't have Big John to worry about no more. I'll cut your eyes out myself.'

'Hey, we're businessmen. This is business, isn't it? We're going to make a lot of money. Dying people all over the world standing in line for a shot at a new life. They can't wait for all those generous donors. And the guys we have as customers have the cash to make it happen. They don't have to stand in line. That's the service we provide, Sal.'

'You are a crazy motherfucker, Marco.'

'I'll be in touch.'

I take my bag. I put a hood up over my head, and I leave by his back door, just the way I came in here.

Chapter Twenty-Six

The Karrioses were in their early seventies, but the old man, Niko, had jet-black hair with only a trace of gray on the sideburns. The mother, Elena, showed the cruelty of age more readily.

Doc and I had tracked them down. They lived in Kankakee. Quite a little ride south of the city. We again had to clear things through the local coppers, but everything worked out smoothly.

We sat in their two-bedroom home in a not-very-fashionable area of this town. He was a retired brakeman for the railroad, and she'd worked as a checkout person at a grocery store for thirty-six years. They'd come here as immigrants, Niko told Doc and me, but they wanted better things for their son. They wanted him to be a doctor, but the boy decided to join the Army when he was in his twenties, instead of finishing college. He wound up as a medic in the Gulf War, but he came home very different, Elena told us.

'He never talk to us no more. He just live here a little while after the War is over and then he leave without telling us anything. He take his bags and he leave. We don't hear from him again . . . We was close, Marco and me.'

I looked up at the wall with the photographs. There

was Marco, and there were his two parents, in several of the shots.

But there was also a photograph of a young woman in several of the pictures.

I rose and walked to the wall with the photos.

'Who is this?' I asked the two older people.

Elena Karrios stiffened.

'She . . . she was our daughter.'

'Does she still live around the city?' Doc asked.

'She . . . she's dead. She been dead a long time,' Niko responded.

'So Marco had a sister,' I mused.

She was blonde and stunning. Marco was photogenic, but his sister outclassed him by a wide margin.

'Yes,' Elena said. 'She was Marco's sister.'

It seemed it was difficult for her to get the words out. She almost spat them at the two of us.

'Were they close?' Doc questioned her.

The old man squirmed in his seat, next to Elena Karrios.

'You could say they were close,' Mrs Karrios admitted.

'How'd she die?' I queried.

Elena looked me squarely in the eyes.

'It was an accident.'

'Accident?' I returned at her.

'Yes. A car accident. She and her husband die in a car wreck,' the old woman murmured. Tears came to her eyes, but she did not break. 'All a long time ago. Hard to remember, now.'

'Is there anything else you can tell us about Marco?' Doc wanted to know. 'If we catch him, he won't hurt anyone else, and maybe no one'll hurt him.'

'You catch him, they kill him in prison. With what? Lethal drug?' Niko said.

'They might,' Doc told him. 'But it'll be easier if we get him before John Fortuna's people catch up with him. You know who John Fortuna is and you know it was his sister who Marco . . . killed.'

'Yes. I read papers. I know who she was . . . But we

cannot help you anymore . . . My wife . . . my wife is sick. Her blood pressure is too high. She could have stroke. Please . . . no more.'

I got up and thanked them, and then Doc and I began the long trip back to the city.

We finally set up a meet on that following Friday. It was at Fortuna's place on the North Side. It was one of those Italian-American 'societies' that the Outfit has in a lot of neighborhoods where a crew is in charge.

All it said was 'Italian American Club' on the window of the joint. Doc, Jack Wendkos and I were meeting with Jackie Morocco. He had refused to sit down with the FBI unless they brought him in with a warrant. He knew my cousin Billy was on the run, so I guessed he figured he had some leverage over me.

He made his entrance like some kind of Hollywood star in a movie. He walked in with the long coat draped over his shoulders, unbuttoned, and some thug took it off him before he sat with us in a four-man booth. He planted himself next to Doc, sitting on the outside.

'Lieutenant,' John Fortuna said as a greeting.

He was about six-four. Tall for a Sicilian. He had the dark brown, glossy hairdo and a swarthy Mediterranean face. He even looked like an actor. But if you knew his reputation, you didn't disbelieve when he spoke.

'I want the killer of my sister found. I'm willing to cooperate.'

Someone arrived at the table with four tiny coffee cups and four tiny saucers. Fortuna drank his brew as soon as it arrived. The three of us left our cups untouched.

'I want you to leave him to us,' I told Fortuna.

'I never thought of doing anything but,' he said.

I was surprised he didn't laugh at his own lie. But everyone at this booth knew John Fortuna was in heat for the blood of The Farmer.

'I don't want that FBI involved with Karrios,' he said.

'The case is ours,' Doc affirmed.

'Good. I know they want me because they think I'm somehow involved in this business, but I want you to know I had no involvement with Marco Karrios. His business is *infamnia*. You know what I'm saying, Lieutenant?' he asked me.

I looked in his eyes and wondered how good an actor he really was, because I was almost convinced *he* was convinced that he had no connection to The Farmer's operation.

'I want that motherfucker in a cage. To die is too easy for him. I want him in a cage like the *animale* he is.'

Chapter Twenty-Seven

The hospital was ten minutes from my house. Natalie was sitting in Emergency, her arm wrapped in gauze. Her face was ashen. She leaned back against the bench as if she was likely to fall down if she tried to stand up.

I sat down next to her, but I didn't dare ask her how she was feeling. I could see she was shaky.

'What'd the man say?'

'Take me home, Jimmy, will you? He says I shouldn't drive because of the painkillers. Whatever he gave me, I feel like I'm riding the airwaves.'

I got her to her feet and guided her to the exit.

'You couldn't stay in forensics.'

'No, Jimmy P. I could not.'

'So what's the story – I mean your version?'

'Kelly and I got called into a domestic. We walk in the front door, uninvited, because the battle's going on between common-law lovers. We enter and all we see are arms and legs flying, like a barroom brawl. She's got a broken bottle, and I catch it on the forearm. Sixteen stitches. I lose a quart of oil. No big deal.'

'What about Danny Kelly?' He was the other uniform, her partner.

'He is very big-time pissed when he sees me leaking on this domestic's rug. He pops the sweetie with the jagged-bottle piece. He nails her on the kneecaps. The bout is over. But hubby is angry that dearie is injured and rolling around the floor. Comes at Danny and me with a broom handle. Danny repeats the swat to the old man's kneecaps and down *he* goes. Now everybody's moaning and groaning, me included. Then our backup arrives and I still got enough in my tank to make it to the hospital and then you show up with your own personal cavalry . . . You look tired.'

'*I* look tired? You ought to catch your own act.'

It was three-forty in the morning. We were into the dregs of winter. It seemed like the change to spring would never take place. We had ice and hail and snow. It had been a putrid March. And our wedding day was set for April 23rd. Natalie had us running in circles trying to complete all the details for the ceremony.

I picked up her injured arm and I kissed the fingers sticking out of all that gauze.

'You're going to need plastic surgery.'

'Yes.' She nodded. She finally started to cry.

'I will not do this,' she muttered. But the tears came anyway. 'One month till the wedding and this bitch has to screw me up. I'll have a scar on this arm and you won't want me.'

'You say that again and I'll swat your fanny.'

She straightened up toward me and kissed me.

'You're not all turned on by perfect forearms, then?'

'Not especially, Natalie, although I'm not happy this sweetheart hurt you . . . When's the plastic surgery?'

'Next week.'

'What really pisses me off is this wench cut me off tonight. Now it's really personal.'

'I wouldn't worry, Jimmy. I think I can still manage to generate a little heat for the both of us.'

She straightened up and let me have it again, right on

the lips. I picked her up and carried her as gently as I could into her bedroom.

It hit me when I was going through some casework downtown. Plastic surgery. That had to be Marco's next move. It was radical, but it was the only thing that was going to keep him on the streets – unless he tried to leave the area or the country. Which would he try? A new face or a new location? I asked Doc Gibron.

'New face ... But who'd do him now that he's so famous?'

'There's a guy. Some rich bastard up in the burbs. Lake Forest, I think,' Billy told us. He had relocated to a crib in Cicero. He'd been moving every week, he told us.

'Guy named Richmond. John's got a fuckin' lien on his property, you might say, but I don't know the reason ... You think Farm Guy wants a new puss, is that it?'

I thanked my cousin and told him to keep mobile. When he caught my drift, his smile turned to something a lot more somber and serious.

'When do you expect Dr Richmond in?' Doc asked the nurse.

'He's taken a two-week vacation. I think it's to the Caymans, but I'm not sure. It's odd because he never confirmed his destination and he always leaves me a number where I can reach him. You know, in case a patient needs to reach him.'

I thanked the good-looking redhead and we departed.

'You think the good doctor has straightened her nose and enhanced her features?' Gibron asked me.

*

167

We tried Richmond's house, but we got no answer. We walked around to the rear of this multi-million-dollar estate where he resided in Lake Forest. We knocked at the rear entrance but there was no response.

Doc saw the jimmy marks near the door handle. When he pressed that handle, the door popped open. So Gibron went back out front and radioed for backup from the County Police. We didn't need a warrant because I thought we had probable cause to enter Richmond's home.

County pulled up in five minutes flat. They didn't tolerate creepers in this neighborhood. Burglars, thieves, breaking-and-entering experts.

The County deputies entered the house with Doc and me at the back door. We walked in with our weapons drawn. It was unlikely the guy who'd broken in was still here, but you never knew. We saw no car parked close to this three-acre lot.

There was nothing on the main floor. They had an old-fashioned spiral staircase that I assumed led to the bedrooms above us. I led the way up, but we were not shouting out that we were down there. Doc and the pair of County deputies were behind me.

The smell hit me as soon as I'd reached the halfway point on the spiral staircase. I began to hurry upward. My pulse and heartbeat were beginning to skyrocket.

I found the girls first. They had separate bedrooms at the top of the flight. They were young teenagers, perhaps fourteen or fifteen. Their throats had been cut and they had died in their beds. Their eyes were closed as if they had expired in their sleep. The four of us walked in and out of the two bedrooms and headed down the hall.

The doctor and his wife were in the master bedroom. Their throats had been likewise slashed. Dr Richmond had had his hands cut off. They lay at the foot of the bed. Mrs Richmond had fared worse. She lay on top of the bedspread with her intestines exposed and her head nearly severed. I was betting that she was missing some of her

168

major organs, but I'd leave the examination to the ME. The strangest item here was the fact that there appeared to have been no struggle. The teenagers looked like they simply never woke up, and the couple in this room seemed to have never been aroused into a struggle either.

'He used the ether on them. At least they never saw what hit them,' Doc offered as an explanation.

'You're probably right.'

One of the County deputies was new on the job, so he ran toward the closest toilet. The other deputy appeared to be turning a shade of green.

I nodded for him to take a walk down the hall too. It was not something just any stomach could handle.

'He didn't stay out of circulation very long, did he?' Doc asked. 'Or maybe he was pissed about the job the physician there did on him. Chopped off the doc's moneymakers.'

'I think he was making sure Richmond was out of play. Then he decided to take advantage of the missus. She's about mid-thirties, no?'

'Yeah, Jimmy. But it's hard to tell age on a slaughtered animal. She doesn't look quite human, the way he left her.'

'Fortuna was right. This guy's an *animale*. We probably ought to let Jackie Morocco's people handle him.'

Doc looked over at me and didn't even blink. He knew mindless anger and frustration when he heard it.

We made the calls and pulled all of our people in place. The Medical Examiner, the forensics people – both city and County.

It was our guy Karrios, of course. So County would let us in the door. I didn't know of any outfit outside the CPD that would want The Farmer dumped on them to handle alone. And the FBI would shortly be on scene as well. I called Terry Morrissey, the agent working with us, and he said his group of investigators would be arriving soon. Dr Richmond's estate would be loaded with strangers.

'Why'd he have to kill the girls?' I asked my partner.

Doc grew distant at the question. He went into hibernation with the deaths of two young black girls a few years back, and now I was sorry I asked the question.

Doc got out his little notebook and Bic pen and went to work.

'Jesus Christ. He hacked up the guy's whole family?' Billy asked. This time we were in Oak Lawn, on the southwest side.

'Two little girls. Just becoming young women,' I explained to him. 'Billy, it's time you told us who The Farmer's contact was. It's too late to worry about getting whacked by whoever it was in the Outfit. And I have the honest feeling that Marco Karrios doesn't deal with Big John directly. So how about telling us who it was who opened business with the capo's crew.'

Billy lit a cigarette. I never saw him smoke before.

'Put that fuckin' thing out. You'll gag the three of us,' Doc commanded.

Billy stubbed out the butt.

'Oh man. This'll make sure they button my drawers, Jimmy.'

'You're dead if we don't get them before they get you. You're smart enough to figure the move here, Billy,' I told him.

'Oh man, oh man. You'll find me with a fuckin' cattle prod up my heinie.'

'Come on, come on. It's too late for all this shit,' Doc reminded him.

He picked up the dead cigarette out of the ashtray and rubbed it to dust.

'It's Sal Donofrio. That's this guy's connection – but don't think Big John doesn't know what his troops are up to, Jimmy. Fortuna's no fuckin' cherry in this. He's just pissed his old squeeze, his sister, got whacked on the deal. What you said about John maybe not knowing about The

170

Farmer's business? That's bullshit. Sal ain't smart enough to pull it off . . . They say Fortuna's got crocodile tears. Remember that, when we were kids? He can fool you that he's all sincere about something, and then he bites your fuckin' head off. Like a crocodile. He ain't clean on this thing, Jimmy P. But he's got a personal thing with this guy Karrios now. And he's got the people to find the son of a bitch maybe even before you do, and if he does, I'm fuckin' dead. You guys gotta win this one, coz. I'm beggin' you.'

I'd never seen him so desperate. I would have liked to assure him that we'd get to Karrios and Fortuna, but I couldn't lie to him. He was right about the miserable odds.

'Hello, Sal,' Doc said, as we sat down in the interview box downtown.

'You guys get randy, I'm lawyering up,' the short, powerfully muscled Sicilian told us.

'We're dutifully threatened,' Gibron conceded.

'We know you're hooked to Karrios,' I said to him.

'Case closed. I want an attorney.'

'Listen, asshole. Your lawyer's not going to save you from Jackie Morocco when Big John finds out you been doing business for a second time with Karrios. He doesn't know that you put Marco onto the plastic surgeon, does he? He'll figure it out. We did. Then what? You're going to need some cosmetic surgery yourself when the Big Dog finds out you been cutting your own deals . . . And what happened? Did Marco threaten you? Is that why you were so hot to start the business back up again? . . . When we catch up to Marco Karrios, and we will, he's going to dump you right into John Fortuna's lap. Either way you jump, you're dead.'

'I want my lawyer,' Donofrio repeated to me.

'Sure, Sal. But there's one deal that might save your ass.'

171

He didn't ask for his counselor this time.

'We put you away safe after you give us John Fortuna. We got the FBI standing right on the other side of that one-way mirror. They'll get you into witness protection, John goes away for life, and we have our hands free to deal with Marco and Marco only . . . Now, before you give me the code-of-silence rejection, you better think about what's best for you. Marco didn't tell you he was going to whack the doctor and his whole family, did he? He probably made you think the two of you are still business partners the way you were. You can't be stupid enough to think he's going to let you go on breathing when he can try to set up his own business with his own contacts. You know how bright this piece of shit is. You don't think he can fly solo, without you and the crew? You that dumb, Sal?'

Donofrio sat motionless. Then he sat up and folded his hands in front of him.

'You got paper on me? 'Cause if you don't, I'm leaving.'

Doc opened the door. It appeared at first as if Sal was debating on getting out of his chair. But he finally did and he walked slowly out into the hall. Just as he was about to disappear, he turned toward Doc and me. It looked like he had something to tell us. But the moment passed, and then he turned and walked out.

'That was our best shot at him. I really thought he might take the deal,' Doc said.

We were sitting in my tiny office upstairs. We could never sit in Doc's cubicle because it was too full of novels and collections of poetry. The place was as cluttered as a teenager's bedroom.

'We have to watch him. Billy says he's the connection, then Marco's got to contact him. Until and unless we're right and he eliminates the middleman. You think Sal's days are numbered?'

'Well, he better check on the status of all his insurance.

172

He's a bad risk. But I'm betting on the crew boss to make Sal disappear before Marco does. Marco's got his new appearance going for him, and Richmond was the only pair of eyes that knew what the new Farmer looks like ... We need an artist to alter Karrios's face. Slap a beard and a mustache over the old visage. Straighten his nose. Color his hair. Whatever. We'll be flying blind, I know ... I think our best bet would be to try and catch him when he hits Sal. Even Sal knows it's the logical move. I say we use Donofrio as bait, without Sal's permission.'

We walked downstairs to where the FBI had set up temporary headquarters. Terry Morrissey was in his office.

'We need big-time surveillance on Sal Donofrio,' I told him.

'We're already setting it up. I was just about to come upstairs and let you know.'

Doc turned his stare from the freckled, red-headed Federal Agent and gave me a non-believing flip of the eyeballs.

'No. No shit. I really was ... Sal's the guy. Marco still might need him before he sets up his own shop on the Internet ... I assume that's what you two were just talking about before you got here?'

The FBI was maybe not as inept as Doc and I kept telling each other. Apparently, at least they have their moments.

'Sal's the man. Karrios wants to be the last man standing,' I told the agent.

Chapter Twenty-Eight

I secure an apartment on the far northwest side. I'm so far out on the northwest that two more blocks and I'm into a suburb. But it's close enough to where I want to be. The city is crowded. Its population makes a great place to hide. I'm called a predator in the media, and I suppose there's something correct in that name because I am a hunter, after all. That's the nature of my trade.

But this homicide police guy – this James Parisi – has been saying things about me that are uncalled for. He's called me an 'animal' and several other things that are very unflattering. As I say, when we killed in the Army, it was our duty. But when I don't have the government's sanction, I'm some kind of jungle creature. And all the press about the mutilations. None of my victims – except that snotty cunt stewardess and that bitch I lived with – felt any pain. I anesthetized each of them with the ether. Even the plastic surgeon's wife.

It was almost too easy, breaking into the doctor's home. The cheap bastard didn't even have a security system. I guess he figured deadbolts would keep the boogyman out. I was inside the back door in seconds. And if he'd had a dog, it would've also added to the challenge. I don't like dogs.

I went up his stairs and discovered the two girls first. I couldn't very well leave them parentless, could I? And the shock of discovering mom and dad all over their master bedroom couldn't have given the two youngsters a good start in life, so I figure what I did was an act of mercy.

All those women and children we killed in Panama and in the Gulf. By accident, the government says. They were casualties of war. And in that same way the surgeon's daughters suffered from being in the wrong place at the wrong time. Did their white skin and their upper-class neighborhood excuse them from becoming those casualties of combat? I don't think so. It's just that the media is horrified when Americans die violently.

I don't really spend a lot of time in self-justification. I've read Nietzsche. I understand the concept of the Übermensch. He was right. There are a number of men who are above the laws of the herd. I'm not entirely philosophical in nature, but I understood enough of Nietzsche's brand of existentialism to see that living under any jurisdiction is living under illusion. But, as I say, I don't spend sleepless nights trying to rationalize my life. Does a wolf rationalize every throat he tears out? Every lamb he slaughters? Why are men any different under Nature?

This Parisi cop irritates me. I'd like to meet up with him and his family at some point, but it's a bit too risky to anger the police by killing one of their own. I can't over-stimulate public outrage because it tightens the loop on my hunting grounds. Next thing I'd know, all the women in the city will be packing heat. I'm trying to conduct business, for the most part, so I suppose it's time for a brief interlude.

In order to fill the other two orders for our European clients via Thailand, I met with two prostitutes, separately, on the west side of the city. I took them to my apartment, I anesthetized each of them on those two occasions, and I extracted what the order called for – liver, lungs, and heart. I dumped each of the bodies on different lots on the west side.

I don't normally do niggers, but, as I said, it was a rush order. Since we're talking in seven figures, there was no time to be as selective as I normally am.

The creative geniuses at the FBI and at the Chicago Police Department have made it very public about how the previous 'victims' were white females in their thirties. The nigger whores were probably in their early twenties, and I tried to make my

175

cuttings as crude as possible. It could be that they'll think someone's doing a copycat. I hope so. It's not very clever to be predictable.

By this time Parisi and his cohorts will have conducted the inevitable interview with my parents. And by this time the police will have learned from my mother and father that I came home 'changed' from my military service. And then Parisi will have noticed a photograph that contains a new player in the Karrios clan. He will have inquired who she was and what she had to do with my growing-up. But my parents will not have told them anything specific about Marina. They will not discuss anything as personal and as delicate as our previous 'situation'. They would not and could not. Marina's been dead for many years. She was killed with her husband in a car accident on the couple's way to their honeymoon. They might have mentioned the accident to Parisi or the FBI or some Sheriff's deputy, but they wouldn't have disclosed anything further. No. They've buried Marina deeper than any cemetery plot. She's gone and she's been disappeared.

My parents would've used the 'Greek immigrant' story with the investigators. They would've shared with them how they had wanted me to become a professional man, a doctor, so that I could become someone greater than a railroadman and his cashier wife who still sported Greek accents after living here for more than five decades. The old retelling of The American Dream. That's what my life was supposed to have become. Now they live in obscurity in a small town that has more than its share of poverty and failure. They live on two small pensions that fulfill all their requirements. He'll read a Chicago paper, which will occupy him for most of the morning. She will clean house and tend to all of Niko's needs. That's Elena. Traditional. Everything about them reeks of tradition. Greek Orthodox Church. Big deals on Easter and the other Church holidays. Lamb on the Resurrection. They both live just to be buried someday somewhere near Athens, their birthplace.

It's difficult to shed the past. Marina didn't have to worry any longer about what preceded meeting a semi head-on on a Wisconsin highway at three in the morning. The police thought

176

that Aaron, her new spouse, had fallen asleep at the wheel, but nothing was ever proved. I just wish that Aaron could have survived so that I could've gotten close to him before he died a natural or accidental death.

But it was not to be.

I've still got her photograph. I will never let go of it, although I keep saying I don't live in history. She was beautiful. Perfect. No statue could recreate the way she appeared. You could look at Marina from any angle you liked and she had no bad sides. She was sweet and gentle. Her touch was like a moist breeze on a sultry night. Her glance could make anyone's heart palpitate. Her form was pure. She was a blonde Greek. A rarity, my parents used to tell me. Ancient Greeks had blondes until the mixing of the breeds took over with all the bloody fucking conquests. But Marina was a throwback. I'm blond, too, but I'm more what they call dishwater. Marina was a very golden hue.

Now, of course, my hair is much darker. My beard and mustache have to be colored to match what's on top. I wear glasses with clear lenses. I wear hats quite often. More often than I ever wore them before the operation. I've also put on fifteen pounds of muscle by working out regularly with free weights at my apartment. My chest and upper torso have all expanded noticeably. I'm in the finest physical condition of my life.

I can see Parisi or one of his partners touching the frame of Marina's picture at my parents' home. I'd like to slice those digits away. He's doing recon on me, gathering research. He'll be looking into my family, but he'll receive no great aid from my mother and father. They won't let him have anything that would help him to track me.

I have business to attend to. Apparently Sal's two shots to the back end of Billy Ciccio didn't take. I hear Billy Cheech is still alive, but I hear he's on the move constantly, burrowing into various safe houses. But I'll catch up to him. It is inevitable. Sal is secure for the moment, although I sense he's becoming nervous about his future. He's probably figured I'm on the way to flying solo in this business. I know more about our computer links than he does and I'll be able to secure my own transporta-

tion for the goods I market. The jet to Europe and southeast Asia is really all I rely on Sal for, at this juncture. He will become expendable soon.

And I have to dispense with John Fortuna before very long. He does not allow people to do business in his name unless he receives tribute. Which we've never sent his way. Since the demise of his dear sister, Mary Margaret aka Ellen, it's him or me. Which suits me fine. I'll have no need for the Chicago version of the Mafia just as soon as I set up my own network. With a new face and an almost new body, everything is about to fall in place. The final stage is to recruit new field operatives. Men who can do the removals for me. When I branch out, it will confound Parisi and his friends and condemn them to sheer misery, I am confident. I'd like to be a fly on the wall of their offices when it all occurs.

I should not bring Marina to the forefront because when I do, I suffer. I do not have a great threshhold for suffering. I'm not a big fan of endurance. That's why I use the ether as often as I do. There are only some occasions when I enjoy watching misery. But there are no instances when I prefer to stick pins in my own flesh. Marina tests me to my limits. I wade in my own figurative blood when I call her to my consciousness. I don't know why I even keep her picture, except that I somehow could not survive without her portrait somewhere near my person.

Her lips were full. Her body was elegant and pure. She was too good for life, so she lost it, naturally.

I really would like to meet with Lieutenant James Parisi. I would like to meet with anyone who is close to him, as well. I could stand to give him a dose of the pain he doled out to Elena and Niko. He'd enjoy giving me a lifetime behind a wall of bars.

There are things to take care of first. Perhaps later. Maybe one day I'll meet face to face with Lieutenant James C. Parisi, Chicago Homicide.

Chapter Twenty-Nine

My son was a little old to be ring bearer, but I wanted him to be part of this ceremony. Michael carted the jewelry to the front of the church without complaint. Kelly, my daughter, served as a bridesmaid.

Natalie's family had gathered from out of state, and the small cluster of people sat behind us here in St Anthony's Church on the North Side.

Doc Gibron was my best man, and one of Natalie's friends from the Department, Sharon Olsen, was maid of honor. Except for Doc and me, everyone was *young* in this church, outside of a few oldsters in the pews. Doc's wife Mari, the pediatrician, sat in the crowd with Doc's adopted little girl. The red-headed Captain, my boss, was there too.

It all went by in a blur until Natalie lifted her veil. I began to have images of the dead. My wife, Erin, who had died of breast cancer two years ago, and Celia Dacy, the woman I had loved who had lost her son and her life because she had tried to square things for the murder of her boy Andres.

But their images departed, and there was no one else next to me except my new wife, Natalie. Tears tracked her cheeks, so I tried to smile at her.

I looked over at her once-scarred forearm, but the

179

plastic surgeon had worked magic. I moved toward her and our lips met when the priest, Father David, told me I could kiss the bride. Our kiss went on and on and I felt almost embarrassed until Natalie pressed against me with all her strength. Then I heard the applause coming from the pews and I decided to give them their money's worth. I turned, still locked to Natalie, and I saw that they were giving me and her a standing 'O'. That was when I had to come up for air.

I came out for a little oxygen at the reception at Dominic's, a restaurant on the near North. Doc and I walked outside as I left Natalie to handle the fifty or so guests inside. It was a fragrant Saturday evening in early spring. Late April, just past Easter and the Resurrection.

'You are a very lucky hombre,' Doc said.

There were a couple other guests out here taking a smoke break, but we walked a few paces away from them at the entrance to Dominic's.

'You going to be able to handle things for two weeks?'

He was in charge while I took two weeks with Natalie in Wisconsin. We were going up north, near the UP where there was still snow.

He smiled at the absurdity of my query. Doc was my teacher, my mentor. He was the Big Dog and no one else was close to his status yet. I hoped to be, someday.

'I don't like that this guy has gone quiet,' I told my partner and my closest friend.

Jack Wendkos came walking toward us.

'Congratulations, Jimmy,' he said as he offered me his hand.

Jack was probably becoming the only other close friend I had in the Department. Everyone else but Natalie was just a coworker. I didn't get close to too many people. I never had. I'd stuck primarily to family. The outer ring seemed too distant for me, most of the time. I could tell these two men anything and feel comfortable. Working with Jack previously helped develop our newer and closer relationship, and I'd worked with Doc since I'd started in Homicide.

'We were talking about The Farmer's downtime,' Doc informed the junior partner.

'I don't think he's been down,' Wendkos told us.

'You think he did the black prostitutes too,' I offered.

'Yeah. I think he's trying to be cute by going away from his usual type of victim. I think he's filling orders again, Jimmy. I think he might have been in a pinch when we almost got to him out on his farm, and I think things were backed up and he had to come up with the best goods he could. You notice he's never sliced open a male, not to fill a request, anyway. He didn't remove anything he could sell with Dr Richmond.'

'It sounds likely to me,' I responded.

Doc grunted some kind of half-hearted affirmation of Jack's theory.

'I still think he'll go for Sal. And for Big John too,' Doc said.

'The FBI has more fucking electrical wire rigged on those mobbed-up fucks than Vegas does on its electric billboards,' Jack added.

'Here we are at a festive occasion and we're talking shop,' Doc admonished. 'Let's go back in and I'll get loaded. Mari's driving tonight.' Gibron smiled.

We walked back toward the restaurant. Doc pulled me to a halt, and Jack stopped as well.

'I don't like it that your name's popping up in the newspapers and on TV all the time. I think this guy might begin to think it's between you and him, James.'

'Yeah, Doc. And he's right. It *is* between him and me. And all my troops, too.'

'He wouldn't be that fucking bold, would he?' Wendkos asked.

'Not likely. He's probably no more inclined to go after

181

a policeman than Sal or Big John Fortuna would be. But I think you should be careful, Jimmy. This guy's beyond "attitude",' Gibron warned me.

'You didn't make public where you and Natalie are headed?' Jack wanted to know.

'*You* don't even know, do you?' I asked Wendkos.

'No. Hell, no.'

'Doc doesn't know either,' I told him. 'Just my mother and the Captain have the number where we'll be.'

'I'm putting someone on your mom and kids, Lieutenant. Please don't argue with me,' Doc said.

The concern in his eyes frightened me a little.

'Okay,' was all I could muster. 'We got manpower on everyone else. It can't hurt, can it?'

Neither of my partners answered. Doc broke the ice by grinning and leading me back into Dominic's before my wife had to begin a detective career by looking for her old man.

Chapter Thirty

I visit cemeteries professionally. I don't make a habit out of coming to them on my own time. Except to visit the markers for three people. My old man, Jake, who'd been a homicide lieutenant, was one of the three. He was buried on the far southwest side at Birch Tree Cemetery. My mother owned the plot where she'd be buried next to my father. Jake Parisi fell down twenty-six steps at our family home, and I went through a lot of pain and therapy about whether my mother intentionally shoved him down those stairs or whether the whole deal was accidental. I suppose it was the detective in me. But I thought I'd come to terms with a question that had no answer. (My mother wasn't sure herself if she didn't subconsciously mean to waylay the old man, who could at times be a verbally abusive drunk.) And then there was the question of my parentage. It wound up that my biological father was really my Uncle Nick. Early in my mother's marriage it seemed that one of my parents wasn't able to produce offspring. My mother went to a doctor, but the old guy refused. She got a clean bill of health. So my mother assumed it had to be Jake's swimmers that weren't pulling their weight. Later on I learned that my dad had had mumps in his late teens, which my family doctor explained to me might have caused him to become sterile. Whatever, my mother conspired with my Uncle Nick to produce a child. Nick had loved my mother before Jake got into the picture, but Nick took off to the Southwest when he was young to try and make a fortune in petroleum. Which didn't pan out. He was gone two years, and so Jake married Eleanor, my mother, before Nick could return and start things up with her. Because Nick still loved my mother, he finally agreed to do what artificial insemination does today. Their thing worked out, but I didn't find out about my true genetic makeup until I was forty years old. It was a long story, and it was so ridiculous it was true.

So I was copacetic with all of it now. I knew my real father, but I visited the man who brought me up, here at his current resting place.

Then there was Erin, who was buried at the other end of the city. My beloved wife. Still was beloved, always would be. I didn't think Natalie had a problem knowing Erin was still inside me and would always be in there. And Celia Dacy. The woman I agonized over because of the difficulty we had nailing the sons of bitches who had killed her kid, Andres, that caused her to seek the vendetta against those same gangbangers who had snuffed her boy's future. She was black, and that was a problem between us. It was a difficulty for both of us. But it wasn't a matter of prejudice for either Celia or me. It was the climate, the city, that we shared.

Celia lay on the South Side, not too far from my dad's resting place.

I visited the three of them every few months. I prayed over them because I was a practicing Catholic. There were moments when I had a lapse of faith, so then I thought I was wasting my time and my efforts for the three of them. But I visited them regularly. It was a need, I supposed. My own need to do it was a sort of ritual I performed for them, to let them know somehow that they were not forgotten. That I held them inside like some kind of

184

flickering candle that I was afraid would be extinguished if I didn't continue to visit them.

Marco Karrios made a trip to their resting places a necessity. It was getting hard to keep up with the number of holes in the ground Karrios was helping to dig. The bodies were adding up. And with all the people who were assigned to pop him, he still wandered loose. With a new face. This time we didn't have any survivors to tell us how his appearance had changed.

We had just returned from the honeymoon. I worried for two weeks about my mother and two children. I called them twice a day from the Upper Peninsula resort where Natalie and I stayed, and I thought the calls began to disturb my mother. She had also become aware of the round-the-clock surveillance on our house. She read the paper and she knew about The Farmer. She was the widow of a Homicide detective. Eleanor knew about the assholes we tried to arrest and sometimes didn't. My mother kept her own loaded .38 in her nightstand. It was a habit she'd picked up when Jake Parisi had still been alive.

She said everything was all right. She repeated it each time I called until she became a bit irritable about my obsession with their safety. It was, as Doc said, unlikely that Karrios would try to get up close and personal with a policeman, but it was also clear that Marco was a ruthless motherfucker who was willing to cross over and do ridiculously dangerous things. He had killed a female lawyer in the foyer of her upscale Gold Coast apartment building. He had killed the security guard and had raped the woman on top of the guard's dead body. So how was fucking with a cop too scary for him?

When I got home, I called the security specialists that Doc had recommended before I'd left on the honeymoon. I put out several grand for their primo operation. Our home became one big bug of technology overnight. Natalie, my mother, the kids and I all had to learn how to punch in and out of there.

The last thing I did was buy a dog. Michael had been whining for a canine for a long time, so here was his chance. I bought us a Shetland Sheepdog, a sheltie. He was perfect. Neurotic, a barker. (Anybody in the nearby vicinity? Dog went fucking nuts.) My mother said I'd have to take him to obedience school to shut him up some, but I thought I'd wait until Karrios was playing pick-up-the-soap-in-the-shower-room in some high-security shithouse. We named the dog Merlin. Like the magician. The pooch was smart and he was friendly and very territorial. Which was what convinced me to buy him. He was like a sawed-off version of Lassie. And Michael was thrilled.

My blood pressure was up. I'd had a physical just before we left for Wisconsin. They changed my prescription to something the doctor called 'the adult dosage'. Our family physician was a wiseass.

I thought my pulse had come down a little after making love with Natalie in an overpriced cabin for two weeks – a fortnight, the old-timers called it. But it began to surge once I returned to shift. Natalie and I were both on the midnight run. We both slept during the day while the kids were at school. My mother was very quiet because, as I said, she was married to a cop and she too was a veteran of the midnight shift.

I visited the cemetery alone, but I invited Natalie to make the rounds with me. I told her I didn't want to do anything alone anymore. I told her I was thinking seriously about jumping at retirement in five years when I hit fifty-five, but she didn't seem to take me seriously. Then I explained I'd be getting out of her way, since she wanted to work in the department where I did business. Homicide. She said she couldn't picture me not working with stiffs, but I tried to convince her that she was all I needed.

I came home after visiting the three burial plots of Jake, Erin, and Celia. I had to punch in our security code. Then I got in without it sounding like a prison break off The Rock or Joliet in 'a thirties gangster movie. Merlin was yapping behind the door until he saw me. Then he wagged his tail and wet the carpet. He was not quite housebroken yet.

Natalie walked up to me in her robe and nothing else. She let the robe come apart in the front.

'Oh! What about—'

'Mom's gone to the mall and then out to dinner with her cronies. She said not to wait up for her. I'm off tonight, so I'll watch the kids.'

She'd become *familia* instantly. She thought of Eleanor as a second mama, and the kids were damn' near her own by now. Kelly and Michael had taken to her instantly.

'I got to go on shift about 10.30,' I reminded her.

We'd be hunting for our boy again, aided this time by an artist's multiple renderings of Karrios's possible new mug. What good that would do us, I wasn't certain.

'Would you like to be a father, Jimmy?'

She made me push her back to arm's length.

'Oh! You said we'd wait about five years. Get your career going. Remember?'

'I can have a baby and a career. Women do it—'

'All the time. But I think we should wait and let the idea percolate and settle in.'

'You afraid the marriage won't take, Jimmy?'

She saw the hurt in my eyes.

'I didn't mean that. It was stupid . . . Let's have a baby. Let's have twins. Let's do it all at once.'

She kissed me and pressed her warmth against me. She started helping me take off my own clothes. I was down to my jockeys when she halted.

'You *do* want a baby with me, don't you, guinea?'

'Yes. You know I do.'

'Then let's not wait for anything anymore. Let's do everything and do it right now, and if we're lucky enough, we can keep on doing it again and again. By the time we're through we'll have little guys hanging from the curtains.'

She'd said she wanted two when we'd discussed this

187

earlier, but now she was carrying me away with her. When she got a load of taking care of one child, I was sure the enthusiasm would wane. It had with Erin, after Mike was born. Two sure as hell were enough.

When this proposed little guy was sixteen, I'd be ... Damn. Daddy would be baby-sitting in a wheelchair. They'd be setting my gray beard on fire and I'd be helpless to stop them.

Natalie had me pressed against her. She was backed up against the dining room table. We were naked and doing our best to fulfill her reproductive intentions by the time we hit the bedroom.

Jack Wendkos said the relationship with the geology professor was progressing nicely, whatever that meant. Doc was still in love with his Indian-born second wife Mari. He was still adjusting to parenthood, and he was still wistfully telling me he was going to retire next year and write his Great American Piece of Literature that he'd been threatening to do since forever. He'd had a couple dozen short stories published in literary magazines that catered to MFAs, he called them – Masters of Fine Arts graduates. But he wanted to break through to the big time, like all writers really do, he said.

It seemed that family and friends had diverted my complete attention from finding this bloody bastard who was quickly reviving all kinds of interest in Jack the Ripper. There'd been a lull since my honeymoon, and it appeared that there were those who believed that Marco Karrios had opted for new hunting grounds.

'It'd be the smart move, Jimmy,' Jack Wendkos suggested while Doc and he and I were cramped inside my work space. I was looking out that window toward the Lake. This portal was my only favorite thing about my office. I'd been whining to the Captain to give me a grown-up's office, and he'd promised me he'd see what he could do.

'He may have something here, Holmes,' Doc agreed.

The irony about calling me 'Holmes' was that Doc despised Arthur Conan Doyle. Doc preferred mystery writers like Ross McDonald and James Lee Burke. 'Holmes' had just become a generic name tag for someone who looked about as British as Tony the Pizza Guy at Fabrizzi's Restaurant in the Loop. No one mistook me for an Anglo, I was saying.

'Smart move? Since when has this guy done anything all that bright?' I asked them. 'Yeah, he's clever about saving his ass, but he takes way too many chances. And I think he thinks of this city as home. In fact, I'll bet he's almost sentimental about this town. And the Doctor – the FBI profiler – said he likes to hunt where he feels comfortable. Look, he's only gone outside the North Side twice. The geology teacher that Jack's in love with . . .'

I saw Wendkos color darkly.

'Shit, what's the matter with you?' I asked. 'You got great taste . . . And the two black hoos he did, which he did no matter what the fuck anybody else on this floor thinks.'

The prevailing scenario was that the black prostitutes had been killed by a copycat.

'Other than those three women, he's a homeboy. I'm excluding Mary Margaret Fortuna – Ellen Jacoby – because that was a domestic beef for Karrios.'

I watched them for their reactions. They didn't seem to have a dispute waiting for me.

'You think he's trying to put us to sleep,' Doc proffered.

'Yeah. I think he's trying to charm the snake with all this soothing-interlude crap. He's setting up for a move. Even though he's no dago, he's learned something from them. Maybe from his brother-in-law or common-law brother-in-law or whatever. You put your enemy at ease just before you whack him. We let down our guards, he goes on a spree. Pretty soon that Victorian London killer, Saucy Jack, starts looking like a piker compared to the numbers Marco's putting on the boards.'

189

'You think he's going to be that hard to catch?' Jack asked.

'How 'bout that Unibomber!' I teased.

'That's the FBI,' Doc tried to explain.

'Maybe. But we still haven't been on the same page or the same block of ground with this prick yet, so I don't think we got any room to dis our federal friends at this point.'

'Then all we really have is to hope he makes a move at the Big Tuna – Jackie Morocco – or at Sal Donofrio,' Doc said.

'Or at me or my cousin. Marco's a very knowledgeable sociopath. He can hit a number of places, and he knows by spreading us thin he can wear us down and maybe even out.'

'You're painting a really gloomy scene here, partner,' Jack lamented.

'It *is* a gloomy scenario at the moment . . . There are two coppers in my household. So let's say I send my family off with Nick, my uncle. He's not a player. The Ciccios don't know about Nick. He wasn't a copper like my old man and he never had anything to do with the Ciccio family. He's an unknown, so my mother and kids'd be safe with him out in Elmhurst, where he lives. That's a decent distance. The kids'll be out of school in a few weeks. No problem there—'

'What're you talking about, Jimmy?' Doc wanted to know.

'I'm trying to say I make myself available to the electronic media. I tell them over and over what a limp-dick psycho Marco really is. I make up a lie about how he's despised by his own mother and father. I say he was sexually abused by his fucking uncle. Whatever. I make it very inflammatory. This guy's overly emotional. He can fly off the handle. We know that about him. If I can get him to come for me, we'll be placing him inside the closest thing we've got to a controlled environment. And that's my plan.'

'You talk this over with Natalie?' Jack queried.

'Yeah. She's a cop and a very fine one too.'

'It's ridiculous, Jimmy. Why don't we just ride with the vendetta Marco's got against John Fortuna?' Doc demanded.

'We got to shove this rectal birth out of the hole. Or his list gets longer. He's a businessman too. He's going to kill because the money's too good not to ... We've got Interpol working on the European end, and they say they might have some good news for us soon. But there's no promise about results from them. We've got to hook Karrios before he carves a bigger chunk out of the female population of this city. And I'm not reflecting pressure from the Captain or the people above him. This comes straight from yours truly. Enough is enough!'

I slammed my desk top, and the THUMPPP! startled me too.

Doc looked right into my eyes.

'You or your new wife gets hurt, I'll never forgive you. I love you, paisan, but if one of you catches a cold on this, I won't be able to let go of it. I'm telling you true, James,' Gibron said in the stoniest voice I'd ever heard come out of his mouth.

'This idea of mine might already be in The Farmer's skull, Doc. We all talked about it before. I'm just going to turn up the heat.'

He shook his head, but he put up his palms in defeat shortly thereafter.

'Playing who's-got-the-balls with a conscienceless dildo like Karrios. There is no percentage ... I assume I'm wasting my breath?' Doc conceded.

I nodded my head slowly at my senior partner.

Chapter Thirty-One

I see you, but you don't see me.

I watch the home where John Fortuna lives, in Skokie. It seems rather humorous somehow that the local Sicilian chieftain lives in the midst of all these Jews. Most of the guineas tend to cluster in their own neighborhoods, but Fortuna lives in what was his father's house. His father, I am told, was a dentist and had no connections to the Outfit at all.

Wherever Jackie Morocco goes, he is accompanied by no less than six goons. Then there is the FBI surveillance, which I'm sure he's aware of. The federals are always around. But none of them knows my new face, which makes it possible for me to try and get close to Fortuna.

John does not believe in electronic security. I've heard him say he pays men to do that kind of work. So when I walk up to his home on this Thursday night – actually it's an early Friday morning – I see that the two FBI agents are asleep in their van, parked a half-block up the street. There is a light on in Fortuna's front window. The house itself is inauspicious. He doesn't show his money by the appearance of the dwelling or by the neighborhood he lives in. It's part of the reason he's always been low-profile. He's not like that guy Gotti in New York. There's none of that flamboyance.

I'll try the back way into the house. I saw three of his associates go in, around midnight, but I think that's the total number of crew assigned as his bodyguards. I assume they work in shifts of eight hours, one awake at all times. So that means at least one of the bodyguards is sitting up, keeping the vigil. I'm betting the one sentry is in that living room where the light burns. It's 2.48 a.m. John Fortuna should be asleep at this hour. He's not a public womanizer, either. Other than what Ellen told me about him fucking his own sister, all those years ago, I don't know much about his private life. He lives a rather solitary social life also.

I pick the dead bolt on the back door only to find there's a chain, but I'm able to get my gloved hand inside far enough so that I can find the chain and its bolt. I maneuver my knife until I find the metal piece that houses the bolt, and then I wedge the tip under that housing. I'm able to dislodge the chain and bolt because the screws that secure them must be loose. In under two minutes I'm inside.

I've never been in Fortuna's home. I've only seen him on the street or at one of the Italian-American 'clubs' that he frequents. He never had any particular use for the man who was fucking what used to be his sole property. I think he would've wanted Ellen to live here with him if she would've agreed to it, but she despised her big brother. It wasn't consensual sex that she engaged in with him. He brutalized her and beat her and tortured her from time to time, but no one in her family would believe that the Big Boss was capable of incest. Ellen said the dentist and his wife were staunch Catholics who could not believe such a thing was possible – until Ellen ran away and got married. She never talked directly to John Fortuna again. But she did set me up with Sal Donofrio.

I make my way toward the living room. I see one of the bodyguards sleeping in the chair in front of a television with a picture but no sound. He's making it too easy. I stand by the lamp. The table on which it rests is next to him, on his left. I don't recognize this one. I'm about to cut his throat with my nine-inch blade when a voice tells me very softly, very gently, to stop.

I pivot and I see the Boss himself.

He's got a nine-millimeter pointed at my head.

'Why don't you sit down? We can talk.'

'No, thanks.' I smile.

'I don't think I know you, do I?' Fortuna asks.

'You don't know me.'

'Your voice sounds familiar, though.'

The sleeper in the chair is finally aroused.

'You awake, Vito, you sleepy fuck?' Jackie Morocco rasps.

'Jesus, John, I'm sorry—'

'Shut the fuck up . . . Look who just popped in. If I'm not mistaken, it's the limpdick who lived with my sister Mary Margaret. And the same guy who slaughtered her like an animal.'

There's no use denying any of this. He's recognized my voice. He's heard it often enough when he's tried to contact his sister at our apartment in the city.

I edge close to the lamp when he turns his attention to his failure of a bodyguard.

'I ought to shoot you and him, Vito, you lazy fuck. When I get done with this animale, *I'll take care of you.'*

Vito gulps but doesn't try to defend himself. There's no copping a plea with Fortuna.

'You want to drop that nice big knife? What the fuck is that? Some kind of hairy-assed scalpel? You were a medical student, weren't you, limpdick?'

The bodyguard stands, next to me, and it diverts Fortuna's attention just long enough for me to grab hold of Vito, yank him in position in front of me, and use him as a shield just as John lets loose with two rounds. The sound of the two shots is deafening in the small living room. The impact of the two slugs knocks Vito and me backward, but I'm able to grab hold of the lamp, rip it out of its socket, and fling it at Jackie Morocco's head. The room goes dark, two more shots explode toward the already dead body I'm still holding in front of me, and when I hear Fortuna coming toward me in the dark, I use Vito's head as a ramming tool and I shatter the picture window behind where the lamp once was. I dump Vito and I make for the

194

opening. I jump out onto the lawn, and two more rounds whine close by me, but I'm not hit. I take off on the lawn and bolt in the direction opposite to the location of the Feds' van. I'm down the street now but I don't hear any more gunfire. I run and run until my lungs want to explode. When I'm certain there's no one still coming after me, I cut through several backyards and make my way back to my own vehicle, using a circular route. I arrive at my car, and the street is quiet. My heart is beating so rapidly and loudly that I think my chest will rip open from the buildup.

After about three minutes of catching my breath, I'm able to start the car and pull away from the curb. I begin the long ride back to my new apartment on the far northwest side. My knife sits next to me on the seat of the automobile. I never let it out of my sight when I go out. I keep it always within easy reach.

Chapter Thirty-Two

The Feds told us about John Fortuna's nocturnal adventure. Terry Morrissey came into my office as Doc and Jack and I were trying to figure out a plan of attack to draw The Farmer to my house.

'Apparently he's not intimidated by John Fortuna and his crew. He managed to get one of John's bodyguards blown away by the capo himself. Then he busts the window out using the dead guy's noggin and he runs out into the night. Fortuna's only able to ID Karrios because of the voice. He said he didn't get a good look at Marco, though, because all there was was a low-wattage bulb in the lamp behind The Farmer. He remembers glasses and dark hair. At least, the hair was darker than the blond topknot he used to have.'

'He'll color it again and he'll ditch the glasses or buy himself a different pair. Maybe he'll shave his head,' Doc told the Special Agent.

'You're probably right,' Morrissey answered. 'We might as well dump all those new artist's renderings.'

Then he smiled and walked out of my cubicle.

'So how do we get Karrios to your house without getting you and your wife hurt? You know the Captain won't allow this thing to fly.'

I looked at Jack.

'He's not going to be told about any of this.'

'I don't like it either, Jimmy,' Wendkos said. 'It just isn't done. You don't get personally involved with these guys. You don't let them get into your head, and I have to say I think that's what's happened here. I'm not trying to sound like a wiseass, but—'

'He *has* got into my head. I *dream* about the son of a bitch. If Natalie weren't a cop, I'd never allow my house to be the center of a thing like this. But we've got a guy who takes anyone who's after him as a personal opponent. It's not like I'm a policeman to him. It's like I'm a competitor. He's got to beat me and beat me personally. He's got to get into all our faces. That's the way I see Karrios, and I think it's our best chance of stopping his string. I don't need to repeat his body count for you, do I, Jack?'

'You're not playing fair, Jimmy.'

'No, Jack, and neither is Marco . . . So what do we do? Put him in our ballpark or hope we get lucky by catching him at work? This guy had the balls or the stupidity to go after John Fortuna in his own fucking home, so what would stop him from trying the same thing with me?'

Jack looked at me. Then he lowered his eyes. I looked at Doc, and Gibron smiled at me.

'Should we get to what kind of party favors we'll bring to this little festive gathering we're planning?'

The landlord called at three in the morning from Berwyn. I heard the address as two coppers from Burglary got the call. One of the Burglary detectives told me the landlord called the wrong department because he'd just got a call from the uniforms on scene in the western suburb. As soon as I heard the address, I knew what he was talking about.

'This is your department, Jimmy,' Frank Loggia, the detective, told me. 'There's been a killing. It's your kind of thing.'

When he showed me the address, my heart dropped down out of my chest.

The yellow tape was already up. The county police were present, along with the locals. The Berwyn cops called in to us once they found out the ID of the victim.

Doc and Jack and I all identified ourselves and then we were allowed inside the second-floor apartment.

I saw my cousin Billy taped to a dining-room chair. His wrists were bound, his ankles were bound, and there was a strip of that gray duct tape circling his head horizontally, covering his mouth. His eyes were wide open, the eyeballs almost popping out of his skull. He sat naked in the chair.

Billy'd been castrated. His genitals had been dumped on the floor in front of him. It appeared that he had bled to death.

Doc and Jack went to work, checking out the scene, but we knew what we had before any of our work had begun.

I crouched in front of my cousin. There were no other wounds on him. I saw a piece of paper sticking out from beneath Billy. I gently maneuvered the sheet out from under him without touching anything else.

There were a few words printed on the sheet. In pencil. They were crudely rendered, like the writing of a child learning to print.

'See you soon.'

That was all there was of a message for me.

'I say we trash the project. This guy's too smart to come after you at your house after trying to get to Fortuna and after wasting Billy,' Doc said.

'I told you. This guy is competitive. It's a task for him. It's like an obstacle. Look where he's already been. He'll still make a run,' I told Gibron.

Wendkos shrugged when I looked over to him. We

were at dinner break at Garv's in Berwyn since Berwyn was where our call about Billy had come from.

'He walked past the FBI and right into John Fortuna's home. He doesn't give a shit if we know he's coming. Let me try and speed him up. That's all. He's going to come to me, but I don't want him doing some other woman in the downtime when he's gearing up for a Chicago policeman. Let's get him going toward me.'

'The Captain won't have it, guinea. You better keep all this in this room,' Doc reminded me.

'Yeah, this is just between the three of us. We put all kinds of people around my house he might try anyway. The FBI didn't scare him off. But he might be a little more overly confident if he sees the door swing open. It's his little door of opportunity. I think he'll move fast because he thinks we think he won't because he got a scare at Fortuna's. Big John pumped four rounds into Vito before Marco got his ass out that front window. Anybody else would knock off while they're still in luck. But not our guy ... Something else I want us to clear up is what's what with that missing sister of Karrios's. She's been out of the picture for years, the parents told us, but I still don't like the way they became all sullen and protective when I asked them who she was. I have the feeling that she's important to Karrios. Very important.'

'One last time, dago. You and Natalie and the kids and Momma Parisi all get aboard a flight and take off for the island of your choice. Don't come back for a month. I guarantee Jack and I'll haul Karrios's ass to the lockup before your tour of Tahiti or wherever is over.'

'No. He will be coming around by my house. I'm not going to let him move me out. Or my family. The kids'll go with my mother to Nick's. We'll have some people assigned to them around the clock too, and Natalie and I'll go along like it's just another week at the shop. Now let's quit dragging it and get our man in motion.'

*

199

I talked to the *Tribune* first. A reporter named Martinson. I met him at the Billy Goat Tavern downtown. It was the bar made famous by John Belushi on *Saturday Night Live*. 'Cheese bugga cheese bugga, no Coke. Pepsi.'

I sat in a booth with this red-headed, freckle-faced journalist. He looked like a kid, but he was in his mid-thirties and had won the Pulitzer twice. He'd been doing a piece or two on the serial killings The Farmer had committed, and I'd turned him down for interviews twice already.

'What changed your mind, Lieutenant?'

The waiters even did the 'cheese bugga' thing when they took your orders. It must have been good for business.

'I'll take any edge I can get.'

'What edge would you mean, Lieutenant?'

'I want you to report some falsehoods.'

He looked at me and then he laughed.

'Now why would I do that?'

'To catch a killer.'

'What lies do you mean?'

'I mean that you print some things that I know will light Karrios's ass end up. I want him mad at me.'

'Why?'

'Will you give me your word on confidentiality?'

'Again, why?'

'Because we're trying something very unorthodox to nab Marco Karrios, and if you tell anyone about it, my ass'll be in the wringer with the people I work for.'

Suddenly it dawned on him.

'You mean you're using yourself as bait. You want to anger him into coming after you. That's ridic—'

'Sure it is. I'm banking on his pride. His vanity. The guy has a new face that no one alive has seen, except for John Fortuna. And Fortuna didn't get a clear picture of him. He was too busy trying to shoot the son of a bitch in the head.'

'You mean that mob guy who was shot was—'

'Yeah. And that's part of the confidentiality. That story was released that way so I could set this up, and I'm asking for your help in getting to Karrios before you and your fellow writers have another dead white woman missing her vitals to write about. You follow all that?'

Martinson nodded.

'I want him to attack me and my wife. My wife's a police officer too. We've moved my family out somewhere, so it's just the two of us.'

'You're involving your wife?'

'She's already involved. Just like every other swinging dick with a badge. Natalie's got her eyes wide open. She's all for it. She knows this guy will eventually turn up in our neighborhood even without the invitation. We just want to expedite, get him off the fucking streets ... Are you willing to spread bullshit for the cause?'

'I can't knowingly print inaccurate material. It's called ethics.'

'Yeah. But you don't know it's bullshit. You got it from a very reliable source in the police department. I'll be the guy who simply misinformed you ... But some of this stuff is true. Some of it is assumption. You got a way with words, don't you, Martinson? Say it was "alleged". Say it any way you want, but I need your help. All the falsehood comes from me, not you. I'll give you first shot at an interview when we clamp this cocksucker ... Will you help me out?'

The guy with the two 'cheese buggas' and the two Pepsis arrived at our table.

Chapter Thirty-Three

Martinson did the deed. He gave me the whole deal. Everything I told him about Karrios made it into his next column, two days later. He had the business about what a sexual-psychotic Karrios was. How he probably couldn't have normal 'relations' with a woman. How he had engaged in necrophilia – sodomy with a dead body. He laid it on thick. We were going to need to put a man on Martinson for his own protection.

Then there was the suggestion that there was something disturbing happening in Karrios's family home. I left that part purposely vague because we were still not sure what it was that was wrong in that direction. Doc and Jack and I were on our way to Kankakee at the moment. I wanted to ask Mrs Karrios what it was that was off about Marco and his sister.

It was another long drive to reach them. When we got to the door, we found Niko Karrios. He let the three of us in. But there was no Elena this time. We asked him where she'd gone to.

'My wife . . . my wife die yesterday afternoon in hospital. She have stroke. My son . . . my son, he kill his mother.'

We sat down on the couch across from the old man.

He was beginning to tear up, so I was hoping to make this brief.

'We just have a few questions, sir,' I told him. 'Please accept our apologies—'

'He *kill* his mother just like he kill all those other people. He put a knife to her heart . . .'

'Do you feel up to telling us a few things?' Doc asked.

'I tell you,' he said angrily. He glowered at the three of us, one at a time. 'I tell you whatever you want and you catch him. You put him in cage where he belong . . . When he come back from Army, he like animal. Cold in the eye. You know? I don't know him no more. It was like . . . it was like he belong to someone else.'

'I wanted to ask you about his sister,' I said.

'What about Marina?'

'Did he have an unusual relationship with his sister?' I asked.

The old man sat up as if he was about to stand, but then he settled back.

'I don't care no more. I don't care. He don't belong to us. He dead to us a long time ago . . . Marina was not his sister.'

'What are you telling us?' Jack asked him.

'Marina . . . Jesus help me. He not mine anymore. He never was *mine*.'

'Can you help us just a little bit more?' I asked him.

'Marina was his mother, not his sister. We knew he was her baby. Marina was ours, Marco was hers. She fall in love with boy when she fifteen. This boy leave her with child. She too young to get married, so we take Marco as ours, go to Kansas City when she have baby. Nobody know about it except Elena and me. Marco find out when he leave for Army.'

'You think that's what made him quit school and leave home, you're saying,' Doc tried to clarify.

Niko winced in pain.

'No. That was not all . . . They . . . they – Marco and Marina. They don't act like brother and sister. Not like mother and son, either. They . . . Jesus help me.'

'Are you trying to say that they had a sexual relationship, Mr Karrios?' I asked him.

He couldn't even nod. The tears streamed down his face.

'I throw him out. I make him leave. He never want to leave Marina. His own mother. It make me sick to remember. Sick.'

'We'll leave you alone now,' I told him. The three of us rose. But he stopped us.

'I want to kill him when I find out. I never tell his ... I never tell Elena ... I find them together, Marina and Marco, when I come home sick from work one day. He was sixteen. I beat hell out of him. I think it would stop then, but I know it don't. It was the way they look at each other. After he get out of high school, he go to college for two years, then he drop out. He come back and start up all over until Marina get engaged to a man name Aaron. Marina is killed in car wreck with husband, but all Marco want to do is kill Aaron. But Aaron is already dead. I throw Marco out when he twenty. He keep going into Marina's old room again and again. It make me sick to have him in house. I make him leave. I never see him since ... But you catch him. You tell him he kill his ... grandmother. You tell him. Will you tell him for me?'

'We will,' Doc assured him.

'You tell him,' Niko insisted.

'So Marina's the tickler in his throat,' Jack said as we made the long drive back to Chicago.

'He's hooked on Mommy. She went out and got married on him. How could she've done a thing like that to poor Marco?' Doc said from the back seat.

'Momma's no damn' good ... I'll bet she was thirty-something when she died,' Jack told me and Doc. 'He keeps on trying to bring her back so he can even up on her over and over again.'

I didn't say anything because, just as he sickened Niko Karrios, Marco nauseated me too.

204

'You going to give this to Martinson?' Doc asked me.

'As soon as we get back,' I replied.

'Sonny will really be angry. He'll be looking for his knife. We better get a round-the-clock for the journalist . . . Sal's under surveillance, John Fortuna's guarded by the best that money can buy, and your front gate's still open, Jimmy. Right?' Doc summarized.

'Natalie and I take turns sleeping. But we took Merlin the wonder dog to Nick's in Elmhurst. He makes too much noise, and I wouldn't want to see the pooch get hurt by that prick's knife. Michael couldn't take it. He loves that goddamned neurotic dog.'

'I don't like being perched two blocks from your house,' Jack said.

I had them keep a big space between me and Natalie and them. I got four detectives for a nighttime shift on my house while Natalie and I were working days. I bucked Doc's advice about approaching the Captain. I went into the redhead's office and I laid it out. He said we should be surveilling my house anyway because he agreed Karrios might want to take out his most vocal irritant – me. So we had the manpower, but we didn't want this weasel to get cold feet. He'd been very careful about hitting the plastic surgeon and about hitting my cousin Billy.

There were moments when I wondered just how personal all this had become. When I went to Billy's funeral, when I saw some of my other cousins I hadn't talked to in twenty or thirty years, things began to well up inside me. Blood told. Not everyone in the Ciccio clan was mobbed up. There were doctors, lawyers, mechanics, nurses, and a variety of blue-collar laborers in the family. I was with them a lot more often when I was a kid. Billy's background, the shitty way he'd lived his life, didn't negate the blood tie.

The vendetta was an emotional, mindless act. It was not what my church taught; it was not what I believed in or wanted my children to believe in. Most murderers I encountered on the job were still human beings. Fucked-up human beings, granted, but human people. They killed out of rage and out of a variety of other reasons, but few of them did it simply because they *enjoyed* it. Karrios was one of those creatures for whom the word 'sociopath' was created. There *was* absolute evil in the world. You didn't need a divinity degree or a PhD in philosophy to figure it out. I dealt with a lot of fucked-up people, but I could almost understand why they did the terrible things they did. Karrios was one of those exceptions. He was like a rogue virus. One of those mutations of nature. His DNA was all messed up and he crawled on the same planet with all the uprights. I could picture myself blowing his brains out. Perhaps I would rather gut-shoot him so that he'd suffer a little bit of what his victims suffered.

Of course I couldn't hurt him physically unless it was self-defense. But God forgive me, because I truly hoped that when we met he'd give me a reason to blow him in half. I had to speak for my cousin and for all the other people he had murdered. I could visualize the scenario. I could see him bleeding. I was holding the gun to the head of his wounded body, in my mind's eye, and I could feel the tension of the Bulldog's hair trigger. It would be so very easy to simply squeeze off just one more round.

Like the man said, you never knew what you were capable of until the opportunity presented itself. So I'd be seeing Father David, the priest who'd married Natalie and me, at confession this Saturday. Maybe he could help me since I was wondering if I could help myself anymore.

I was back on midnights when Terry Morrissey came bursting into my office at two in the morning.

'The wiring has gone off the scale. There's an intruder trying to get into Sal's house.'

The three of us, Doc, Jack and I, were in the Taurus, and Terry Morrissey and three other Federal agents were in their vehicle, headed toward Sal Donofrio's house. The agents who were surveilling Sal had spotted a guy walking the neighborhood at a very late hour. He had walked past Donofrio's home three times, the Federals on scene had reported. Sal was still unaware, at least officially, that he was being watched.

We pulled up behind the four-door Chevy that was staked out there. Terry got out of his car alone. We were parked directly behind him. I got out and left Jack and Doc in the Ford.

We walked up to the driver's side of the Fed's car.

'What've you got lately?' Morrissey asked Jim Phalen, another Chicago-area special agent. Carl Lux was his partner, sitting on the passenger's side. Lux looked like he was ready to z-out. He didn't appear excited about the prospect of nabbing Marco Karrios.

'White male. About six feet, maybe a little over. About 180 pounds. Glasses. Too dark and too far away to make his face. But I don't think he lives in this neighborhood. We've been here ten days and I've never spotted him before.'

'Where's he now?' Morrissey asked.

'Down at the end of the block. I think he goes down about two or three blocks and then circles around. But he stopped twice right out in front of Sal's and looked awhile before he continued making the rounds.'

'So you don't think he's a solid citizen with insomnia,' Terry asked.

Lux started to giggle. I thought he was finally waking up.

'You want to grab him when he comes back, Jimmy?' Morrissey wanted to know.

'I got a bad feeling on this guy, Terry. I don't think Karrios is big on indecision ... But let's check him out anyway.'

We went back to our cars and waited. Ten minutes passed, and then a figure appeared, and he was headed toward Donofrio's. Morrissey had already called for backup. There was a fed car behind this guy and another pair of Fibbies in the alley behind Sal's. We were surrounding him.

We got out of the vehicles quietly. Marco was not known for carrying anything but a knife, but we didn't know what he had on him tonight.

As soon as the figure became aware that five cops were approaching him from the south end of Sal's block, he decided to try the other way. But now there were four dark images trotting toward him from the other direction. I got the feeling he was going to bolt toward someone's driveway or yard, but he stood still instead. We were on him in seconds.

'Put your hands over your head,' Morrissey commanded.

The man followed the order. Lux patted him down and found a .22 pistol in his coat pocket.

We took him to the Loop. He could have been Marco Karrios. He had the same body size, but it was anyone's guess if he was the right guy because he didn't say anything until Morrissey asked if he had a license for the .22. Then he said he did. He said he was contracted by a private investigation agency to protect Salvatore Donofrio and that his name was Anthony Manigotti.

We took his prints to confirm his ID. In half an hour we found out that his prints didn't match Marco Karrios's. We called his 'agency', but we recognized the 'owner'. It was Philly Donadio, one of John Fortuna's soldiers. The private-eye agency was a front for muscle. Everybody in the department knew it, but their business paid taxes to the IRS and no one had caught them with phony paperwork yet.

We released Manigotti one hour later.

A half-hour after we cut the 'private eye' loose, we got a call from Sal Donofrio himself. He was calling from his cell phone. He said he was on the way to the hospital.

208

'That motherfucker Karrios busted into my house. But he had bad luck. He got a chunk out of my forearm, but I think I popped him high on his torso with a .38 slug,' he told me on the phone.

I told him to shut up and get to the emergency room.

'I moved my old lady out. I hired help, and you goofy fucks pick him up and Karrios is out there waiting for his chance,' Sal told us while the emergency physician was stitching him up. 'You want a songbird, you got one,' Sal continued, once the doctor had left the room. 'You guys still give me that deal?'

'Why now, Sal?' Doc asked.

'I have to live without my wife. I can't go nowhere. I can't do business. This fuckin' guy is like a ghost. He fooled all of you and got into my house. It's a good thing I got insomnia. I been carryin' the piece around the house like it's the fuckin' remote control for the tube. I can't get no peace. This guy's wearin' me down, and that piece of shit Fortuna has put a hit out on me because he found out Karrios and me paid him no tribute. But I ain't sayin' anything else until I get a piece of paper with signatures on it.'

He looked down at his bandaged arm.

'Motherfucker's got me so's I can't even take a decent shit. I been takin' bran and everything, too. Prune juice. The whole fuckin' nine yards. It's over. I've had enough. I want immunity.'

Doc looked over to me.

'*Prune juice*,' he repeated.

'I'm next,' I told Gibron and Wendkos. We were taking a walk around the Loop as a break from all the paperwork and interviewing with Sal. The FBI were part of the interview process since they put up all the manpower on Donofrio. A federal prosecutor made the final deal with

Sal. He had delivered John Fortuna and he had handed over Marco's contacts with Europe. We called Interpol and they said arrests were imminent. As for Karrios ... we got a post-office box number and a lock box in a bank where Marco put some of his money. We were putting people at those two locations to try and snag him. But I knew as soon as Marco discovered Sal was missing, he'd figure out what had just happened and he'd avoid checking in for his mail and chump change.

None of the hospitals had a record of a gunshot victim that would match the description for what Sal said had happened to The Farmer. We had all the medical centers under alert. There had been wounds to tend to that night, but none of the wounded even came close to our guy in size and shape. They'd all been positively ID'd.

'He's self-medicating,' Doc said as Jack and he and I circled State and Lake.

'How many places can he go for an antibiotic?' Jack wondered.

'He's not a doctor. He'll have to forge something,' I said. 'But we could get some help from some Academy manpower. We could have those kids canvass every all-night pharmacy in a ten-mile radius of Sal's house. I'm guessing Marco's still in the city, still living somewhere on the North Side. We could take a chance that he's living upscale, so that would mean the northwest area. It's a very faint chance but we might get a sighting.'

Doc said he'd take care of it. Jack said he'd call the Academy and try to round up a hundred or so volunteers to canvass the drugstores.

'He'll have to come in and present a prescription. He'll probably have an idea of where to go to get a doctor's pad. He's smart enough not to check into a health center. He knows we'll be watching there,' I told the two detectives.

'But he's hurting, Jimmy. And he's likely very angry at you and at Martinson for the lovely article you two concocted. He'll have to move fast, and there's also the chance that he just won't be able to get himself any penicillin. If we're lucky, nature'll kill its own fuckup.' Gibron smiled.

Chapter Thirty-Four

The bullet has gone clean through the top of the flesh of my shoulder. But the bleeding was severe, and I barely made it back to my apartment before I collapsed on my single bed.

When I awoke, there was a bloodstain beneath me, soaked all the way into the mattress. But my bleeding had ceased and there was caked black blood over the entry and exit wounds. I checked myself in the mirror. Having been a medic saved me from having to run to a hospital. I have to have an antibiotic, however, or infection will surely set in. The problem, of course, is that I can't go to a doctor. The only physician I could've trusted is the dead plastic surgeon. Ironic, isn't it?

I've been around enough doctors to know how to falsify a prescription. It isn't all that difficult. I've done it before to get Ellen some painkillers in a dosage that her family physician would never prescribe. I've got a pad I had made up which uses a real doctor's name. He's in family practice. I've only forged his name twice, and both times I was successful in securing something with codeine for my lovely ex-lover, the sister of John Fortuna.

I've been hitting an unlucky streak, it seems. I missed Fortuna and Sal Donofrio, and Sal has put two holes in my shoulder. And when I opened the newspaper recently, I read all about my Marina and me. Written by some hack named

Martinson. The list of those people I need to encounter is apparently growing. Parisi has been quoted numerous times in Martinson's column, and I really need to talk to both of them.

Marina was the last insult. Martinson wrote about her as if he thought he knew her. No one knew her as I did. I loved her more than anything I have ever cared about. She was the only human being who made my life temporarily livable, so naturally she was taken away from me.

Then I get the information from Elena that Marina is not my sister as I had been told so very often. I was informed that she was my biological mother. But it made no difference to the way I felt and the way I still feel about her. She was mine and I was hers. It made no difference that we had something that is considered a taboo. Incest. It's supposed to be a word that freezes your blood. We were having incest all along, even when I thought she was my older sibling. Why would a change in identity alter our relationship? It didn't, at first. But then she met Aaron Blassingame and she confided in me that she had fallen in love. She told me that what we had was wrong, was evil. She broke me in two and shattered everything I dreamed of having. I told her we could share an apartment when I got out of school. When I got into medical school we could cohabit somewhere in the city. Who would give a damn who was living with whom in a city of millions? We could always say we were married or go with the brother-and-sister story and share a two-bedroom apartment. No one would give a shit. We wouldn't have to explain anything to anyone.

But she'd developed a serious case of conscience, she said, just as I was finishing my second year at the university. It couldn't go on any longer, that which we'd been sharing since I was seventeen. She told me she knew it was unspeakable from the beginning, but she had a special feeling for me that went beyond the maternal. Marina said she couldn't explain it to me, but she felt for me as she felt for no other. She would love me always, but she couldn't go on sharing a bed with me. The pressure on her from herself was too great. Marina couldn't live with the growing shame. It had to stop, and it suddenly did when she met Aaron.

213

I can't say I hated him. He was a decent young man. But he took her away, and that was reason enough to despise him.

I didn't kill them. Niko and Elena had it in mind, though. The police even talked to me. But there was nothing to the accusation, and they let me go. I still think Niko believes I was involved. My brushes with the law after my military service convinced him I was a criminal. Reading about Elena's death, I can't say that I miss my grandmother. But I will never be able to heal the hole that Marina punctured my chest with the night she died in that wreck. It is, therefore, her fault. If she'd gone away with me somewhere where Elena and Niko could never find us, my life would have taken a 180. None of this would have been necessary, I'm certain. Marina's the one who put the knife in my hand. I could've finished medical school. I wouldn't have become involved in selling drugs . . . Truly, all of that self-hatred would've been avoided and I could've lived a traditional life if I could've simply had one very non-traditional relationship.

The herd crushed us. It moved her away from me and eventually got her killed. She would never have been on that highway and in that car if it hadn't been for her conscience attack. But the cattle closed in on her and made her go their way. Now she's dead and I'm alone, and when the hate becomes too virulent, I use my knife. No, I'm not just in it for the money, no matter what the police like to say about my being a sociopath, that generic term for anyone who escapes categorizing.

They all pushed her away from me, and I can't see her or touch her or smell her again. But I can make them pay. I can transpose Marina's face onto all those others, and when the rage builds to its apex, I can carve them like beasts in a slaughterhouse. Each time I do one of them, my anger increases. I know I'm not getting even, but it does vent some of my spleen. Besides, they are the people who separated us. They and their ancient desert-prophet codes.

Enough. I have two physical holes in my flesh that need tending to. I have to find an antibiotic to stop the infection. I have to clean myself up and go to a pharmacy. Somewhere close,

214

because I still might fall on my face from the loss of blood. I'm very weak. It'll be awhile before I'm back to full strength.

Then I'll meet with Martinson and Parisi. I don't care if I'm caught or killed. There really is no good reason to keep on. My contacts have been severed before I could get my own operation up and running. I literally have no income coming in, although I have at least a half-million stashed in my lock box downtown. The police and Sal and John Fortuna are all seeking me out, and I understand the weight of the odds. One of them will find me eventually. There's no sense in running because Fortuna and the police have universal manpower. All I can do is make a final gesture to them. All I have is one last statement, if you will.

I get up slowly and make my way to the bathroom. My shoulder is throbbing. I need to get cleaned up, dressed, and get to that drugstore before the fever I have at the moment knocks me all the way out. I'm hoping the shower will revive me.

I struggle to get my blood-soaked T-shirt off. Then I strip the underwear off as well. I manage to turn the water on in the shower, and I get into the stall. The water assaults me with a cold spray. The shock almost sucks my breath away. I can feel the wooziness coming on, and I grip the cold-water handle before I go down flat on my face. My grip on the handle becomes weaker and weaker. The lighting in this shower stall is becoming progressively dimmer, and suddenly I'm on my knees and I'm bleeding again.

This is just a shoulder wound, I keep telling myself. It's nothing fatal. Then why is it that I feel like I'm never going to wake up when my face meets the floor of this stall?

My face does meet the floor. My eyes are a few inches from the drain. I'm hunched up like a Muslim at prayers. I want to get up. I need to rise. I know if I stay here that red trickle going down the drain will become a river of my own blood. Who knew that those guinea bastards would be awake so late? Who knew that Sal Donofrio would be waiting for me with heat in his hand?

I reach out and put my fingertips over the drain. I figure I'll be able to save my blood, somehow keep it from dribbling down and out into the city's sewer system. It's a ridiculous notion.

215

But I'm getting very sleepy and I cannot move. I can't get to my feet. Everything I've ever desired in my life is joining that scarlet rivulet. The bright red stream flows past my eyes, downward, downward, downward . . .

Chapter Thirty-Five

Natalie sat in the kitchen while I was asleep. She said it gave her a better visual of the floor plan in our house. She could concentrate on keeping watch if she was not in the same room with me.

The kids and my mother had been gone two weeks. We both missed the three of them terribly. I felt as if Karrios was already here, an intruder in my home. I liked it when everyone was here, when I could see all of us together. When the kids were out of the house, I suffered anxiety attacks wondering if they were all right and if they'd arrive home safely. The Elmhurst police force had cooperated with us and had put a man with my family at Uncle Nick's – I still couldn't call him Papa or Dad. I called them frequently. They were lonesome for their friends and their home surroundings, but I couldn't put them where Karrios might show up.

I didn't sleep well. Maybe it would've been better if we'd kept the security system running and the dog at home. But then a smart little dick like Karrios would sniff out the trap. The way he'd got to Sal had impressed me with his patience and his alertness. No, he wouldn't try to come in unless his way was cleared. I was hoping he'd figured that I was confident that he wouldn't dare attack a policeman. It just wasn't done. Certainly not by his former associates, Fortuna and Donofrio. They wanted to fuck with a cop, they threw some money around. Killing lawmen was just too messy. And it generated unbelievable heat. You could buy a cop and get away with it, but you killed one of the brotherhood, there was no hole you could hide in. It was the one taboo that most of the Outfit would not mess with. It was just not worth the problems you'd suffer after the fact.

But Karrios was not Sicilian, he was not in a crew, and he was not the usual workmanlike thug. He was beyond that ballpark. He'd loved his own mother, she'd died on him, and since he couldn't have her again, he was punishing women who fit into her age and physical categories. They were surrogates for his abuse. I was no shrink, but that was the only way I could figure him.

He had to show up soon. There'd been no progress in canvassing all the pharmacies. No one'd come in with a bogus prescription for a bug zapper. We'd given all those places a general, and vague, description of the 'new' Marco Karrios as well. We had a hundred Academy kids who had volunteered to keep going round to the drugstores for as long as we needed them to.

I rolled over and I saw that Natalie was out in the house somewhere. It was three in the morning. We were still working days. We figured our being at home at night would edge Marco even further in our direction. But, like I said, it had been two long weeks.

I heard something like a thud that seemed to come from the kitchen. I snapped myself up to a seated position. I wanted to call out for her, but I didn't want to announce that I was awake.

I got up out of bed and threw on a pair of shorts and a T-shirt, and I picked up the Bulldog from the nightstand. The gun was kept in easy reach now that my kids were out of the house.

I walked slowly toward the kitchen with the piece palmed in my hand. When I got to the room where my wife liked to keep watch, I didn't see her. There was only

218

a fluorescent bulb lit. It was over the kitchen sink. I walked back toward the front of the house, toward the living room. It was dark. No one there.

I was beginning to feel my pulse take off from the launchpad. I wouldn't be taking my hypertension medication until seven in the morning, and I could feel the invisible fingers applying pressure to the back of my neck. I thought I was going to explode if I didn't see Natalie in about ten seconds.

I ran up the stairs to the second floor, where the kids' bedrooms were. Nobody was there. I came back down the stairs and checked if she had missed me in transit somehow and was back in our bedroom. Still no one. I went back toward the kitchen. It was still unoccupied.

Then I heard another thud coming from below, in the basement.

I cocked the .44 Bulldog. I opened the door that led downstairs. It was a few paces beyond the kitchen, toward the back door. I flipped on the light switch and began to move down the stairs very lightly. But there were a few inadvertent creaks in spite of my careful steps.

The only light came from a forty-watt globe hanging from the ceiling. We rarely went into the basement unless it was to clean or to look for something in storage. I heard another quiet thud, and I aimed the miniature cannon into the darkness.

'Natalie?'

There was no reply.

There was a flashlight at the bottom of the stairs on a workbench. I found it and flipped it on, but the batteries were dead and I got no light from it.

I walked into the basement, away from the stairs, and immediately stubbed my toe on a piece of copper pipe that was lying in the middle of the concrete floor. Which caused me to snap my head up in agony. Which, in turn, caused me to whack the overhead bulb that hung from the ceiling of the basement. Which caused the light to bob eerily throughout the cellar, creating shadows and flashes

219

of light that bounced off the various items of junk we had on the walls down here.

In one of those flashes I saw a face. I yanked the pistol upward as I grabbed hold of that bobbing goddamned forty-watt bulb. I aimed the fixture toward the face, and I saw it was our front-lawn Santa Claus statue. I had almost whacked the fat, jolly guy with a .44 slug.

I was convinced there was no one down here but a resident mouse. Now I'd need to buy a goddamned cat to even the odds against the fucking rodent.

I headed back carefully toward the stairs. Suddenly I heard footsteps above me. It sounded as if they were moving rapidly across the kitchen tiles. Moving faster now, I reached the top of the basement stairs. I shoved open the door with the Bulldog stuck out in front of me.

There was still no one in here. The light remained on, but the kitchen was deserted.

I tried the bedroom on the main floor once more. Nobody. I trotted upstairs. Nothing. I came down into the living room and it was as it had been. Dark. Unoccupied.

Someone was playing hide-and-seek with me and it'd gotten beyond irritating.

'Natalie, goddammit!'

The only place left was the backyard. I walked through the kitchen yet once more and opened the back door. I walked down the steps onto the cool concrete, and I felt a shiver work its way up my back. There were cops down the alley and cops down the street aways, but I hadn't used my handheld, back in the bedroom, to call in the troops.

I walked out toward the back fence, toward the alley, and the grass was wet and freezingly cold. I stopped at the fence and looked both ways. Nothing that I could see. The surveillance guys were supposed to give us about a block's space so Karrios wouldn't be scared away before he tried to get inside.

I turned and walked back toward the house. I was heading for our bedroom. Something was wrong. Natalie didn't play games like this. She wouldn't run out of the house without telling me something was up.

I reached the porch at the back of the house and walked back in through the door. I had the gun clamped tightly in my hand, and I could feel those intangible fingers grabbing at the muscle on my neck. It was damn' near throttling me.

I walked into the house, turned on another light inside the kitchen, headed right toward our bedroom to retrieve the handheld radio – and then there was another muffled sound coming from the front of the house. This time I bolted toward the front door, threw it open, aimed the piece in front of me—

Right at the noggin of my red-headed bride, who had her own nine-millimeter pointed squarely at my neck.

'Jesus Christ, Natalie! What're you *doing* out here?'

'Whew ... Jimmy, God. I thought I heard something out on the front porch. When I came out here the first time, I heard something coming from the back of the house. So I ran back into the yard and then I thought someone was back out here, messing with me ... I finally found two cats who were rolling around in the throes of romance. They were having a mobile go of it, from our front porch to our backyard. You didn't hear all the yowling?'

'I thought that prick was in the house. I thought he had you, because I couldn't find you.'

'From now on I'll wake you up if I think I hear something out of the ordinary.'

She led me back into the house. The invisible grips on the base of my skull were finally released.

'You have great legs, Jimmy. Anybody ever told you that?' she said as she shut the door and tripped the dead bolt.

Chapter Thirty-Six

We were summoned once more, near the university where Karrios had assaulted the geology teacher Jack'd become more than attached to. This time the request came from that same County Sheriff we'd dealt with when we went out there previously.

Sheriff Espinoza met us at the cornfield that lay beyond the farmhouse where Marco had mangled Ellen Jacoby.

There was a tractor sitting out some hundred yards from where Espinoza was waiting for us. We pulled the Taurus to a stop by the house, and Jack and Doc and I got out of the vehicle. We walked over to the Sheriff.

'They found something in the field. They were plowing it up to put in some kind of late crop, and they found a body. Her name was Dee Dee Tremont. He buried her stuff with her. I guess he figured she'd be safe out there, but when he left this place the owner of the property decided Karrios wasn't likely to be coming back. So the owner was going to try and use the land again until he sold it to someone else.'

We walked out to the yellow markers that surrounded the remains. When we arrived, there were three deputies keeping watch over Dee Dee Tremont's body, or what was left of it.

'It's his work, all right,' Doc confirmed.

There was not much left to work with, but we could see that the body'd been mutilated, slit up the middle. The

222

insects hadn't left much, but there was enough flesh still left on it to indicate that it was a good bet that someone else hadn't planted this woman out in a corn field.

'You guys have anything new on this Karrios?' Sheriff Espinoza asked.

'He's been underground. He got himself clipped by a wiseguy, and we're sort of hoping he died from the wound,' Jack explained.

'That'd be too bad, if you really think about it,' the Sheriff said.

'Why?' I asked.

'Because it'd wind up like the way it did for that guy in England. You know. The real Jack the Ripper. The killings just stopped because the son of a bitch disappeared. He never got caught. Can you imagine how those Scotland Yard types must have felt, not knowing if the bastard might come back and start things up all over again?'

We began to walk back to our car. The County ME had already made his examination. This was just a courtesy call for the three of us. Espinoza's people would handle the rest and would share any information they came up with. It wouldn't be of much use to us because we already knew who killed Dee Dee Tremont. But something might be found on her that could help us.

I thanked the Sheriff for letting us in on what had happened in the cornfield. We got back in the car and headed east, back to the city.

Dee Dee Tremont had been in the missing-persons file for some time. Her parents had reported her as gone, weeks ago. We investigated and found that she'd been seen last at a bar on Rush Street. Since it had been a while, all the bartender could remember was that the guy she left with fitted the general description for Marco Karrios. Nothing else we found out helped us locate Marco.

*

223

We got a call from the Fire Department. When there was arson involved and when someone had been killed in a fire, we were contacted.

The fire was on the far northwest side, at the edge of the city limits. Jack and Doc and I were off again in the Ford. It took maybe a half-hour in light early-afternoon traffic to make it out to the location. When we arrived we saw not much left but debris. It looked like Berlin after an Allied night raid in early 1945. The building was a skeleton. It was a three-flat and, even though it was brick, there was not much left of the outside of the structure.

The Fire Captain was standing out in the street, waiting for us.

'We had to wait a few hours for the heat to subside,' Captain Danson told us. 'That's why there was a delay in getting ahold of you. I couldn't get anyone inside that place for a while. Whatever set it off must have been highly flammable. I mean, the heat was intense. The investigator from arson thinks someone used an accelerant . . . The body's on the second floor. We needed a hoist to get the investigator up there. The stairs were gone. He said there's very little left of whoever it was on that floor. Not even teeth. It was an extraordinarily hot blaze . . . But they found the occupant's car on the street. We know it was his because the landlord came out and pointed it out for the investigator. That's why they called you, Lieutenant Parisi. The guy on the second floor fit the general description for Marco Karrios. Wasn't that his name? . . . Well, we figured you might want to get prints off the vehicle. They've got it blocked off. It's over there.'

He pointed about a quarter of a block to our left.

The three of us walked down to where two patrolmen were guarding the car. We showed them our ID and they let us take a look. We inspected the interior – the door was unlocked. We checked out the trunk. Doc popped it with his burglar's tool. There were clothes and a few other objects. But we'd need a print man to find out if these pieces belonged to Marco.

224

We walked back toward the fire scene. The blaze must've begun when the other tenants were at work. It was lucky they hadn't been in their beds.

'Self-immolation?' Doc asked, as we looked at the smoldering rubble.

'Could've been the ether. Could've just been suicide. That'd be the way this cheesedick'd leave. With a big burst of glory,' Jack suggested.

'Why suicide?' I asked them.

'He's got a lot of people after him, Jimmy,' Doc concluded. 'Maybe he was cut off from his cash, too. And he was hurt pretty bad. After Sal disappears in witness protection, he must know we're watching his lock box. We cut him off, and maybe he figures his string's run out. Fortuna's not in prison yet, and Big John has a contract out on him.'

'We need to see the landlord. Right away.'

Jack went over to the Fire Captain. The fireman pointed to a short bald man standing out in the street near the three of us.

I walked over to the landlord with my partners.

'Mr Strezcak,' Jack said. 'We're with the police.'

The bald guy looked up. He was depressed by the waste of his property. It was all over his sad mug.

'We'll need a description of the man in that second-floor apartment,' I told him.

'Why would he torch the place?' the short man groaned. 'Jesus Christ, he could've killed all of those other people—'

'Please, sir. We could use that description right away. I mean now,' I explained.

So the four of us went for a walk down the street.

Karrios had darkened his hair, added a mustache and a beard, and had put on about twenty pounds, we found out. Strezcak worked with our sketch artist for about an hour until the artist came up with a match of Karrios's new face. We got copies of it out as soon as the sketch was finished. The landlord moaned again about the loss of his property and the potential holocaust that might have occurred if all the other occupants had been home.

'Upstairs has two little girls. Jesus Christ. What kind of a maniac would do a thing like that?'

Then he left.

'He's right,' Doc added. 'What kind of a loose joint would kill himself the way Marco did?'

Fifteen minutes later we got a call that confirmed the prints on the shirts and pants and underwear that had been left in the car. It was Karrios.

'You can sleep again at night, Jimmy P,' Doc grinned.

'They can't do a positive ID on the remains, they said,' I reminded him and Wendkos.

'From the remains they can still come up with a general body size, Jimmy,' Jack said.

'No prints. No dental. That cop out in the boonies, Espinoza, was right. It's like the guy in London. He disappears and no one's sure he's really gone.'

'The odds are with us this time, guinea. It's him,' Doc said. 'He didn't have the balls to keep up his act. Too much hot wind on the back of his neck. It was Karrios, Jimmy.'

What Doc had concluded about the body was substantiated by the remains of the crispy critter they found in the shower stall on the second floor. If the Fire Department had arrived later, they would've had a one-level building – everything would've fallen to the ground. They had to remove the remains by using a cherry picker that the arson detective used to get close to the body. It wasn't a very heavy body to remove. Most of it was ash. There were only fragments of a few bones remaining. The teeth were so badly burned up that they couldn't use a dental scheme to prove who it was that was in that shower stall. All we really had was the stuff we found in the automobile. I couldn't get myself comfortable about any of it. I thought Doc and Jack were simply trying to stroke me so that I'd stop worrying about Marco, but I didn't think they liked it either that we hadn't got a positive ID. They put on a good show for me, however.

We were at yet another lunch at Garvin's in Berwyn. Jack was about to be reassigned to another case because our Captain had decided that the red names of all those female victims were going to be changed to black lettering. This case was on the books, the Captain insisted. No one was more relieved it was over than our boss. He had had considerable heat blown at his ass over Marco Karrios.

'We've got a multiple homicide on the far North Side. We've got singles on the west side, and that's about it. The caseload seems to be clearing up a bit. Chicago is becoming the safest city in the Midwest.' Doc grinned as he sipped his glass of Sprite.

Garvin came limping down the bar with our Italian beefs. It was new on his menu. We were his guinea pigs, the barman explained.

'Why don't you take your vacation now, Jimmy? You still have two weeks left, don't you?' Doc proffered.

Garvin slammed the plates down as he always did and then he gimped back toward the kitchen.

'We're saving the time to go visit Natalie's mother over Christmas.'

'Oh yeah? Well, I'm thinking about heading to the islands. The Caribbean, you know, mon?'

'I can picture you there. You're the one with the fish-white gut.'

'There's a reason God made us white . . . Take a leave of absence, Jimmy. You look all tired out. And your b.p.'s still up, isn't it?'

I looked over at him but I didn't answer.

I couldn't come down from all this. It was the way it was after firefights in the Vietnam War I was in. You came out of some scary-assed situation where you were on nothing but adrenalin for a few hours, and it was almost impossible to come down from the screaming high where you were. Booze didn't calm me. I didn't use drugs because I never had any use for them or for the people who used them. Nothing would calm me; nothing but a lot of time.

It was that way when Celia Dacy died. It took a few months before I was able to even talk to my current wife Natalie after that business was resolved.

'You need to get out of town, bro. The Captain'll grant you the leave. Shit, you must have three months of unused vacation time coming.'

'I've got eighty-four days accumulated,' I told him with a smile.

'Jesus Christ, Jimmy. You're a hoarder. That's what the hell you are.'

He chomped into his Italian beef.

'This guy Garvin is a genius, dago. Christ, he's outdone himself again . . . Hey! Old man! Can you hear me back in that kitchen?'

We were back on swing shift the next week. We were both working afternoons first, but after this week, Natalie wouldn't be matching my time off.

I'd thought about Gibron's idea of taking off for a few weeks, but Natalie's schedule wouldn't allow it. And I was certainly not going anywhere without her and the kids. We were in the middle of the summer heat of late July, and my family had finally arrived home, here on the North Side. My mother was back, of course, but I thought she would've preferred to spend more time with Nick. She'd always been in love with him. It just didn't work out for them to wind up together. Since she was the widow of his brother, there was no chance for them to be together at the end of their lives. But I thought she saw him on the sly from time to time.

I heard things in the night. I couldn't relax and fall asleep. I kept dreaming Marco was alive and that he was going to make good on meeting up with me. It was unfinished business for him if he was still alive.

I repeated to myself constantly that it had been Karrios in that fire. Doc was right: he came to the end of his string and he killed himself. Without any worries that he might burn alive everyone else in the three-flat. That would be Karrios, though. He wouldn't care about bystanders. The thought gave me some reason to calm myself. It was precisely how this dick would've done himself. The flames were glory. The spectacle was a final 'in-our-faces'. We could not catch him. Here I was, he was telling us. He left the car behind to ensure we'd know who it was.

We still didn't have the report on the accelerant. We still didn't know if DNA would help confirm his identity. The inferno had done a complete job on the corpse. We wouldn't be able to find evidence of the wound Sal had inflicted on him, but we did have military health records. They took blood from him as they did with all GIs. We'd just have to see if there was enough left to complete a worthwhile test. The forensics people were not optimistic on this point.

Natalie rolled to her left, and I could see that she was smiling.

'Your energy level's back up. See? Our evening walks have lowered your blood pressure and have increased your get-up-and-go.'

'Sometimes I got the get-up, but no go.'

'Cut it out, Jimmy. You are a wonderful lover.'

'I never asked you if I was your first.'

'You weren't, lover.'

I looked over at her, but she had removed the smile.

'I didn't reckon that you'd saved it for me. Don't get angry at me, Natalie.'

'I'm not. I thought I saw disappointment on that swarthy dago face.'

'Hey. I wasn't a virgin. Why should you be? You're a grown-up.'

She reached over and tickled my throat. She knew it drove me nuts. Then she giggled.

'Never loved anybody but you.' She grinned.

I wished I could tell her the same thing, but I didn't lie to her.

Her face went serious again.

'You think he's still alive, don't you?'

'I wish I knew for sure that he was dead, that's all. It's like they're saying in the media. No solid identification. I know they're using that just so they can keep this fuck's legend alive, but it still disturbs me a whole goddamned lot.'

'You've got to calm down, baby. You can't let him keep you in his hooks. That's why he did himself the way he did. He knew you'd be bothered by it. So don't let him get away with it . . . By the way. I missed.'

'Missed? Missed what? . . . Oh Christ . . . How long?'

'A few weeks, Jimmy. But my little friend tends to show up on time. I just thought you'd like to know.'

'You think you're pregnant?'

'I haven't had the pukes in the morning yet.'

'What do you think, though?'

'I think you should get over to me and make it a unanimous decision.'

'You can only get knocked up one at a time, Natalie.'

'Please, Lieutenant. Tell me more. Tell me all about it. Instruct me.'

I rolled toward her and I kissed her. She had the ability to distract me. She had the power and the ability to do what no one else seemed able to do.

'What do you suppose the odds are, Natalie?'

She came up off the bed and changed places with me. They called it 'female astride', I believed.

Then she looked at me with those killer eyes and told me:

'It's over. He's dead. He's gone. Life goes on and so do we.'

She lowered her face slowly toward me until she filled my field of vision. She was all I could see.

230

Chapter Thirty-Seven

Fortuna grudgingly accepted our invitation to have a sit-down downtown. He was under indictment, but I heard he was also trying to set up a deal like his soldier Salvatore Donofrio. Sal had gone into hiding and John wanted to squeal for a deal on the current Don, Santos Marichante.

Fortuna sat with his lawyer inside the box with Doc and me. Jack was out on the street with a new case and a new partner.

'You have anything you want to share about the death of Marco Karrios?' Doc asked.

'Only that I wish I'd tossed the match that burned him to dust and charcoal.'

His lawyer, Tony Amonte, tugged at Jackie Morocco's sleeve.

'I don't give a shit. The motherfucker was a piece of crap and I wish I done him myself, but I didn't . . . Is this why you dragged me all the way down here? Because I thought I was being cooperative in the investigation of my sister's murder.'

Doc looked at me. He knew this was a waste of time. Big John Fortuna now belonged to the Federal Bureau of Investigation.

*

I still had trouble sleeping. I had a prescription my family doctor gave me to help me out, but those damn' pills made me woozy in the morning. I didn't think they mixed well with my b.p. prescription.

It was Saturday morning. My kids and mother were going off to the beach. They were leaving early – about nine. I was going in late because I was planning on working late. Natalie was staying home. It was her day off, and she was planning on cleaning the house from top to bottom. It was about 8.45 already. My mother had the two kids in tow and they were on their way out the door. They were using the van. I'd taken Doc home in the Taurus and I'd kept it at my place so I didn't have to bum a ride into work.

The kids and Eleanor told Natalie and me goodbye. They scurried toward the Plymouth in the driveway, and they were gone. I walked back into the bedroom because I knew I'd forgotten something. I couldn't scratch it back into my memory. Natalie said it was the onset of senior citizenship, and then she kissed me as I left the house.

The Taurus awaited. Doc and I still had four outstanding cases to turn to black.

It was sunny, hot, and humid. Just what you expected of the end of summer. The heat'd die hard.

I looked out at my front lawn and saw that it needed a serious watering. I didn't have much grass, but I liked taking care of the front and back of the house.

Looking down the street, I saw that the neighbors' lawns were in scraggly straits, too. The outside was deserted. It was only nine a.m. and it was already eighty-two degrees and sweltering. The only life on the block was some tall female who was apparently selling 'Katie Ann Kosmetics'. I saw her violet-colored company car at the very end of the far block. She had a straw hat covering what looked like yellow-blonde hair.

I got into the company car and I backed out of the driveway, thinking I should've gone with the kids and

Eleanor to the Lake. I hadn't been to the beach a single time this summer. Too many dead bodies to deal with.

I drove the mile and a half to the Stevenson in-bound exit. When I got on, I saw I had been gulled into believing that this Saturday traffic would be light. After I'd gone a half-mile along I-55, I was in the middle of a jam. I saw helicopters hovering over the eastbound lanes, about a mile ahead of us. I turned on the talk-radio station and a DJ finally revealed that there'd been a massive accident up ahead. Just my luck. Heat, humidity, a poorly working, inefficient car air-conditioner, and a wreck that could hold me up for an hour and a half.

But I was coming in on my own to work this Saturday. It originally was one of my days off. I started to daydream about Natalie, naturally, wondering if she was pregnant. Then my mind wandered to changing my wife's hair color. What would I like to see her change to? Brunette? Black-haired? Blonde?

Blonde. A tall, statuesque, yellow-haired beauty. Just like the blonde on the street, selling the cosmetics.

Tall, she'd been. Very tall. She'd been far down the block, but even from that distance she'd looked a little . . .

The heat rose to my temples. I looked ahead and found the traffic still moving inch by inch. There was no getting anywhere in this mess. Even if they'd cleared the wreck, there'd be a half-hour gapers' block. I couldn't get to the next exit by sitting here. So I pulled over onto the shoulder just as the anxiety level inside me exploded to critical.

It was him. It was Karrios. That son of a bitch was working his way down to my house. He was working his way toward Natalie. The golden hair, the yellow topknot. It was the color he would pick . . .

I got on the radio to downtown and I ordered up a small army to get to my place. But I was still the cop closest to Natalie and my house – and I was headed in the wrong fucking direction.

I was able to zoom up the shoulder for about three

blocks. Then I came to a stalled car and I was stuck again. Three lanes creeping at about an inch every five minutes and a blocked shoulder.

I tried to patch in a call to my wife via the radio in the Ford, but when they connected me, she didn't pick up. She liked to play the stereo full blast while she vacuumed. I'd already bitched at her about the noise this morning.

It would take me too long to run back home. It was a couple of miles.

So I got out of the car and left it sitting behind the stranded VW Bug that was spouting steam from beneath its upraised hood. I ran across the three lanes of creeping traffic, climbed over the rail, ran down the ditch that separated the eastbound traffic from the westbound, and stepped onto the westbound outside lane. These guys were going medium speed, perhaps forty. The traffic had become sluggish because of the show they'd just passed on the opposite side. The gapers hadn't decided it was time to resume normal speed.

I tried to step out onto the lane and tried to flag someone down, but no one would halt in front of me and my flapping arms. Marco was down the block by now. Maybe he'd gone directly for Natalie after he'd seen me leave the house. He could count. He knew four of us had left the premises, and he'd know my wife was still there. You could bet he'd done a surveillance on the house, now that the police watch on my place had ended.

I finally stepped out into the middle of the road. There was about a two-block gap between me and the late-model red Corvette that was headed directly at me. The inside two lanes were clogged with traffic, so the guy in the Vette had nowhere to go but right at me. He was travelling at the speed limit or thereabouts, and it was not certain that he'd be able to avoid hitting me, but he jammed on his brakes so fast that the car began to fishtail and screech. The other two lanes heard him hitting the brakes and they thought there was an accident ahead that

234

they somehow hadn't seen yet, and they started screeching to a halt as well.

The driver was a young kid, I saw, as he came to rest about ten yards in front of me.

'You fuckin' nuts?' he screamed at me in a rage.

'Get out of the car. Police emergency!' I shouted. I showed him the ID, but I kept myself planted right in front of him.

'Fuck you! I ain't gettin' out!' he raged back at me.

I removed the Nine from my shoulder holster.

'Get out of the car, Junior.'

I could see his face blanch immediately, and he hurried out the driver's side.

'Are you really a cop?' he wanted to know as I walked past him and got into the Corvette. I showed him the badge once again, and then I laid rubber.

The traffic ahead was still thick. It was as if everyone'd gone slow-motion after witnessing the carnage back toward the Lake on the eastbound lanes. Everyone seemed to love a good accident.

It was two miles to the exit where I got off for my house. I cut two angry drivers off, making my way to the left lane, and I caught sight of two raised middle fingers as I went by. Road rage, they called it.

I placed the nine-millimeter on the passenger's seat.

My wife. Oh God oh Jesus, my wife. My possibly pregnant wife. Natalie.

He couldn't have taken very long to get down to my door. No one would be on the street to see him skip all those other homes. He'd make a beeline toward Natalie.

Was he carrying a bag? Christ, I couldn't remember.

I didn't have a radio in here so I couldn't try calling her again. And now the inane thought reentered my head that I'd forgotten something in my haste to get out of the house. Why I remembered something as stupid as—

I hit another snag in traffic just as I was six blocks from my exit. I yanked the Vette over into the right lane and cut off some more unhappy motorists. I got over onto the shoulder and I was sailing until I saw another guy with his hood up in front of me, a hundred feet away.

I screeched the Corvette back into the inside right lane and sideswiped a Chevy Blazer. The Blazer jammed on its brakes, but I kept going. I swung to the shoulder once more and it was clear, finally, all the way to my exit ramp. When I saw the traffic backed up on the ramp, I swerved around to the right shoulder on the exit and I passed by a number of honking, angry drivers.

Finally I was into city traffic, a mile and a half from home. I bobbed and weaved and blew through a stoplight and then a second stoplight. When I tried to whip through a third red light, someone nailed the rear end of the sports car and I did a 180 in the middle of the intersection. I straightened the expensive hot rod out, aimed myself in the right direction, and took off again. I was still alive and untouched, but the Vette had taken a good pounding. The young man I'd left behind on the Stevenson was going to be mightily pissed off.

Natalie. Jesus, Natalie. Don't answer the fucking door!

Halfway down the block, a pickup truck pulled in front of me and I thumped into his ass end because I had no time to evade him. Smoke billowed from the Vette's engine. I thought it was on fire, but no flames erupted from under the hood.

Then I couldn't get the car into gear. I shifted into first and then second and then third, but nothing happened. I couldn't get the Corvette to budge.

Natalie, don't open the door!

The only gear that worked was reverse, so I pulled the car around and headed down the block backwards. When I reached the next corner, a bus slowly pulled out in front of me and I had to literally jump on the brakes to avoid losing any kind of mobility.

The passengers in the back of the bus were staring out the back window watching an idiot in a red Corvette squealing his tires and tearing down the street in reverse right behind them. My neck was becoming very tired, as I had to turn sideways and look over my shoulder. I couldn't just use the rearview mirror. It was dangerous enough doing it this way.

Then the bus driver must have noticed the clown in the red car speeding up behind him in reverse, so he stopped the bus. I jerked the vehicle to a halt, tore the steering wheel to a 180, and then managed to work my way backwards around to the side of the bus. I looked out my driver's side window as I passed the stunned bus driver and his fares.

There was an open street in front of me – or behind me – as I continued peeling backwards in reverse. Another pickup pulled deliberately out from the corner in front of me and again I wasn't able to swerve quickly enough because of the awkwardness of the steering. But after I thumped violently into the Chevy pickup's rear with the tail end of the obliterated Vette, I thought I'd somehow managed to loosen up the transmission of the red wreck. When I came to a stop, I tried to force it into first gear, and miraculously the Vette lunged forward. I went through second and third as if the vehicle had never been damaged, and finally I was driving the smoking car the right way down the block. When I reached eighty m.p.h., traffic increased and I had to slow down. But I wasn't going slowly enough to avoid another rear-end crash, so I attempted to slide the Corvette between two cars in this four-lane traffic. It didn't look like there was enough room, but there was open street in front of the two poke-asses in front of me. I hit the accelerator hard and tore between a new Cadillac and a beater Mercedes. There was the terrible sound of screeching metal as I simultaneously sideswiped both vehicles. I was nearly stuck between them, but the Vette had enough guts to shear itself away from these two outraged drivers who were shouting several kinds of obscenity at me. I didn't have time to respond.

More smoke was pouring out from beneath the red hood.

Don't open the door, Natalie!

I could hear grinding coming from the guts of the automobile. This beautiful ex-sports car was about to give up its ghost and I was still too far from home to run for it.

Third gear gave out, and I was chugging along at a greatly reduced speed. I tried ramming it into second gear, and it worked, but I couldn't get it going past 40 m.p.h.

Yet one more hillbilly with a pickup pulled out from a corner and cut me off. I thought they must have had some kind of obligation not to know about right of way, but I had no time to change myself into a traffic copper.

When I tried to pull around this latest stumpjumper and his Ford pickup, the driver, with full beard and John Deere ballcap, looked over at me with a brown smile full of fixings from a mouthful of chewing tobacco – and proceeded to try and run me into oncoming traffic in the lane to the left of mine. He brought his much-dented truck over and made a hit on my passenger's door. I couldn't believe this asshole was trying to push me into a head-on collision!

Reflex kicked in and I pulled the Nine from its resting place on the seat next to me. I aimed it at the billy-boy in the beater Ford. We were both doing forty-five, and it was fortunate the street was clear ahead of us. When he saw the aimed piece, he literally stood up in his cab and jammed on the brakes. So I sped away from him.

Now second gear was grinding away, just blocks from my house. More smoke billowed up in front of me and it was becoming more difficult to see anything. I had to hang my head out the window to get any kind of decent visibility.

Second gear gave out, and I downshifted into first. The best I could get out of the damn' thing was twenty m.p.h. It felt like I was moving in slow motion, as though the car was trapped in amber.

Then I tried third again, bypassing second, and the car

lurched up to speed once more. It was a miracle. I thought maybe these toys really were worth their high price tags, afterall.

I got it up to fifty-five in this thirty-five m.p.h. speed zone and again I hit traffic. There was no way around or between this gaggle of cars, however – until I saw that the sidewalk was unobstructed with pedestrians. So I swerved over to the right and tried to jerk my way onto the sidewalk. As I did, something went loony with the steering. I felt the steering wheel give just slightly, and suddenly the Vette had tipped to the right and I was driving on two wheels – the right front and back. It was like in one of those Demolition Derby stunt shows. But I had never performed in an automobile before, and I thought my bowels had finally loosened sufficiently for me to dirty my underwear. I sped down that unoccupied sidewalk, tilted precariously on those two wheels for the better part of a block. Then I decided I was going to be killed or kill some unwary pedestrians anyway, so I rammed my shoulder toward the driver's door and I was able to bring the Corvette back down on all four pegs.

I was beyond the logjam on the street now, so I veered the car off the sidewalk just as three women appeared in front of me. They screamed as I screeched the red, boiling-over Vette back onto the street surface. I had missed the three middle-aged females by about twenty feet, I reckoned.

Third gear was grinding again and I understood my luck was about to vanish like the smoke in front of me that was swept aside by the slipstream of the Vette's motion. Amazingly, there were no police cars in pursuit of this maniac in a stolen red Corvette that was accordioned on both sides, flattened front and back, and driven by a gun-waving lunatic who'd aimed his handgun at a civilian in a pickup truck.

Don't open the door, Natalie. Don't open the door.

As this vehicle lurched and shuddered toward my home I thought about my wife being pregnant. I thought

239

about her finally recognizing Karrios as she opened the door for him. She would think it was just a blonde woman selling perfume. Just a summer day with a door-to-door female peddling her wares.

The road was open ahead of me. People weren't on the streets. They were at jobs, at their workplaces. Life was going on in a normal way for everyone but Natalie and me. No one else had a mad savage waiting at his or her front door. Just me. Just Natalie. If I were in any other profession, I'd be biding my time until my vacation at the Wisconsin Dells. You spent two weeks in the water and watched the waterskiers perform.

I thought I saw a flame erupt from the hood.

It was just a matter of blocks now. Just feet and inches.

Don't open the door, Natalie.

My beautiful red-headed wife. This would make three losses consecutively for me. Then I thought what a selfish notion that was, coming at that moment.

He would hit her with a mouthful of ether. That was how The Farmer operated. He would neutralize her with a cloth soaked in the stuff, and then he would strip her and . . .

When he was through, when he was spent, if indeed he could have an orgasm . . .

Jesus, Natalie, don't open the door!

He would take his time with her. There would be no rush. She would be unconscious, so he would begin to do the things he did with all of his victims. Yes, he would work slowly.

I slammed my hands three times on the steering wheel. I could muster no more speed out of the red car, but my luck was holding with the still-empty street before me.

Then I definitely saw a slight flame from beneath the crumpled hood. This ride was about to explode. And then The Farmer would have an open field ahead of him. I wondered if he sensed I was onto him. He probably hoped I was, just so I could speed home as I was, just so I could see his signature and Natalie's mutilated body.

That beautiful body that had lain with me just hours ago. That body that contained my seed and my offspring too, I thought. That would be the final coup for Karrios. To kill our child.

My street's corner finally appeared ahead of me. An old man in a large Crown Victoria was in front of me just before I turned onto our street. He was dragging his ass, so I swerved around him and passed him.

'You stupid bastard!' the Second World War-vintage geezer shouted at me.

There were clouds of black smoke rising in front of me as I made toward my house. This was my street now. Karrios had invaded my home.

Now I was just a couple of blocks from home. The tires screamed in agony. I was going so fast I almost flipped the car as I swerved. But I got back on all four wheels, and I could see my house down the block. The violet-colored 'Katie Ann Kosmetics' car was parked right next to my driveway, on the street. I was coming on so hurriedly that I couldn't stop the car fast enough, and I crashed the front end of the Corvette into the ass end of Karrios's vehicle.

I charged on out of the Vette with my nine-millimeter in hand. I got to the door and I could hear loud music from inside the house. I started looking for my keys, but I remembered I'd left the goddamned things in the ignition of the Ford. They were on a ring with my car keys. *Son of a bitch – I couldn't get into my own house!*

I raised my foot to crash in the door. The music was blaring so loud that I could feel the vibrations out here on the stoop. Just as I was about to kick my way into my own home I heard the explosion of a single round of gunfire.

I shattered the door handle with one kick from my right heel. The door flew open and I saw a tall, golden-haired woman standing in the middle of my living room. She had a scarlet hole in the dead center of her back. Somehow she was able to turn to me. It was then that I saw the

241

nine-inch blade in her right hand. Natalie had clipped her just above the waistline. The blonde was gut-shot. A lethal hit.

But I saw also that the tall woman still had the strength to lift that knife and lurch toward me. As soon as she raised the blade, I aimed the nine-millimeter and let loose with two rounds. The shots were audible above the noise of the Rolling Stones CD that my wife had blaring on the stereo – the song was 'Sympathy for the Devil'. The impact of my two shots jerked the blonde backwards violently onto our couch. There were two holes in the tall woman's throat, and then the blood began to cascade out of the wounds. Again, she tried to rise. I heard the same kind of explosion I'd heard just before I burst in. I looked over and saw the smoke coming out of the barrel of the Bulldog that my red-headed wife still had in her hand, aimed at the chest of Marco Karrios in drag. The slug had torn through him and our new couch. The guts of the pillows were floating in the air behind the couch right now.

Karrios made no further attempt to rise. His eyes went dead. His blood began to ooze lazily down onto his summer dress.

The army of cops I'd called out was inside the house just a few minutes after Marco stopped breathing. The first thing I had done was to remove the knife from his grip. It was not really a knife. More like a scalpel for epic-scale surgery. I dropped it on the coffee table, and then I carefully approached Karrios and took his pulse. There was none. The ME would make it official, but I was glad anyway when my backups arrived and watched Marco so he wouldn't somehow rise up off that couch.

I went over to my wife. She still had the .44 Bulldog firmly clamped in her grip. The hand, however, dangled at her right side.

I took her into the kitchen after one of the uniforms removed the wig from Karrios. When he took the golden hair away, we all saw the face that'd been plastered on the new renditions of the Marco Karrios posters. Here was the face that Dr Richmond – the late doctor – had created.

I sat Natalie down at the table and I was finally able to extricate the pistol from her grip.

'You . . . you forgot it this morning, Jimmy.'

'I know . . . Are you all right, baby?'

She nodded slowly.

'How . . . how did you know it was him?' I asked.

She looked up at me slowly.

'He . . . she . . . Karrios must have rung the bell. The dog started barking like crazy, loud enough for me to hear it over the stereo, so I knew there was someone out there . . . I looked through the peephole in the front door, and I saw this very tall, muscular blonde woman outside. I was just about to open the door when I saw something else.'

'What, Natalie?'

'I saw an Adam's apple.'

'An Adam's apple?' I asked.

'Yes. A pronounced goddamned Adam's apple. It was jiggling in his throat when he said "Katie Ann Kosmetics". Then I knew who it was. His arms were a little too well defined, too.'

'Why the hell'd you let him in?'

'It's what we prepared for, wasn't it, Jimmy? I'm a cop, aren't I?'

Now her tears began. She started to shake.

'He was dead, Jimmy. I couldn't let him come back to life, could I?'

I came around to her side of the table. It was then that Doc entered our kitchen.

'Well, it's the Fighting Parisis,' he smiled. 'I'll come back later.'

I stopped him.

'You can stay. We need the good company.'

'I apologize,' Doc said. 'I should've listened to your intuition, guinea.'

243

He patted my shoulder and then sat in the chair I had just got up from.

'So Officer Natalie Parisi got her man.'

'She knew who he was when she let him in,' I explained.

'Christ, Natalie. The hell you do that for?' Doc grinned.

My wife started weeping again.

'Oh, Jesus, I'm sorry,' Gibron apologized.

'It's okay, Doc. It's okay. It's my first shoot and I'm just a little unnerved.'

'She recognized his Adam's apple,' I told my partner.

'No shit. Really? Oh ... oh yeah. The Adam's apple. That was very astute, Officer Parisi, ma'am.'

My wife smiled weakly.

'Listen, I better get out with the crew ... You know, he didn't make a bad version of his mommy. Maybe a little too much dark hair on his forearms ... You gonna be okay, Natalie?'

Doc's face turned serious.

'I think so. Give me a minute,' she sniffled.

Doc walked out of the kitchen and into the living room.

'Are you okay?' I asked again.

'I'll be all right. I'll have to talk to our people, won't I?'

'Yeah. And me, too.'

'You forgot your .44. I'd just picked it up and was going to lock it up back in the hall closet when ... when that son of a bitch rang our doorbell. I put the piece in the front pocket of my robe. You know, the gray robe that I wear when I clean?'

I nodded.

'Then I looked out that peephole and I saw him, and I almost didn't notice anything until that thing moved in his throat. It bobbed up and down. And then I remembered what you said about his mother. The blonde hair. I wasn't going to let him in, but I had to, Jimmy. I turned off the security system by the door, and I swatted Merlin the dog out toward the kitchen. He's such a coward that he scooted away and hid behind the refrigerator.'

244

I looked and saw that the mutt was still cowering there, next to the fridge, having made a watery mistake that I'd have to clean up.

'He'll never make a hunting dog,' I told Natalie.

Merlin wagged his tail and continued to shudder.

'I had to let him in. It wasn't courage, Jimmy. It was fear. I was afraid he'd go off and start it all over again.'

She sobbed and I took hold of her again. But she calmed down, slowly but surely, and by the time a detail of on-scene investigators arrived she was able to go back into the living room with me so we could get on with the usual questioning.

Chapter Thirty-Eight

I look into the red-headed woman's eyes, and we connect. But there is something else going on. She reaches into the robe's pocket and pulls out an enormous handgun. It is squat and ugly, and I know now that this is as far as I go. I've shown her my knife, and now she shows me the pistol.

Marina, I think.

This is as far as we travel. I won't let her arrest me. Parisi's wife is a cop, but I won't let her take me. So I hoist up the blade and as I reach arm's length above me, I hear the bullet's boom. The impact shoves me back about three feet, but somehow I'm still standing.

Marina, this is where it ends.

The door behind me crashes open, I turn around and see him, her husband, and I try to lift my weapon again. But he aims at me and shoots twice. The bullets strike me below my chin and this time I'm flung backward and down, onto the couch.

Again I try to rise, but I hear the boom of the squat handgun, and I see feathers flying about my head.

Marina, this is all there is. I'm looking for you, expecting to see you, but there is nothing. No sound, except for the closer and closer buzzing of an insect. It sounds like a fly is wafting about my head.

Marina, where are you?

The insect circles closer and closer, but it is getting too dark to see. It is a summer morning. It has to be fully light outside, but my eyes begin to fail.

There are two figures in front of me, but all I can hear is the approach of a common housefly.

Circling. Coming nearer to me. Closing in.

Epilogue

The man in the fire was identified by one bone from his leg and one bone from his forearm. From those two items our people were able to establish his size and weight. I didn't understand how, but they were able to approximate the height of Karrios's victim. Then DNA came into play and we had a match with a man who was reported missing about a week ago. According to our investigators, he was a homosexual who liked to consort with dangerous men. He apparently ran into more than he bargained for.

Karrios was cremated at his father's request. There was no burial, so Niko took the remains home with him.

The newspapers were full of the story about Marco's metamorphosis into his mother/sister. They were constantly bothering Natalie and me at home and at work. Natalie was not used to media attention, but now she appreciated what most of us in Homicide had to go through from time to time. She needed the experience for her future as a plainclothes officer.

The Captain said my wife might step up to Burglary as a detective within two years. It could happen that fast because of her newfound celebrity. She was the cop who shot Liberty Valance, the boys and girls in Homicide teased her. She put The Farmer down – with a little help from the old man.

The kid who owned the red Corvette was suing the city and me, but our attorneys said the young man was now talking deal, so it'd cost Chicago and the Department something in five figures. The car was totaled in the run back to my house. The engine still ran, just about, but the body was wiped out.

Doc was still threatening to write the Great American Opus, as usual, and Jack Wendkos was living in transit, back and forth to that university. The lovely professor was trying to convince him to move out there and commute, and he was trying to get her to take a teaching job in the city.

My wife, Natalie, continued to walk a beat in Hyde Park. She also continued to take that at-home test for pregnancy. It was a morning ritual, regardless of what shift she was working. We were currently on days, so we rode into work together.

My blood pressure had subsided once The Farmer was deep-fried and turned to ash. The family doctor was hopeful that this was a trend toward better things. But I was compelled to exercise more and to eat the right things. My wife was part of the conspiracy to change my life. I lost eight pounds in three weeks, and I needed to buy new pants.

Natalie had gone to her gynee and asked about her peak periods of ovulation. When we arrived at one of those window-of-opportunity moments, we had to excuse ourselves from anything we were involved in and retire to the bedroom to take advantage of one of her peaks.

So far we hadn't produced the proper color on my wife's test kit. This morning I wanted to sleep in because I was taking another of the eighty-three days vacation time I had coming. Natalie's romantic hold over me had worn me out.

My caseload was somewhat under control – we had three outstandings, still in red ink. But it was better than it had been. Karrios was enough for a career, all by himself. I was almost looking forward to no-brainers. To a series of slam dunks.

I was hiding beneath the sheets when I heard Natalie's voice. Faint, at first. But then she became louder and clearer. The voice came from the bathroom, where she did her daily test. My heart started to beat a bit more emphatically when I heard her.

'*Jimmy! Jimmy! Get in here, Jimmy! Get in here right now!*'